CANCELLED

Putnam Co. District Library
525 North Thomas Street
Ottawa, OH 45875

CANCELLED

DANGEROUS DECEPTION

DANGEROUS DECEPTION

Janet Tanner

This first world edition published in Great Britain 2006 by
SEVERN HOUSE PUBLISHERS LTD of
9–15 High Street, Sutton, Surrey SM1 1DF.
This first world edition published in the USA 2006 by
SEVERN HOUSE PUBLISHERS INC of
595 Madison Avenue, New York, N.Y. 10022.

Copyright © 2006 by Janet Tanner.

All rights reserved.
The moral right of the author has been asserted.

British Library Cataloguing in Publication Data

Tanner, Janet
    Dangerous deception
    1.   Governesses - Fiction
    2.   Romantic suspense novels
    I.   Title
    823.9'14 [F]

    ISBN-13: 978-0-7278-6407-9
    ISBN-10: 0-7278-6407-6

Except where actual historical events and characters are being
described for the storyline of this novel, all situations in this
publication are fictitious and any resemblance to living persons
is purely coincidental.

All Severn House titles are printed on acid-free paper.

Typeset by Palimpsest Book Production Ltd.,
Polmont, Stirlingshire, Scotland.
Printed and bound in Great Britain by
MPG Books Ltd., Bodmin, Cornwall.

The old gypsy woman's dark eyes narrowed in her wizened, weather-beaten face, as the pair of girls, laughing together, arms linked, approached her. A tremor ran through her skinny body. The crowds who had come to revel at the fair on the village green were unreal to her suddenly, their shouts of merriment hushed so they were no more than the sighing of the wind through a field of corn. She heard only the laughter of the girl, saw only her smiling face.

And all around her a cloud of darkness, a shadow which the bright summer sunshine could not penetrate.

The basket of lucky heather, picked that morning to sell at the fair, slipped unheeded from her hands. She stepped forward like one in a dream, grasping at the girl's arm.

'Missy! Missy!' Her voice was a dry croak, like the creak of an old dead branch, but her tone was fraught with urgency. 'I must speak with you.'

The girl stopped, startled, and tried to draw away. But the crone's bony fingers held her fast.

'There's trouble ahead for you – terrible trouble. You must beware or your whole life will be in ruins . . .' The old woman's eyes were far away, yet narrowed with concentration as she strove to make sense of the overwhelming feeling of foreboding that had come over her the moment she had set eyes on the girl, make the cloud that surrounded her take shape and form so that she could understand it. But the pictures were hazy, and the words that were forced from her cracked and dry lips came from she knew not where.

'There's a man . . . no, two men. One is handsome, the other is rich. But they spell danger for you. Darkness – and danger. You must avoid them at all costs. For between them they will bring about your ruin.'

1

'Oh, for goodness sake!' the girl's companion burst out. 'Why can't you just tell her she'll travel to foreign lands and meet a charming stranger, as your kind usually do?'

The old woman shook her head. 'I say only what I see. I can't spout platitudes just to please.'

'Then we don't want to hear your horrid predictions.' The girl glanced down at the basket of heather, lying forgotten at the old woman's feet. 'And we don't want your heather, either. If we need it to bring us good fortune, we'll pick our own, thank you!'

''Twould do you no good, anyway, my dear, if you don't heed my warning,' the crone muttered. ''Tis not strong enough magic to overcome the evil that lies ahead.'

'Come on! Don't listen to her!' The second girl tugged at her companion's arm.

'If she don't listen, on her own head be it.'

'I'll set the constable on you, frightening decent folk so!' the second girl flared over her shoulder as she led her friend away.

The old woman stared after them, two girls in their best summer gowns, for all the world as carefree as birds on the wing.

But the one, at least, had reason to face the future with apprehension. The old woman hoped desperately that she would heed the warning, though somehow she doubted it.

She had seen stubbornness along with the alarm in that pretty face. Once her mind was made up, it would take more than the garbled words of an old gypsy to make her change course.

She was walking away fast now, her hair bright in the sunlight.

But the dark cloud went with her.

Book One

Imogen

One

If I live to be one hundred and one – a very unlikely eventuality, I must concede – I shall never forget that bright golden day in the late summer of my twenty-first year when my life changed forever. Every detail of it is etched in my memory as clear as if it happened just yesterday.

I can see the sun slanting in at the window of my grandfather's study, making a bold, sharply-edged pattern on the great oak desk where I sat working to transcribe his spidery scrawl into a neat enough hand to be read. I can feel the impatience that burned in me to be out in it, feeling its warmth upon my face, hearing the bees buzzing in their last urgent efforts to gather nectar from the flowers before they faded and died for winter, watching the swifts and the swallows gather for their long flight to warmer climes. I wanted to be anywhere but here in the dim, dusty study – it always seemed dusty to me, no matter that I cleaned it every day and polished the desk until it shone like a mirror, for Perkins, the maid, could not be trusted not to muddle up or mislay any of Grandpapa's precious papers.

'They are just scribblings to her,' Grandpapa would say. 'She'd have them in the waste-paper basket as soon as look at them. You take good care of them. You know how important they are, Imogen.'

I knew how important they were to him, certainly, though sometimes I doubted their importance to anyone else. Grandfather was a scholar, a former schoolmaster; now, in the twilight of his life, he was writing his memoirs, and though there were parts that were interesting, I could not imagine that the world would stop turning if they never saw the light of day.

But it was not for me to question. The memoirs were

Grandpapa's passion; it was my task to help him prepare them for publication. He had asked me to do so, and so I did – that much I owed him. He and Grandmama had taken me to live with them after Mama died when I was ten years old. They had fed and clothed me and kept me in comfort; they had given me warmth and affection, helped me to overcome my grief and adjust to my new life. And besides, I had nothing else to do. I had no employment to fill my days, for they did not consider it fitting for me to work for my living, and no social life either, for theirs was a very secluded existence. My quiet and scholarly grandfather had never been one for forming friendships; he lived for his books, and my grandmama's only concern was making him happy, keeping a good table and a smoothly-run household.

I was grateful to them, of course, though I could never quite understand just why they had whisked me away from my stepfather's house in Bristol with such alacrity when my mother had died. Perhaps my stepfather had said he no longer wished to have responsibility for my upbringing, and if that was the reason, I could scarcely blame him. I was not, after all, his daughter, and he had two children of his own to care for, albeit some years older than me. But my grandparents merely told me that my place was with them, that for all that he had been my mother's husband, he was not a blood relation as they were, and beyond that they would not go. Certainly I do not remember my stepfather raising any objection when they came to take me home with them to Devon, but to be honest, I was in such a state of shock and grief at the loss of my mother that I was not very aware of anything.

I had lived with them now for ten years and I was grateful to them, of course, for all they had done for me. But that did not stop me from wondering sometimes how different my life might have been if Mama had not died and I had remained with my stepfamily in Bristol. And it did not stop me from wishing, on that warm afternoon in late summer, that I could be anywhere but the dusty confines of Grandpapa's study, transcribing page after page of dry notes.

Little did I know that my wish was about to be granted – and in the most unexpected way!

I had just reached the end of Grandpapa's latest sheaf of notes, laid down my pen, and was daydreaming a little, when the door opened and Grandmama came into the study. That in itself was an unusual occurrence; generally they left me to work undisturbed, and in any case, Grandmama usually took a nap at this time of day.

Now, however, she was very much awake – and rather flustered, judging by the pinkness of her cheeks and the fact that her afternoon cap, usually set with perfect precision on her soft silvery hair, was a little awry.

'You have a visitor, Imogen,' she said without preamble.

I frowned, puzzled. 'A visitor?'

'Yes. Someone who has come a long way to see you.' She touched my arm; I felt her fingers trembling. 'I think you should prepare yourself for a shock, my dear.'

'Whatever do you mean?' Though my mind was racing, my hands were automatically neatening the sheaf of Grandpapa's notes, placing a paperweight on top of them so that no unexpected draught should blow them away. 'Who is it, Grandmama?'

She hesitated a moment, as if she were unwilling to tell me; as if she had difficulty in bringing herself to speak the name. Then:

'It's your stepbrother,' she said. 'It's Miles Voisey.'

Miles! I could scarcely believe it! In the ten years since Grandmama and Grandpapa had brought me to live with them in Devon none of my stepfamily had ever been to visit me, nor I them. From the moment I had left the house in Bristol that had been my home ever since my mother had married Raymond when I was just five years old, I had never so much as set eyes on any of them, not Raymond, nor Miles, nor Rosalie, his sister. It was as if they had ceased to exist, except of course in my memory, and I thought they had, in all likelihood, forgotten about me.

Now Miles was here in Devon, come to visit me, if I could believe what Grandmama was saying – and unlikely as I would have thought it, Grandmama had no reason to say such a thing if it were not true.

A little bubble of excitement formed deep within me – an

7

excitement I knew I must hide from Grandmama, for I felt instinctively she would be hurt if I made my pleasure too obvious. But though I tried to conceal it, a sparkle must have come into my eyes, for Grandmama's hand tightened warningly on my arm.

'I think he may have some disturbing news for you, Imogen.'

A shadow of alarm fell across my pleasure.

'What . . . ?'

'It's for him to tell you,' Grandmama said. 'Leave your work and come down now. Miles has come a long way and doubtless he will want to make some headway towards whatever lodging he has arranged for himself on the return journey before darkness falls.'

Her tone left me in no doubt – she did not want Miles under her roof a minute longer than was necessary. But although her coolness – and Grandpapa's – towards my stepfamily had puzzled me for many years, I did not waste time now thinking about it. I was too anxious to see Miles – and learn what it was he had come all this way to tell me.

'He's in the parlour,' Grandmama said as I followed her down the two flights of stairs from the upper room where Grandpapa had his study. 'I'll leave you to talk to him alone, Imogen.'

I nodded, and pushed open the door.

Miles was standing by the window, looking out, so that his back was towards me. Then, realizing that he was no longer alone, he turned and we were face to face for the first time in ten years.

'Imogen?' he said wonderingly. 'Is it really you?'

'It's me,' I said.

'The last time I saw you, you were a little girl! Now, you are a beautiful woman!'

'Hardly beautiful,' I said truthfully. My mouth, I always thought, was too large, my nose too tip-tilted, my eyebrows too heavy and my hair too straight. But certainly I had changed a good deal from the gangly child I had been when Miles had last seen me.

And I could well understand his astonishment, for I was

8

experiencing much the same sense of unreality. When I had left Bristol he had been fifteen years old, still a boy, and that was how he had remained in my mind's eye.

When I thought of him, I had seen him still as he had been then, a little shorter than his friends of the same age, a little stouter, with an untidy lick of hair that was forever falling into his eyes, and a rather round face. At some stage, however, he had shot up in height so that he now towered above me, though I was considered quite tall for a woman. The puppy-fat had turned to muscle, so that he was now powerfully built but perfectly proportioned, and the round-ness had gone from his features too.

Miles had grown into a very handsome man, and though of course I would have known him anywhere, yet it was still difficult to believe this was the boy I had grown up with, the boy I had once seen crying because his friends had teased him that no girl would ever look twice at him.

'You've changed too,' I said.

'Hardly surprising!' He came towards me, taking my hand in his. 'It has been ten years, after all. I should have made the journey to see you long before now, Imogen. Can you forgive me that I have not?'

'It's a long way,' I said. 'In any case, I am as much at fault. I have never been back to Bristol.'

'No one would have expected you to,' Miles assured me. 'No, the fault is entirely mine. Though I've thought of you often, and the fun we used to have.'

I was a little surprised by that. As I remembered it, Miles had never had much time for me. I had always thought he considered me something of a nuisance, the little half-sister he was often instructed to look after when he wanted to be off with his friends on some adventure or other. It was hardly to be wondered at, of course – an energetic growing boy lumbered with two younger sisters – and maybe I had been oversensitive to what I had seen as his resentment of me, the cuckoo in the nest.

'I've thought of you, too,' I said. 'Of course I have! How are you all? Is your father well? Have you married? Has Rosalie? What do you do for a living?' The questions were tumbling out, one after the other, when suddenly I remembered my manners. 'Oh, I haven't offered you any refreshment!'

'It's of no consequence.'

'I'm sure you could drink a dish of tea, at least!'

'No, really. I am booked into a good hostelry where I'm sure I'll get a hearty meal and a pint or two of good ale. It won't do me any harm to wait for that.' He patted his stomach, which, now that he had drawn attention to it, I could see was indeed still a little round from good living, though much leaner than his former portly build.

At that very moment, however, as if she had been party to our conversation, Grandmama came in with a tray laden with milk, tea and sugar, and some scones and jam. Uncomfortable as she might be with having Miles in her house, her own standards of offering at least a little hospitality had prevailed.

She did not remain in the parlour, though. With a nod at Miles, she went out again, leaving me to pour the tea. We both sat down.

'So tell me how you are all faring,' I said, handing him a cup – one of Grandmama's Sunday best bone china set, I noticed.

'Papa is in poor health, I'm afraid,' Miles said, taking it. 'There was an epidemic of some vicious infection that spread like wildfire in that hot spell we had – brought in, no doubt, on one of the foreign ships in the docks. Papa caught it. He almost died, as did many others, and though he pulled through then, it seems to have weakened his heart. We fear we could lose him at any time.'

'Oh, I'm so sorry!' I was shocked. Raymond had always seemed so strong and full of life – it was hard to imagine him close to death.

But given the lack of contact over the years I could scarcely believe that Miles had travelled so far to tell me this in person, and remembering Grandmama's warning of disturbing news, I wondered anxiously what else had occurred of which I knew nothing. The question burned on my lips, but I thought it best to leave him to tell me in his own way – and his own good time.

'He can no longer carry on his business, of course. That

is a great sadness to him – it was his life, as you well know.'

I nodded sympathetically but said nothing. In truth, I had never quite understood what Raymond's business was. I had some vague idea it involved dealing in art, amongst other things, and certainly the walls of his house had been hung with paintings and drawings which had fascinated me as a child, but that was the extent of my knowledge.

'You didn't follow him into the business then?' I asked.

'No. I work as an accountant in the city.' He smiled ruefully. 'It doesn't bring in the rewards that Papa garnered in his heyday, but it keeps a roof over our heads.'

'Do you still live in the Leigh Woods?' I had fond memories of the house high above the Avon Gorge, so close to the city, yet quiet and secluded and surrounded by trees.

'Papa and I do, yes.'

'So Rosalie has married?' I asked.

Miles's face darkened. For a long moment he was silent, and I felt a little tremor of dread crawl over my skin. This was it, then, the disturbing news of which Grandmama had spoken. Something had happened to Rosalie. Oh dear Lord, surely he was not about to tell me she had caught the fever too, and died of it? If he was, I could not bear it!

Though my relationship with Miles had always been a little tense, I had adored Rosalie. Four years older than me, she had been everything I yearned to be – impossibly pretty, self-assured in a way I had thought that I could never be, and a little wild. Rosalie's daring had led her into scrapes more often than I could count, yet somehow she was always able to extricate herself from them. No matter how much trouble she found herself in, she could always escape the consequences – and the threatened punishment – with her winning ways. Her father had been putty in her hands, and even my own mother would merely shake her head, hiding a smile as fond as it was exasperated, and exclaim, 'Oh Rosalie, whatever is to become of you?'

Oh, how I had longed to be like her – brave and gay and beautiful, not plain and timid and anxious to please, as I was. I had followed her around like a puppy-dog, lost in admiration and hoping against hope that some of her magic might rub off on me.

Now ... I gazed numbly at Miles, dreadfully afraid of what he was about to tell me, not wanting to think the unthinkable, yet somehow trying to prepare myself for the worst.

'Rosalie married, yes,' Miles said at last. 'A little over a year ago. Do you remember the Palmers at Upton Stowey?'

'I remember their house, certainly!'

Upton Stowey was a village some hour's drive into the beautiful countryside that surrounded Bristol. I had been there on several occasions with my stepfather, visiting Sir Harry Palmer, a landed gentleman and the owner of a number of profitable coal mines. Upton Stowey House, where the Palmers lived, had seemed to me a magical place. It was a huge rambling mansion, reached by way of a drive that ran through a deer park, and was fronted by a broad gravel turn-around with fountains and carefully tended formal flower beds. There were portals round the great front door and the windows on the front of the house reached right down to the paved terrace, hung with heavy drapes of deep blue velvet.

I remembered Sir Harry too – a daunting figure of a man to a young girl, tall, broad, bewhiskered and clad in a smoking jacket and matching cap. But he had not been a young man – to me, at ten years old, he had seemed as old as Methuselah, and even with the perspective of a grown woman, I guessed he must have been approaching fifty then.

'Rosalie did not marry Sir Harry Palmer, surely?' I exclaimed in disbelief.

'Not Sir Harry, no,' Miles said. 'His so-called great-nephew – Bradley Palmer, he styles himself, though I doubt that is his rightful surname. Do you remember Sir Harry and Papa fell out not so long before your Mama died and you left?'

I shook my head. 'No, I don't remember that.'

'Well, they did. Papa was dreadfully upset, but I suppose you were too young to notice. I'm not sure of the rights and wrongs of it, but it was all Bradley Palmer's doing. Most likely Papa told Sir Harry what was only too clear to the rest of us – the man is clearly a chancer and a charlatan, eager to worm his way in as Sir Harry's heir. As you know, Sir Harry never married and has no close family. Bradley Palmer made himself indispensable to Sir Harry and Sir Harry seems never to have seen through him. He has control of the estate now and lives like a lord.'

'And Rosalie has married him?' I said. It sounded to me as if she had done rather well for herself. But Miles's expression was still dark.

'Against all advice,' he said. 'She thought herself in love with the rogue, and headstrong as she is, refused to listen to a word against him. And I am very afraid, Imogen, that she has reaped the consequences of her recklessness.'

Bewildered, I gave a small shake of my head. 'Whatever do you mean?'

'Something has happened to her,' Miles said. 'According to Brad, as he is familiarly known, she has run away. He claims not to know where she is, or what has become of her, and all my enquiries to ascertain her whereabouts have come to nothing. It's as if she has disappeared off the face of the earth.'

Again I shook my head, trying to make sense of what he had said.

'You mean she has run away because he was ill-treating her?' I said. 'But surely she would have come home to you and Raymond!'

Miles's jaw hardened.

'Precisely. I am not sure, Imogen, that one can believe a word that scoundrel utters. I am not sure that she has run away at all.'

I stared at him, bewildered and alarmed.

'Something is terribly wrong, I am sure of it.' Miles's tone was grim. 'And it is one of two things. Either Brad Palmer is keeping her prisoner against her will, or he has caused her some terrible mischief. Whichever, Imogen, I am dreadfully concerned for my sister. And somehow, by whatever means, I have to discover what has become of her.'

The parlour seemed stuffy and airless suddenly; Miles's words hung heavily and I could feel my own heart beating hard in my chest as I struggled to take in what he had said.

'I don't understand,' I said. 'Are you trying to tell me you think that this man has . . .' – the word 'murdered' came to my lips and I rejected it as unthinkable – ' . . . that this man has *made away* with Rosalie?'

13

Miles's face was grim. 'I pray not, Imogen. But given his history, I believe there's a chance that he has.'

'His history?' I repeated foolishly. 'What do you mean?'

'Rosalie is not his first wife,' Miles said tersely. 'Brad is ten years older than Rosalie, and had been married before. She, too, was a beautiful girl – Alexandra Sutton, of the well-to-do banking family. She died tragically a few years ago, supposedly took her own life. But rumours abound that her death was not quite what it seemed. That in fact, she died at the hands of her husband.'

'Why would anyone think such a thing?' I asked.

'Alex, too, disappeared mysteriously. In midwinter. It was spring before her body was discovered – on a bleak hill in the Cotswolds. It had lain there undetected under several feet of snow which had hung even longer than usual. By then there was no way of ascertaining the cause of her death, but there were questions, all right. Brad and some of the staff – loyal to him and afraid for their livelihoods, no doubt – testified that she had been in a state of depression and even a little unhinged ever since giving birth to her little daughter, and had not only threatened to take her own life, but actually attempted it not once, but several times.

'But why was her body discovered so far from home? Why had she travelled to Gloucestershire to make away with herself? And how? A frail woman clad only in light clothing and slippers could never have got so far on foot. She must have had use of a carriage of some kind, or assistance.

'And so the rumours began – that it had been Brad Palmer himself who had taken her there, more likely already dead than alive, and disposed of her where he hoped her body would never be discovered – or at least, not until the elements and the animals had ensured she could not be identified. As it happened, of course, the heavy snow beneath which her body lay all winter had preserved it to a certain extent. When a traveller stumbled across it in the spring, there was no mistaking that it was indeed Alexandra Palmer.'

'What a terrible story!' I whispered. 'But why . . . ?'

'Popular opinion had it that he had killed her for financial gain,' Miles said. 'She was, as I say, a member of a well-to-do family and had money in her own right – all of which, of course, passed to her husband on her death. Brad was well-known as a heavy gambler and big spender, and it may well be that he had misappropriated money from the estate and needed to make up the deficit before Sir Harry realized what he had been up to. Oh, if it hadn't been for his connections in high places, Brad Palmer would have stood accused, I'm sure of it. But because of who he was, it was all hushed up, and officially no guilt was attached to him.'

'But surely if what you fear is true, he would never have done the same thing to Rosalie?' I argued, desperately trying to find the flaws in Miles's reasoning and disprove his dreadful suspicion that Rosalie had met with a similar grisly fate. 'He'd know he couldn't hope to get away with it twice! And in any case, she's not a wealthy heiress. He would hardly have married her for her money and then disposed of her for it too, whatever the truth of what happened to his first wife.'

'Rosalie is not wealthy, it's true,' Miles said, 'but she did have an inheritance of her own from our mother, which she came into on her twenty-first birthday. It was not wealth on the scale of Alexandra's, of course, but worth having none the less, especially to a man on the edge of desperation as he would be if he had been embezzling again and Sir Harry was on the point of finding out and disinheriting him.'

'I can't believe it,' I said. 'I can't believe Rosalie could be taken in in such a way. She was always so sharp, so astute . . .'

'Love makes fools of us all,' Giles said. 'She was in love with him, not a doubt of it – and I have to admit he can be a personable devil. Obviously she wanted to believe he was in love with her, too, and not just the financial bonus she could bring him.' He paused. 'And then again, maybe he was. Maybe the stories of him killing his first wife for her money were just that – stories. Maybe it's nothing more nor less than that he killed her by accident in a fit of rage. He has a terrible temper when he's roused, it's said. And maybe he's done nothing at all – not to Alex, and not Rosalie. I pray that is the case – that she has run away, as he claims, of her own accord, for some reason we are not party to. But . . .' – he brought his fist down hard on the arm of his chair

15

– '. . . where is she, Imogen? Why has she made no contact with me? And don't you think it is something of a coincidence that both Brad Palmer's wives should mysteriously disappear? And that one of them should be found dead and the other still missing?'

'Oh Miles, I don't know . . .' My head was spinning. 'It's just too awful to think that poor Rosalie . . .'

I broke off. I did not for a moment want to consider that my stepsister and friend might have met the same fate as the first Mrs Palmer. Well, she would not be found buried and frozen beneath a snowdrift, that much was certain. The summer months had been long and exceptionally warm. But Upton Stowey was set in the heart of the countryside, where there were acres of thick woodland. There were lakes and disused shafts from the older coal mine workings. Plenty of places where a body could be disposed of and would never be discovered.

I shuddered. Oh, dear Lord, to think that Rosalie might have met such a terrible fate!

'He can't be allowed to get away with it!' I said. 'If he has harmed Rosalie, he must be brought to justice and made to pay.'

Miles nodded. 'My sentiments exactly. And if he has not, if Rosalie is being kept prisoner somewhere against her will, or even if she *has* run off to escape his clutches, we must find her.' He reached out and took my hand. 'Will you help me, Imogen?'

'Of course I will, Miles!' I responded quickly. 'But how? What can *I* do?'

Miles sucked in his breath, and his eyes held mine.

'More than you think, Imogen. It's the reason I've travelled all this way to see you – in the hope that you would feel as I do. Strongly enough to perhaps put yourself at risk in the effort to find Rosalie – or, if needs be, justice for her.'

I frowned. 'What do you mean, Miles?'

His hand still held mine, his eyes still bored into mine. They mesmerized me, almost, those eyes.

'Listen and I'll tell you,' he said.

Two

I waited. Miles seemed to be gathering his thoughts, wondering, I suppose, where to begin.

'You recall I mentioned that Brad Palmer and his first wife, Alexandra, had a child?' he said at last.

I nodded. 'A little girl, did you say?'

'Yes – Janine. She is six years old now, a pretty little thing. Rosalie brought her to visit on more than one occasion, and I thought her bright and quite charming. Rosalie was very fond of her, and of course, after she married Brad, had care of her. Now that Rosalie is missing there is no one to keep Janine company and teach her her lessons and all the things a growing girl needs to learn.'

'Pour little soul!' I said, remembering my own distress when Mama had died. 'To lose first her mother and then her stepmother . . .'

'Not to mention being at the mercy of that devil,' Miles said savagely.

'Oh, he'd never harm her, surely?' I cried, appalled.

'It's to be hoped not. He dotes on her, they say. But who knows what a man of his temperament is capable of?' He broke off. 'No, you're right, of course. It's most unlikely he would ever lay so much as a finger on his own flesh and blood. But all the same . . . being raised by a rotter like him . . . what chance does she have?'

Again he broke off and I saw the raw emotions chasing themselves across his face. Then he collected himself and continued.

'Palmer has been advertising locally for a governess. So far, to my knowledge, he has found no one suitable. Upton Stowey House is quite isolated, which I suppose has deterred some, especially if they are used to life in the city, and there would not be many local girls qualified to teach Janine her lessons as well as look after her – even if they wanted to live and work under the same roof as a man who has been suspected of doing away with his wives like some modern-day Bluebeard. When I heard of the situation he finds himself in, Imogen, I thought of you.'

'Me?' I repeated, startled.

'Yes. Why not?'

'But I am not trained to teach,' I protested.

'Your Grandpapa is an academic,' Miles pointed out. 'Didn't he take pupils?'

'Yes, but . . .'

'Has he not taught you well? Doesn't he entrust you with all his secretarial work?'

'Yes, it's true, but . . .'

Briefly I wondered how Miles knew this, given the lack of contact between us for all these years.

'Brad Palmer would jump at the chance of someone so well-qualified, I'm sure,' Miles said. 'His lack of success at finding a governess locally is, I am sure, of the greatest concern to him. He desperately needs to fill the post quickly, before winter sets in and Janine is confined to the house with nothing to do and no one to take care of her. If you were to apply, he'd engage you in a trice – I'd bet every-thing I own upon it.'

'I'm not so sure,' I demurred. 'And not just because of my lack of formal qualifications. If he has something to hide, he'd never take me on, knowing my connections with Rosalie and with you.'

'I'm sure that's true,' Miles agreed. 'The last thing he would want would be someone with a personal interest in Rosalie's fate poking about in his house and knowing too much of his private business. But if he did *not* know that you were my stepsister – and Rosalie's – then the objection would not arise.'

'Not know?' I broke off, thinking furiously. 'You mean I should pretend to be a stranger?'

'To all intents and purposes you *are* a stranger,' Miles pointed out. 'It is ten years and more since you left Bristol. No one would recognize you – when you left you were just a child. And you would not even be in Bristol, but out in the sticks at Upton Stowey.'

'My name would certainly give the game away,' I said. 'Voisey is not one that is encountered very often. Imogen Voisey might well strike a chord in someone's memory.'

'Perhaps you could use your grandparents' name?' Miles suggested.

'Blackmore, you mean? Might there be those acquainted with both your families who would know that was my mother's maiden name?'

Miles frowned. 'It's possible, I suppose. Why not shorten it, then, to Black? That's common enough not to arouse suspicion.'

'But what about references?' I asked. 'Surely no one would employ a governess without references, and I cannot expect Grandpapa to go along with such a deception and write me one under an assumed name.'

'Leave the problem of references to me, Imogen,' Miles said smoothly. 'If you agree to go along with this, I will provide you with the necessary letters.'

'Forged, you mean?' I asked frankly.

'Needs must when the devil drives,' Miles replied carelessly.

'Oh Miles, I don't know . . .' I hesitated, overwhelmed by the audacity of what he was suggesting.

'I know I'm asking a great deal.' His eyes bored into mine. 'But don't you want to help Rosalie?'

'Of course I do! I just don't see how—'

'I have done everything I can,' Miles said urgently. 'Palmer has taken exception to my repeated questioning – yet another indication of his guilt, in my opinion. The last time I went to Upton Stowey he threw me out and warned me against coming back. I've pursued every possible line of enquiry and met with nothing but yet more blind alleys. But if you were in the house, a trusted governess, you would be in a position where you might be able to learn something that would lead us to Rosalie – or, if the worst has happened, to some evidence of her fate.'

'But supposing this Brad Palmer came to suspect me?' I said.

Miles grimaced. 'That, of course, is the risk of which I spoke. There's absolutely no knowing what a man like him would be capable of if he found himself deceived – and under threat of his evil deeds being exposed to the light of day. I realize that I am asking a great deal of you, Imogen, and I shall quite understand if you do not feel you can place yourself in a position of such risk.'

He shifted in his chair, sitting forward urgently.

'But there's no reason why Brad Palmer should suspect you as long as you are careful and take every possible precaution. I would never have suggested this course of action if I did not believe you to be more than capable of carrying it off. Or if there were any other avenue left open to me to discover Rosalie's fate – and whether, if he is holding her prisoner, there is the chance she might yet be saved. For her sake, Imogen, I am begging you to at least give this some consideration. You, at least, would be prepared, and unlike her, on your guard. And I am not so far away. If you believed yourself to be in danger, you could always get a message to me and I could be there to whisk you away in no time.'

'And how would I get a message to you?' I asked.

'Charles Winters, the estate manager, thought the world of Rosalie, and was loyal to her, I know,' Miles said. 'He lives in the lodge not far from the house and I feel sure you could trust him.' He took my hand, his grip so tight my knuckles rasped together. 'I am begging you, Imogen, if ever you loved Rosalie, do this for her.'

I bit my lip, still lacking the confidence in my own ability to carry off such a scheme, given my lack of expertise in the position for which I would be applying, much less the chance I might learn anything useful in an environment where I would be a total stranger.

But the thought of Rosalie meeting some terrible fate at the hands of this wicked man made me reckless. My memories of her, gay, daring, always kind to me, were fond ones; the bonds that remained from the life we had shared were strong. I might not have set eyes on her for a decade, but the time we had spent together had been my formative years. We might share no blood ties, but from the time my mother had married her father until her death, Rosalie and I might as well have been real sisters.

I knew that if I did not do everything in my power to save her – or, if it were too late for that, to obtain justice for her – I would never be able to live with myself.

I looked Miles straight in the eye and straightened my shoulders.

'I'll do it,' I said.

My grandparents raised objections, of course. Though I omitted to tell them the real reason behind my decision to apply for the position of governess to the daughter of Bradley Palmer of Upton Stowey, yet still they were reluctant to let me go.

'What will I do without you to transcribe my manuscript?' Grandpapa asked.

'I'm sure one of your former pupils would be only too willing to help,' I said. 'And it's almost finished, in any case.'

'It's so far from home!' Grandmama said. 'And I'm not sure that it's fitting that you should live in the same house as a single gentleman. Tongues will wag.'

'Then let them!' I said recklessly. 'Grandmama – Grandpapa – I love you both dearly and I am truly grateful for all you have done for me. But I can't stay cooped up here forever. I'm almost twenty-one years old – I want to see something of the world outside these four walls.'

'And so you will – when you marry and have a home of your own.'

'What chance is there of that?' I pointed out. 'I hardly have suitors queuing at the door. I've never even had a sweetheart – not a proper one, anyway. Except, of course, Robert Linwood, and he scarcely counts.'

Grandmama's lips pursed tight. The affair of Robert Linwood had been one of the few things to cause ripples on the pond of our uneventful lives, a little threat to the concord that existed between me and my grandparents.

He had been a student of Grandpapa's in the days when he still took private pupils, a merry lad with irrepressible curls and sparkling blue eyes. He had professed himself in love with me, and I had fancied I was in love with him too. For a few magical weeks in the glorious summer when I was sixteen, we had stolen away into the garden whenever my grandparents' backs were turned. We had talked and laughed and shared our dreams – and even a kiss! For me the memory of Robert Linwood would forever be of the scent of roses and sun-warmed flesh. And a joyful feeling of floating, light as a butterfly, between scarcely contained excitement and a bittersweet yearning for I knew not what.

But the promise was never fulfilled. Grandpapa had come upon us one day, chastely holding hands and gazing into one another's eyes, and everything had been ruined. Robert Linwood had been sent packing – Grandpapa would no longer have him as a pupil – and I had been confined to the house 'for my own good'. We were not to be permitted to see one another again.

'You are too young to be alone with a boy, Imogen,' Grandpapa told me sternly.

'But why?'

'Never mind why. And don't answer back, young lady.'

'Why can't I be alone with Robert, Grandmama?' I asked later.

Grandmama turned very pink. 'It's not wise, Imogen.'

'But *why* is it not wise? Why am I forbidden to see him? Grandpapa was so angry, but we were not doing anyone any harm. We were only talking . . .'

I broke off. Instinctively I knew better than to mention the kiss. Perhaps they knew of it. A little colour tinged my own cheeks at the memory.

But, 'You'll know when you are older,' was all that Grandmama would say.

I had thought, of course, of defying them and slipping out to meet Robert. I had so enjoyed our clandestine meetings and I was so starved of company of my own age – well, any company really, apart from that of my grandparents. And I think I would have done it too, but I had no way of contacting Robert now that he no longer came for lessons, and in any case, I was no rebel. I was too anxious to please, and be held in high regard, as well as feeling that suffocating sense of duty to the grandparents who had sacrificed so much for my sake. Even my half-laid plans and the little fire of rebellion that smouldered briefly within me had the power to induce in me a backlash of guilt.

And so Robert Linwood became history, just a nostalgic memory, one of the sweethearts I had never had . . .

'You'll meet a young man when the time is right . . .' Grandmama said now – *I don't see how!* I thought, with just a hint of that old rebellion – '. . . and you don't need to go all the way to Bristol to do it.'

It is Bristol they wish to keep me away from! I thought suddenly.

Considering how overprotective of me they had always been in every way, it seemed strange that this one thought should occur to me now, and with such overwhelming clarity. Given their stubborn determination to protect me, wherever possible, from the harsh realities of life in the outside world, it was perfectly predictable that they would raise every possible objection to me leaving to pursue a career of my own away from their influence. Yet quite suddenly I knew without a single doubt that in this case their main concern was that the place I was proposing to work was Bristol. They did not want me there, and they did not want me in contact with the Voisey family.

Not for the first time, I wondered how my mother had come to meet and marry Raymond Voisey. My real father had been a Devon man, or so I had always been told, for I was too young when he died to have any recollection of him. My earliest memories were of living with Mama, Grandmama and Grandpapa in the selfsame house I lived in now. If Mama had lived the same secluded life that had been mine these past years, I could not imagine for the life of me how her path had crossed with that of an art dealer from far-away Bristol. Certainly Grandpapa had no interest in art – apart from a few prints of rural scenes that hung in the parlour, and a sampler and a religious picture in my grandparents' bedroom, the walls were bare of such ornamentation.

Nonetheless, met they had, and my grandparents must have been very upset when Mama had left with me. Bristol was much too far away for them to be able to see enough of us. Perhaps that was why they had clung so to me after I had been returned to them, and they dreaded being out of close contact, especially now that they were no longer young; the reason they were raising innumerable objections to my leaving now.

But I could not help feeling it was more than that. The swiftness with which they had removed me from the Voisey home after Mama's death, Grandmama's obvious displeasure when Miles had come to visit me, their reluctance now for me to take up a post he had suggested, all pointed to some reservation they harboured concerning either the location or the Voisey family themselves.

It might, of course, simply be that I was their only grandchild and they wanted me close to them. And it might be something else, of which I knew nothing. Whatever the reason, my mind was made up. I must do all I could to help find Rosalie, or learn her fate.

Take care what you wish for – the fates may be listening, it is said.

I had yearned for escape from the claustrophobic world in which I lived. And in the most unexpected way, not at all one I would have chosen, my wish had been granted.

I took care, of course, to hide the duplicity of my application for the post at Upton Stowey House from Grandmama and Grandpapa. I made certain they had no sight of the references which Miles obtained for me in the name of Imogen Black – glowing references purportedly from families in the south of Somerset. Who these people were, or even if they existed, I did not know. But I did know that area well enough to be able to talk about it should the occasion arise – we had holidayed sometimes in the Quantocks and Exmoor, and the beauty spots such as Tarr Steps, Blue Anchor and Porlock Weir were familiar to me, as was the village of Dulverton. I only hoped that if the people who had signed the letters of recommendation were fictitious, or unaware that their names had been used, Brad Palmer would not pursue them, or my flimsy story would be exposed as a sham before I even began.

The references must, however, have satisfied him, for a week or two later a letter arrived from him inviting me to take up the position on a month's trial basis.

It was addressed, of course, to Imogen Black, and it was my misfortune that Grandmama saw the envelope before I could secrete it away.

'What's this, Imogen?' she asked, her face puckered with puzzled concern. 'Why are you not using your own name?'

I could not meet her eyes. 'I thought to use yours, Grandmama. I thought it would make you and Grandpapa proud. But Mr Palmer must have made a mistake.'

'It seems very odd to me,' Grandmama said sagely. 'Are you sure it has nothing to do with Miles Voisey?'

My colour deepened; I felt the flush rising in my cheeks and lowered my head. I hated lying and deceiving my grandparents.

'Why should it have?' I countered.

She shook her head. 'Oh Imogen, Imogen! I don't like this at all. How I wish that man had never come here! He is behind this, isn't he?'

'It was something he said that gave me the idea,' I hedged.

'I knew it!' Grandmama's face grew ever more pink. 'Please, Imogen, I beg you to reconsider.'

It was time, I thought, for some straight questions.

'But why?' I asked. 'What do you have against Miles?'

'Miles – nothing personally.'

'The Voisey family, then.'

Grandmama hesitated. Then, all of a rush, she said: 'I don't like them, Imogen. The less you have to do with them the better.'

'But why?' I pressed her. 'What reason can you possibly have for feeling like this?'

Again Grandmama hesitated, unwilling, it seemed, to share her reasons.

'There must be something,' I persisted. 'I've never asked you, Grandmama, why you whisked me away from them almost before my mother was cold in her grave.'

'You were our own flesh and blood, not theirs,' Grandmama said fervently, reiterating the excuse I had heard repeatedly down the years. 'Of course we took you! Your place was with us!'

'And that is the only reason? It had nothing to do with the fact that if you had not, it would have been Raymond who would have had responsibility for my upbringing? I'm a woman now, Grandmama, not a little girl who must be fed fairy tales. I think you owe me the truth.'

Grandmama crumpled the duster, with which she had been polishing the hallstand when the letter from Brad Palmer had arrived, between hands that suddenly seemed to tremble a little more than the customary tremor which was afflicting her with the passing years.

'Raymond Voisey has no honour,' she said. 'His standards and his way of life were not at all a suitable environment for you to grow up in. Oh!' she gave a quick impatient shake of her head, 'he was not the sort of man I would have wished to see your poor mother involved with at all. But she was putty in his hands. So impressionable, so vulnerable . . .'

Because of the life she led – the same life you force me to lead . . . The words hovered on my lips, but of course I did not speak them. I knew I was already hurting Grandmama enough with my plans to leave them, without making things worse by such plain speaking.

'She was not a child,' I said instead. 'Nor even a young innocent girl. She was a married woman with a daughter of her own.'

'She was not a married woman!' Grandmama's colour deepened to a dark rosy flush, and she scrunched the duster even tighter between those trembling hands. 'You were born to her, Imogen, out of wedlock.'

Shock and surprise seemed to drain the strength from my body. 'But my father,' I whispered. 'I have always been led to believe he died, leaving my mother a widow.'

'It was a story we concocted for the sake of our reputation as a decent, God-fearing family,' Grandmama said. 'At the time you were conceived he was unable to marry your mother – he already had a wife and children of his own. Oh, the shame of it! I don't believe I will ever recover from the terrible disgrace. Your grandfather was a highly respected tutor, my father a man of the cloth . . . and my only daughter unmarried and with child. It was a truly terrible time.'

'Was he a Devon man as I've always been told?' I asked. 'Is he still alive? Do I know him?'

And Grandmama frowned, her eyes puzzled in her flushed

face, and spoke the words that left me quite dumbfounded.

'Haven't you guessed the truth yet, Imogen? The identity of the man who betrayed his wife and ruined your poor mother – and us?'

I shook my head. 'No. How could I?'

Grandmama drew a deep trembling breath.

'Your father, Imogen, was Raymond Voisey.'

If I had been in a state of shock already, Grandmama's revelation rendered me momentarily speechless. I stared at her with the same staggered disbelief as if she had just told me, with authority, that the earth I lived on was made of cheese.

Could it really be true? Was Raymond not my stepfather as I had always believed, but my own real father? And if so, why had they never told me? Why had they continued to lie to me after my mother married him? And why had my grandparents continued with the deception? I was a grown woman – to hide such a thing from me was not only wrong, it was utterly needless. They might have disliked and mistrusted him, but surely it was my right to know the truth?

'I don't understand,' I said faintly at last. 'What reason could Mama possibly have for keeping such a thing from me?'

'It's obvious, isn't it?' Grandmama said. 'She was anxious to preserve her reputation.'

'Well, it's not obvious to me,' I said frankly.

Grandmama was becoming ever more flustered. 'Your moral well-being was important to her, and your good opinion too. She didn't want you to know how she had disgraced herself, or to feel inferior because you had been conceived out of wedlock. In any case, once a story has been concocted it isn't so easy to refute it. She had been staying with friends of ours at Porlock Weir, in the south of Somerset, when she first met that man, who was in the district in connection with his business.'

Porlock Weir! South Somerset! The very area that Miles had selected for my bogus references.

'Who were the friends?' I asked.

'The Ramsdens. You won't know them. We cut all contact with them after this dreadful thing happened. We could never forgive them for allowing such a liaison to flourish whilst Sarah was under their roof.'

I breathed a little more easily. Ramsden was not the name on any of the references. But it was vaguely familiar to me, and I wondered if I had met them as a child when we had visited the area for holidays.

'When we discovered Sarah was ruined, we put it about that she had secretly married, there in Porlock, and her husband had died tragically soon afterwards. A drowning, we said. It seemed as good an explanation as any, given that all that part of the world is so close to the sea. I'm not sure how successful we were in concealing her shame. No one ever questioned us outright, of course, but there were looks – and whispers. We cut ourselves off, naturally. Did our best to keep our business within these four walls.'

So – was my mother's behaviour the cause of their reclusive existence? I wondered. Had they been so ashamed they could no longer look their neighbours in the face?

'We hoped, naturally, that that was the end of it,' Grandmama went on. 'We even hoped that one day Sarah would meet some nice respectable man who would be prepared to marry her and take on a child. There would have been no chance of that, of course, if the truth got out. A young widow is one thing – a single girl who had let herself down as your mother had is quite another.'

'So you maintained the pretence,' I said.

'What else could we do?' Grandmama demanded. 'No decent man would have given her so much as a second glance if he had known the truth.'

'But things did not work out as you planned,' I said.

'No. Your mother, I am afraid, was quite besotted with Raymond Voisey. I cannot imagine why, but he seemed to have some kind of hold over her. His sort do sometimes hold a fatal attraction for women, I know, but I had thought Sarah had more sense than to be taken in by him not just once, but twice. They must have kept in touch secretly, I imagine, for when Raymond's wife died he came seeking her out. And this time, very much against our wishes, she married him.'

'That goes to prove, then, that she must have truly loved

him,' I said, trying to find some comfort in all this. 'And he her.'

Grandmama sniffed. From her pursed-up expression I could tell she did not think so – or at any rate, did not want to think so.

'She'd be alive today if she had not married that man,' she said bitterly.

'But she died in childbirth – and the baby too,' I said before I took Grandmama's meaning.

'Exactly! He should have known better than to get her in such a condition!' It was a measure of the strength of Grandmama's feelings that she should say such a thing; under normal circumstances she would, I feel sure, have considered it indelicate. 'She was never strong after you were born. She should not have had another child.'

I bit my lip as the awful memories of the day Mama had died came flooding back.

I, of course, had been kept downstairs, as far as possible from the bedroom where she was confined. But there had been no escaping the terrible screams and moans that had filled the house. I had been so distressed, so afraid, covering my ears and praying for them to stop. But when they did it was because Mama was beyond screaming and moaning. She was dead, and the silence was even more frightening than the screams had been.

I had some vague idea too that something dreadful had occurred before Mama had gone into labour, hazy memories of running footsteps and people shouting at one another, which had alarmed me. But that had all been forgotten in the numbing grief of Mama's death.

With an effort I pushed aside the distressing memories which had haunted my nightmares for months – years – afterwards.

'I still don't understand why they kept the truth from me,' I said. 'Why would they do that if Raymond was really my father?'

'No doubt they were still ashamed of their affair,' Grandmama said. 'No doubt they did not want the children of his first marriage to know he had been unfaithful to their mother. And they preferred to maintain the pretence that

Sarah was a respectable widow. If you had known, so would everyone else, I dare say. I have to admit I am surprised Raymond Voisey gave a fig about such things, but your Mama, hopefully, still clung to a little modesty.'

I stood silent, too overwhelmed by all this to know what to say.

'Anyway.' Grandmama became brisk suddenly. 'I don't want you to go anywhere near Bristol, Imogen. The Voiseys have brought nothing but trouble to our family. And Miles Voisey, no doubt, is as unprincipled as his father. Whatever he has tried to persuade you to do, no good will come of it. Now please, say you will forget all about it like a good girl.'

Suddenly I was thinking again of the business of Robert Linwood, and all the other times my grandparents had controlled my life, keeping me here like a bird in a cage.

Now, of course, I knew the reason why. But that did not make it right. However they worried about me, I must be free to try my wings. I was not a child any more, I was a woman. I was not my mother, I was me. And on this occasion, I was not going to bow to their wishes.

If anything, all that Grandmama had told me had only made me more determined to continue with the plan which Miles had suggested and set in motion.

I had already wanted to help Rosalie because I loved and admired her. Now I had even more reason to do so. For Rosalie was not just the daughter of my stepfather. She was my own half-sister.

'I am sorry, Grandmama,' I said, 'I don't like going against your wishes and I can better understand your concern now. But it cannot change my mind. Whatever you say, this is something that I have to do.'

Three

Upton Stowey House looked exactly as I remembered it – the vast rambling structure of grey Mendip stone softened by the fading light of the sun, turreted and surrounded by parkland where deer skipped among the trees and peacocks strutted on the cobbled courtyard. A fairytale castle, I had thought it as a child. But now I wondered if it was in fact the home of an ogre. For those walls now hid from me the secret of Rosalie's disappearance, and perhaps her death.

Tired as I was from the long journey, first by train and then by way of the carriage that Brad Palmer had sent to meet me, I felt not purposeful, as I had when I had left Devon, but full of apprehension. How had I ever allowed Miles to convince me that I could carry this off, let alone learn anything useful? Brad Palmer would see through me in the blink of an eye, and if he really was as dangerous as Miles believed, then I was placing myself in peril of my life for no purpose at all.

But somehow I drew together the remnants of my courage. It was too late now to turn back. For Rosalie's sake I must steel myself to face whatever lay in wait for me beyond that imposing front door.

I allowed the coachman to help me down, hoping against hope that he would not notice that my hand was trembling. But even if he did, surely he would think it was no more than the understandable nervousness of a new governess, I told myself. And in any case, it was none of his business.

I waited whilst he lifted down my trunk and heaved it up the two broad stone steps. Then, taking a deep breath, I pulled hard on the bell-rope, setting the brass bell jangling.

Without warning, the door flew open. I had heard no one coming to answer it, and at once I saw the reason why.

A young girl stood in the doorway, dressed in a pretty sprigged muslin gown and soft slippers – her feet would have made no sound on the intricate mosaic tiles of the hall, and the door must have been on the latch, for she could never have reached to undo the bolts. Her small square face was serious, but her eyes were wide and sparkling with excitement – the same excitement that had brought her running at the sound of the jangling bell, I imagined.

'Hello,' she said. 'Are you Miss Black?'

I smiled. Apprehensive or not, I could not help it.

'Yes,' I said. 'And you must be Janine.'

She nodded, her eyes darting from my bonnet to my boots and back again.

'Oh good, you're quite young,' she said. 'I was afraid you might be old like Miss Carstairs. She was my governess before Rosalie came and she was . . .' She screwed up her nose and made a sound that expressed disgust.

I was almost laughing now in spite of my nervousness.

'Well, I am very glad you don't find me . . .' I wrinkled my nose, copying the way she had wrinkled hers and imitated the little puff of disgust.

'Miss Janine! Whatever are you doing? Come away in, now, or your father will have you on toast for his supper!'

A maid appeared in the doorway behind the child, a middle-aged woman as round and rosy as a russet apple.

'I'm so sorry, Miss,' she said to me. 'She had strict instructions to wait in her room like a young lady and leave me to answer the door. But she has a mind of her own, this one, as you'll soon find out. Come in, Miss, come in! And you, Janine – off your room with you.' The girl scampered off.

I did as she bid, and as she went to close the door behind me she saw my trunk lying on the step.

'Oh, lawks, has Perry left your things there? He should have waited and brought them inside, or taken them round to the back with him.' She stepped out, calling 'Arthur! Arthur!', but of course it was too late – the coachman had already pulled away, headed, no doubt, for the stables.

'Oh, I don't know!' She tossed her head impatiently. 'I don't know what he can be thinking of! Well, he'll just have to fetch it in when he's stabled the horses. It's not my place to be lugging heavy stuff about, even if I could, which I can't.'

Again I felt a smile twitch my lips, my nervousness evaporating yet more. An excited and expectant child who approved of me because she thought I was 'quite young', a chatterbox of a maid . . . so far this was not the daunting household I had steeled myself to expect.

'Come along, Miss, this way.'

She indicated one of the doors that led off the hall, which was, I noticed, hung with portraits and heavy with the scent of roses which had been arranged in a ewer on the hall dresser.

'Mr Palmer said to show you to the drawing room and he'll be with you shortly.'

And suddenly all my nervousness returned with a rush, threatening to cut off breath and suffocate me. A nerve jumped in my throat and once again I was overwhelmed by the audacity of what I was doing.

A little girl and a maid had no reason to question me or my right to be here. They accepted me uncritically, at face value.

Bradley Palmer would be quite another matter.

The drawing room was large, light and airy, furnished still in the style of a bygone age with elegant spindle-legged furniture, some gilt, some gleaming rosewood inlaid with intricate patterns of mosaic, and the golden drapes at the window reflected the warmth of the late afternoon sun. There was an ornate French clock on the mantle above the fireplace, and some ornaments, but sparsely arranged to show them to their advantage, not jumbled all together as the fashion seemed to be nowadays. And there were more roses in a crystal bowl atop a pretty little table, so that the scent of the hall came with me.

But to be truthful, I took little notice of the room on that first day. I was too busy rehearsing my lines for the part I was playing – and at the same time trying to compose myself so that my nervousness would not be immediately obvious.

How long I was there alone, pacing, making myself be still again, I do not know. It certainly seemed like a lifetime, but I suppose it could only have been a few minutes before the door opened and Bradley Palmer came into the room.

My first reaction was one of surprise. Brad Palmer did not look in the least like the ogre I had prepared myself to face. Though somewhat taller than average, he scarcely towered over me as I had imagined he might, and while his shoulders were broad and muscles rippled beneath the fine lawn of his shirt, he was not barrel-chested either. There were no side-whiskers on his angular jaw, his hair was mid-brown, not the jet-black I had pictured, and it was hard to imagine that those hazel eyes hid any dark secrets.

But, I reminded myself, the devil comes in many guises. And I should have known that Brad Palmer would be a physically pleasing man who no doubt knew how to charm a woman too. If he had not been, Rosalie would never have become involved with him at all, much less married him, especially given the rumours concerning the fate of his first wife and his reputation as a gambler and a chancer. The Rosalie I knew might very well be attracted by danger, but that danger would have to come in a seductive form.

'Miss Black,' he said. His voice was deep, but in no way threatening. 'You had a comfortable journey, I trust.'

'Thank you, yes.'

Again I felt a little surprised, but what had I expected? That he would begin by questioning my credentials without even the pretence of the niceties of social intercourse?

'I hear you have already met Janine,' he went on. 'And you will no doubt have formed the opinion that she is something of a handful.'

'Just childlike, from what I could see of it,' I said.

'Well, I'm sure you are more than used to putting scamps in their place,' he remarked.

At once I felt the guilty colour begin to rise in my face.

'I usually find they respond to a firm hand coupled with love and understanding,' I said, hoping that my reply sounded convincing, given that I had no experience whatever in dealing with children of Janine's age – or any age, come to that.

'A woman's touch. That is something, I am afraid, that has been lacking more often than not in Janine's upbringing,' he said. 'Her naughty ways have been the cause of the departure of more than one governess, and I only hope that you will make allowances for her and stay long enough to bring some stability into her life.'

'I thought I had been engaged for a trial period of a month,' I ventured.

'Such an arrangement seemed a sensible starting point.' Those hazel eyes seemed to be summing me up. 'If things work out well, I hope you will stay a good deal longer than that.'

As he was speaking something caught my eye – a brief glimpse of a fair head above the back of one of the armchairs. Brad Palmer's back was towards it and he had not seen. But though the owner of that head had bobbed down again out of sight again and though she made no sound to betray her presence I had no doubt as to whom it belonged.

Janine had not gone to her room as she had been told to. She had come into the drawing room where she knew her father would be greeting me and hidden behind the chair. No wonder she had darted off so readily when the maid had scolded her! She had been anxious to secrete herself before I, or her father, entered the room.

I felt a flash of amusement – and empathy with her curiosity. I recalled how once I had hidden behind the drapes when Mama and Raymond had visitors, steeling myself against moving a muscle and breathing as shallowly as I could manage whilst being very certain that the thudding of my heart would certainly give me away. Amazingly it had not, but I had had my comeuppance, for I had been trapped there for what seemed like hours, bored by a conversation that was all double-Dutch to me. Eventually, cramped and exhausted, I had fallen asleep and toppled over, falling through the drapes at the feet of the visitors. Raymond had boxed my ears and I had been put to bed in disgrace, where I cried myself to sleep at my humiliation.

I very much hoped Janine would escape a similar fate.

'We'll have a full discussion with regard to your duties tomorrow,' Brad Palmer was saying. 'I am sure you are too tired from your journey to want to go into detail at the moment. Would you care for a dish of tea and something to eat, or would you prefer to go straight to your room?'

'Tea would be very nice,' I said. 'The heat of the day and

the dust from the roads have made me very thirsty.'

I had been hoping that Brad Palmer would go to the kitchen to order the tea, as Grandmama would have done, giving me the opportunity to tell Janine I knew she was there and suggesting she escaped to her room before her father returned and found her, but I had forgotten that this was no ordinary dwelling but a grand house with all the conveniences that afforded. Brad Palmer merely crossed to where a bell-pull that hung in the alcove beside the fireplace and tugged on it. My heart came into my mouth. Would he see Janine when he turned back? From the way the chair was angled I felt sure she would be visible from that side of the room.

'So, how many people are there in the household?' I asked, trying to draw his eyes towards me and away from Janine's most inadequate hiding place.

To my relief the ploy worked. It was in my direction that he turned before returning to his previous position.

'Apart from the staff, just the three of us – myself, Janine, and my uncle.'

'Your uncle?' I queried.

I, of course, knew exactly who he meant, but 'Imogen Black' would not have known, and it was vital I should play my part convincingly.

'Sir Harry Palmer.' He paused, frowning. 'Oh, I do apologize. I've left you standing for far too long, Miss Black. Please, do sit down.'

'Thank you.' I perched on the edge of a velvet-covered chaise, and to my dismay Brad Palmer took a seat himself in the very chair behind which Janine was hiding. She would have to be very quiet indeed if she was to avoid detection!

At that moment the door opened and the rosy-cheeked maid came in.

'You rang, Mr Bradley, sir?'

'Yes. Could we have tea please, Dolly – and some kind of refreshment to go with it? Fruitcake, perhaps, or biscuits?'

'There's scones, sir, fresh out of the oven.' Dolly beamed. 'And clotted cream from the farm, and Cook's strawberry jam that was made this year from the crop in our own strawberry beds.'

'Thank you, Dolly, that would be splendid.'

'I thought you'd be pleased at that, sir. There's nothing quite like fresh-made strawberry jam—'

'As quickly as possible, Dolly, before Miss Black expires from lack of nourishment,' Brad chided her gently.

'Oh yes, sir. Of course, sir. I'll have them here before you can say knife!'

She bustled out. Brad gave a slight impatient shake of his head as if irritated by Dolly's irrepressible chatter.

'Now – where were we? Oh yes, my uncle. Upton Stowey belongs to him – the house, the estate, the coal mines – and half the village too. In his time he ran it all himself with the help of an agent – and very successfully. Now, unfortunately, he is in failing health and somewhat confused, and I have been forced to take responsibility.'

I nodded, but I could not help but remember what Miles had said about how Brad had arrived on the scene and wormed his way in. 'Forced to take responsibility' indeed! Why, it had no doubt been his intention all along! And when the time came, he would inherit everything, I supposed.

'My uncle always takes a rest during the afternoons, but you'll meet him at dinner,' Brad went on. 'I should warn you, though, that sometimes he can be a little confused. He wanders a good deal in the past and it can be disconcerting.' He paused. 'I explained in my letter, did I not, that Janine's mother died tragically when she was very young?'

'Yes,' I said, striving to keep my voice level. 'A dreadful thing.'

A tap on the door, and Dolly the maid entered with a tray of tea, a plate of scones, and dishes of thick yellow cream and strawberry jam. Though I had eaten nothing since breakfast and would, under normal circumstances, have been very hungry, I thought I would have difficulty in swallowing so much as a mouthful, so nervous was I. But I knew too that I must do my best to hide it and not behave in any way that was likely to arouse Brad Palmer's suspicions. So I accepted a plate, piled cream and jam on to a still-warm scone, and took a bite.

As I did so, I noticed the golden head bob up again briefly from behind the chair in which Brad was sitting. The delicious smell of scones, fresh from the oven, was almost too much for Janine, I guessed. But knowing she was unlikely to get one even if she revealed her presence, but rather would be sent to her room in disgrace, must have helped her to overcome the temptation, for she bobbed down again, quiet as a mouse.

'There is one other thing I should mention,' Brad Palmer said as the door closed again after the maid. 'You will no doubt hear from the staff or from Janine herself that I recently married again.'

Breath caught in my throat; I froze, the scone inches from my lips.

'It was, I am afraid, a bad mistake,' Brad continued, his tone cold now, and hard. 'I had thought that Janine needed a mother and that Rosalie would fill the gap in her life. I thought she was genuinely fond of the child and would provide—'

'A woman's touch,' I said, with some irony, echoing the words he himself had used earlier, though I could feel myself beginning to shake with anger.

'Precisely. I was, however, mistaken. Rosalie was, I regret to say, concerned only with herself.'

My fury was almost at boiling point now. How dare he speak so of my sister in an effort to explain her disappearance? The callousness, the bare-faced nerve of it, was breathtaking, and it was all I could do not to fly at him and accuse him of all Miles suspected. But somehow I controlled myself.

'She is no longer here at Upton Stowey, then?' I managed.

'She is not. Which is why I am employing you to do all the things for Janine that I had hoped she would do.' Still his voice was cold and hard.

'Where is she?' I asked, not expecting to learn anything so easily, but wanting to hear what he would say anyway.

His face was set, the deep lines between nose and mouth very pronounced.

'Forgive me for being blunt, Miss Black, but that is no concern of yours. I have mentioned Rosalie only because I feel sure you will hear of her existence from some other source. Rosalie is no longer here. That is all you need to know.'

'And if Janine asks me?' I pressed him boldly. 'What am I to tell her?'

'You will tell her to talk to me.'

So I had come up against a stone wall, just as Miles had. Brad Palmer had not the slightest intention of imparting the smallest nugget of information regarding Rosalie.

Another tap at the door – Dolly again.

'Sorry to interrupt, Mr Brad, sir, but Mr Winters is here wanting to see you. It's urgent business, he says. I did tell him that you were with the new governess, but it did no good. Said I was to tell you he had to see you right away.'

Brad Palmer's face registered annoyance.

'What do I pay the man for?' he muttered, but he rose anyway. 'Tell him I'll be with him in a moment, Dolly.' He glanced at me. 'Will you excuse me, Miss Black? Charles Winters is my estate manager. Clearly there is some urgent estate business I need to be appraised of.'

My ears had pricked up at the mention of the name, and my nerve-endings tingled. Charles Winters was the man Miles had suggested I could turn to if I needed assistance. Had he spoken to him about our plan? And was he as loyal to Rosalie as Miles believed – and as trustworthy? The man was after all an employee of Brad's, and lived in a house that was tied to his work. Supposing he had seen me arrive and come to denounce me to Brad?

'Do please finish your tea,' Brad said now. 'And when you are ready, ring the bell for Dolly. She will show you to your room and fetch a jug of hot water so that you can freshen up, if you wish, before dinner.'

His tone was clipped now; he was anxious to discover the reason for the estate manager's urgent summons. Clearly estate business was of far greater importance to him than acquainting himself with his daughter's new governess. He had not asked me a single question about myself, I realized, and though I was glad of it, I could not help but think it was an uncaring father indeed who would turn his daughter into the care of a stranger without some effort to find out something about them.

Not, of course, that he had the slightest idea that I was already alone with the little girl.

I waited a few moments after the door had closed behind him, then I said, 'It's safe for you to come out now, Janine.'

Silence. No movement from behind the chair. I began to wonder if I had imagined that she was there at all, but I knew I had not.

'You must be very cramped,' I said. 'And there's a scone with cream and jam waiting if you show yourself.'

I might have known the promise of such a delicious treat would be more than she could resist. The fair head appeared again, and a pair of blue eyes met mine over the back of the chair, wide and a little wary.

'It's all right,' I said. 'I don't bite.'

She crept out hesitantly, still watching me with that unwavering gaze.

'How did you know I was there?' she asked.

I suppressed the smile of amusement I could feel hovering about my lips.

'You might fool your father, but you don't fool me,' I informed her.

'Have you known all the time?' she asked.

'Yes,' I responded crisply. 'All the time.'

'And you didn't tell Papa?'

'I didn't see any need to – this time. That doesn't mean I won't tell him next time you do something you shouldn't. I shall decide according to how bad I think it is.'

'I'm never *really* bad,' she protested.

'No?' The smile was twitching my lips again. 'I'm sure you heard your father tell me that you had behaved disgracefully towards at least one of your former governesses.'

'Oh, that was just Miss Carstairs!' Janine said dismissively. 'She was so dull – and so *old*. It was fun to play tricks on her.'

'I don't suppose Miss Carstairs thought it was fun,' I said sternly. 'And I won't either. But neither will you get rid of me so easily.'

She pouted, her rosebud mouth thrust out and down at the corners.

'Be careful the wind doesn't change,' I warned her. 'If it does, you'll be stuck with that horrid expression. I wouldn't like that to be the second lesson you learn today.'

'The *second* lesson?' She could not contain her curiosity. 'What was the first?'

'That eavesdroppers never hear any good of themselves,' I told her, straight-faced. 'Now, do you want a scone before you go to your room – as you were supposed to do?'

She nodded eagerly and I held out the plate to her.

'Here you are then. And be careful of the crumbs, or we'll both be in trouble.'

She took a scone, carefully spreading it with jam and cream and nibbling it delicately before stuffing the remainder into her mouth so that both her cheeks and her eyes bulged.

'Off you go then,' I said, 'before Dolly comes in and finds you here when you are supposed to be upstairs.'

She sidled to the door, still looking at me with a slightly puzzled expression.

'And remember,' I warned her. 'You never know who is watching you.'

As she scuttled silently out, I felt a glimmer of satisfaction. Maybe dealing with Janine was the least of my worries, but at least I felt I had scored some points in the opening round between us.

With everything else that was on my mind, the last thing I wanted was a daily battle with her too. Perhaps now she would be less likely to lead me the merry dance she had clearly led her other governesses.

I certainly hoped so!

Four

L eft alone, I seized the opportunity to take stock of my surroundings, looking for anything that would give me a clue as to Rosalie's life here prior to her disappearance. Though it was far too soon to begin asking the sort of pertinent questions that might bring me answers, I thought that the more familiar I was with the household, the easier it would be for me to know where to begin looking.

The drawing room, though beautifully appointed, was, however, curiously impersonal. There were no books to give me any hint as to where Brad Palmer's interests lay, no pictures beyond a large oil portraying a rural scene, no newspapers or periodicals, no personal effects left lying about.

There was, however, a pretty little escritoire in an alcove beside the fireplace, the sort of escritoire that might be used by the lady of the house, since I felt sure Brad would have a large and serviceable desk in his study.

Had Rosalie used the escritoire? I could well imagine her sitting in this big sunny room to write letters or even a journal. And if so, had she left something in one of the drawers? So far I had not seen the slightest evidence that she had ever lived in the house at all, but there must be some, somewhere. Whatever had happened to her? If she really had run away she could only have taken a small valise containing the barest essentials with her, and if she had not . . . surely Brad Palmer would not have removed all her belongings with such alacrity? If he had done her harm, and wished to maintain the pretence that she had left of her own volition, then surely he would not wish to give the impression that he knew for a fact that she would not be coming back, nor sending for her belongings at some time in the future? Servants could be very astute about such things, and he would be anxious above all to avoid suspicion and speculative gossip.

My heart pounding, I crossed to the escritoire. Like everything else in the drawing room, it was perfectly tidy, no papers in the pigeon holes, nothing on the gleaming rosewood top but a crystal ink pot, stoppered, and two quill pens neatly lined up beside it.

Carefully I pulled out the first drawer: nothing of interest – just a blotter and writing paper and envelopes neatly stacked. I closed it softly and was just sliding out the second drawer when the drawing room door opened.

The sound of it made my heart lurch and my bones feel as if they were melting. To be caught snooping within an hour of entering the house was the very last thing I wanted! How on earth would I explain myself?

I spun round, my cheeks flaming, expecting to meet Brad's accusing gaze.

Instead I found myself face to face with Sir Harry Palmer.

There was no doubt whatsoever that it was he. The sidewhiskers, the brocade smoking jacket and small cap perched on his iron-grey hair were just the same as I remembered from when I had visited with Raymond when I was a little girl. But there the reality parted company with the memory. The Harry Palmer I had known then had been tall and broadly built, a most imposing figure of a man. This Harry Palmer was gaunt and stooped, the flesh of his face shrunken behind the still-luxuriant whiskers, eyes faded and sunken, skin an unhealthy greyish hue. Though both Miles and Brad had mentioned his declining health, yet still it was a shock to me to see him so.

I stood stock-still, my hand still incriminatingly upon the drawer handle of the escritoire, staring at him. And as I did so, a smile came over those haggard features, a smile that was somehow chilling, for it seemed to me to resemble the rictus grin of a death's-head, and he spoke.

His voice had changed just as his appearance had done. It no longer had the richness I remembered. Now it was the dry croak of a dead branch when a high wind threatens to rend it from the tree trunk to which it still clings. But it was what he said that shocked me most.

'Alexandra!' he said.

I was rendered speechless. I opened my mouth, but no words escaped.

'Alexandra!' he said again. 'You have come home!'

My head was spinning. Brad had warned me that his uncle could be confused and wander in the past, but it was most disconcerting that for some reason he thought that I was Brad's first wife, dead these four or five years. Somehow I found my voice.

'I am not Alexandra,' I said. 'I am Imogen . . .' – in the stress of the moment I almost said 'Imogen Voisey', but somehow I recovered myself in time – '. . . I am Imogen Black, engaged as governess to Janine.'

'Oh!' His smile faded, and I could not help thinking that puzzlement suited those haggard features much better than the grotesque expression of pleasure. 'Oh, I thought . . . Forgive me. Of course I can see now that I was mistaken.'

But he was still staring at me as if he had seen a ghost.

I took the opportunity to slide the drawer closed and move away from the escritoire – and whatever secrets it might conceal. They would have to wait for another day, although now I suspected that it had been Alexandra and not my dear Rosalie who had made use of it. Why else would Sir Harry have supposed the young woman he had surprised at it was the long-dead Alexandra?

'I am just enjoying a dish of tea and one of your cook's excellent scones,' I said inanely, in an attempt to rectify the awkwardness of the situation. 'Would you care for some?'

'Oh no . . . my appetite these days is not what it was. You eat them up, Alexandra. You always had a sweet tooth.'

'I am not Alexandra,' I reminded him.

'Oh, you already told me that, didn't you? Whatever is the matter with me? You must excuse me. It's just that . . . oh, I have hoped for so long that she would come home. Such a sweet girl. So beautiful. I miss her so much. Why doesn't she come home? Can you answer me that? Brad loves her so much, and little Janine . . . we all love her. I cannot imagine where she can be . . .'

I gave a small, helpless shake of my head. Clearly Sir Harry had quite forgotten that Alexandra was dead.

'The other one came, of course,' he went on. His voice was slightly less croaky now, as if speaking had loosened it a little, as oil will loosen a creaking hinge. 'But she was not Alexandra, oh dear me, no.'

'The other one?' I questioned.

'What was her name? Rose? Rosamund? No . . .'

'Rosalie?' I prompted.

'Yes, that's it, Rosalie. I didn't care for her. She was impatient with me. Yes, impatient. No, no, I didn't care for her at all.'

I bit my lip. I could well believe that my bold, bright sister had been impatient with the wanderings of this very confused old man. Patience had never been her strong suit. But at least he remembered her. He had not confused *her* with Alexandra.

'She's not here now, though,' I said, feeling a compulsion to talk of Rosalie, wondering even if I might be able to coax some information from him.

'No, she's not, and it's a good riddance,' he replied with surprising vehemence.

'She went away too,' I ventured. Though I could not help but feel a little guilty, for trying to elicit information from him was like interrogating an innocent child who could have no grasp of what I was about, at the same time I was not unaware of its advantages. And I felt safe, too, in trying to do so, for no doubt he would quickly forget our conversation had ever taken place, and even if he did not it was unlikely that anyone would believe it should he repeat what I had asked. They would put it down to the wanderings of a confused mine.

'She went away, yes,' he echoed. 'They all go away. I expect you will go away too.'

'Does it make Brad sad?' I asked, scarcely daring to breathe. 'Does he mind that they go away?'

Sir Harry laughed shortly, a dry cackle that reminded me again of the cracking bough.

'Brad? Oh, Brad cared nothing for her – for Rosa . . .

whatever you said her name was. I told him she was trouble, that one. But he was taken in by her, you see. Thought she'd make a good mother for Janine. He's too trusting where women are concerned. Good with business matters, but too trusting of women. I told him what she was up to – after the same thing as her father. He was behind it all, I shouldn't wonder, and I told Brad so. But he wouldn't have it. Didn't believe me. He should have listened to me. Ah well, she's gone now. And good riddance.'

He was simply rambling, I realized, frustrated. Perhaps his dislike of Rosalie was due to him harking back to his old falling-out with Raymond. Certainly the idea that she had been 'up to something' was absurd. But I decided my best chance of learning anything at all was to play along with it.

'So Brad sent her away when he realized you were right, did he?' I asked.

The faded eyes grew puzzled, intense almost, as if Sir Harry was trying very hard to remember what had taken place.

'Sent her away? Now, let me think . . .'

A tap at the door – and without waiting for a bidding, Dolly the maid came bustling in.

'I thought as how you might not like to ring the bell seeing as you've only just arrived, Miss . . .' She broke off, seeing her master standing there. 'Oh, Sir Harry, whatever are you doing up and about when you're supposed to be having your rest?' Without waiting for an answer, she turned back to me, garrulous as ever. 'He's supposed to have an afternoon nap, aren't you, sir? Else he gets himself in a terrible muddle. Well, he's in a muddle most of the time, but worse if he overtires himself. Mr Brad would certainly have something to say about it if he had been the one to find you down here, sir, and bothering the new young lady too, who's no doubt tired out from her long journey.'

She paused for breath, pressing her hand to her plump pouter-pigeon chest.

'I came to see, Miss, if you were ready to go up to your room, and what do I find? Now I'll be blowed, I don't know which of you I should see to first!'

'Please don't worry about me,' I said. 'I'm quite all right.'

'No, you'll be wanting to freshen up. I know I would if I'd been travelling all day! Sir Harry can sit here for a little while and have a nice dish of tea, can't you, sir?'

She took his arm, steering him towards a chair, and he let her, unresisting as a docile cow. She settled him down, plumping a cushion behind him before pouring some tea and placing the cup and saucer on a little table beside him.

'Now can you manage, sir? Just you drink that and I'll be back in a minute to see how you're getting on.' She turned to me. 'There's nice hot water ready in your room, and that rascal Perry has taken your trunk up for you. Come on now, while he's quiet.' She spoke almost as if Sir Harry were not there at all.

I could do nothing but follow her from the room, utterly bemused by the household I found myself in.

The room that had been allocated for my use was at the top of the house and under the eaves, I imagined, for the ceiling sloped down sharply above the bed and the windows were quite small and high up. But it was a pleasant room for all that, comfortably furnished in pink and with bright rag rugs on the polished board floor which would, I felt sure, feel cosy to my feet when winter came.

If I was still here by then, I thought. Surely I would not be? Surely it would not take so long for me to learn something of Rosalie's fate? Perhaps she would even have turned up safe and well. Oh, how wonderful that would be!

My trunk stood beneath the window and when I had eventually managed to get rid of the chatterbox Dolly I opened it up and took out some of my gowns. Then I hung them in the intricately-carved but narrow wardrobe that provided the only hanging space in the room. Clearly a governess was not expected to have an extensive array of clothes, I thought – just as well that I had brought only two or three day dresses and my silky Sunday best to wear to church on Sundays, and in case of a special evening occasion.

Neither had Dolly thought to unpack for me. Not that I wanted her to – I did not like the thought of some stranger handling my underwear and personal belongings, but for all that, it made clear my place in the household. I was no guest, but an employee just as she was.

47

Like the drawing room downstairs, this room of mine was quite impersonal. There was a china jug and basin on the little marble-topped washing stand and a towel hanging from the rail on the side. There were some little trinket pots on top of the dressing chest – which was also graced by a free-standing mirror – and a family of pottery rabbits on the narrow mantelshelf, but beyond that, there was no stamp of anyone's personality on the room.

But then there would not be, I reminded myself. It was a blank canvas by intent, so that I could dress it with my own things and make it feel like home. As if, under the circumstances, it ever could!

Uncomfortable suddenly, I dragged the little bedside chair over to the window, climbed upon it, and looked out.

The room was at the rear of the house; below me was a cobbled courtyard and outbuildings which I imagined must be the coach house and stables. All was quiet there, no sign whatever of activity, and somehow it increased my sense of isolation. If I should find myself in danger and need to escape, I could not do so from here. The little high-up window, the sheer drop to the courtyard below, the absence of stable lads and estate workers going about their business, all contributed towards making my room a virtual prison cell.

I gave myself a little shake. If I was careful I would have no need to escape. I would learn what I could and walk out of the front door as I had arrived, with my head held high. That was what I must hold on to.

No one had told me what time dinner would be, or how I was expected to know when it was ready, so when I had freshened up and changed into a clean gown I decided I would make my way downstairs.

And not before time, it seemed. As I made my way along the hall, intending to return to the drawing room, I heard voices coming from an open doorway on my left. I glanced in and saw a long table set with pristine white napery, silver and crystal. The speakers were out of my line of vision, but I thought that one of them sounded like Brad.

'Oh, there you are, Miss!' Dolly had come up behind me from the direction of the kitchens. 'I was just coming up to call you, but it seems you've saved my poor old legs.'

'Dinner is served then, is it?' I asked.

'Soon will be, Miss. Just you go in and make yourself at home. Mr Brad's there, and Sir Harry, God bless him. And there's a guest tonight too. I've set a place for Charles Winters. He's the estate manager here, you know, and when he and Mr Brad get to talking about the estate they can't seem to bear to break off. It's only to be hoped they won't keep on about pheasant chicks and the like until they bore you half to death.'

Her discourse could hardly have failed to attract Brad's attention; her constant chatter seemed to be conducted at a volume that could well have carried into the city of Bristol itself!

He appeared in the doorway dressed exactly as he had been before, in a fine lawn shirt, open at the neck, and dark trousers.

'Miss Black! Do come in. I apologize for neglecting you, but as Dolly has just been telling you, I have had business to discuss.'

Well, at least it did not seem that the discussion had been about me, I thought in some relief. I had been so afraid this Charles Winters might not be as trustworthy and loyal to Rosalie as Miles thought. But I was anxious now to meet the man who I had been told I could go to for help should it become necessary.

He was standing in front of the fireplace, a glass of wine in his hand. He was, perhaps, in his early thirties, and it seemed to me that he had something of a look of the Mediterranean about him. Luxuriant dark hair sprang above a broad forehead, his complexion was olive, his eyes dark as jet. Like Brad, he was casually dressed, with his shirt open at the neck, but his trousers were of a coarser fabric, more suited, I supposed, to the line of work he was engaged in. Clearly, though, for all the fine crystal and napery of the table setting, the Palmers did not stand on ceremony – but then, if the two men had been working until they adjourned to the dining room, there would have been no opportunity to change for dinner. Without doubt Charles Winters was strikingly handsome and in every way a fine figure of a man.

Those dark eyes were on me, appraising, but giving me no clue as to whether he was aware of my true identity and reason for being here or not. This was a man who could keep a secret, I thought, unsettled by the intensity of his scrutiny, which appeared to see so much whilst revealing nothing at all.

So mesmerized by him was I that I was barely aware of anyone else in the room until a dusty-dry voice from behind me said: 'Alexandra! They told me I must have dreamed you were back! I told them I had not!'

I turned and saw Sir Harry seated in a chair behind the door. He was smiling again, that same grotesque death's-head smile that had the power to make my blood run cold.

'Uncle.' Brad's voice was patient enough, though I sensed a modicum of exasperation. 'You are mistaken. This is not Alexandra. It is Miss Black, Janine's new governess. Alexandra is dead. You know that.'

'Do I?' The faded eyes were puzzled. 'Oh dear, oh dear, how sad!' He gazed at me intently for a moment. 'Miss Black. I know you, don't I?'

'We met earlier,' I said. 'In the drawing room.'

'Oh yes. You gave me a dish of tea.' He looked remarkably pleased with himself suddenly for having remembered. 'You were kind, Miss Black.'

'Imogen, please,' I said gently. 'I should like it if you would call me Imogen.'

'Imogen,' he repeated, childlike.

'*Imogen*, Uncle,' Brad emphasized. 'Not Alexandra – *Imogen*.' He turned to me. 'You must excuse my uncle, Miss Black. He is somewhat forgetful, and tends to live in the past. Alexandra was my wife and he was very fond of her.'

I nodded, though I thought his phraseology a little strange. Given that he had recently married Rosalie I would have expected him to refer to Alexandra as his *first* wife.

'In fact, Mr Palmer, I would like it if you would call me Imogen too,' I said boldly. 'Miss Black sounds very daunting to me.'

I did not say, of course, that I was a little nervous too that I might not always find it easy to respond naturally to my assumed name!

'Very well – Imogen. Now, may I introduce you to Mr Charles Winters, my estate manager.'

Again I was struck by his phraseology. Whilst he might be in charge of running things, the estate was still undoubtedly Sir Harry's, and I would have expected him to refer to Charles Winters as *our* estate manager.

Charles Winters set his wine glass down on the mantelshelf and came towards me, smiling.

'Delighted to make your acquaintance! Though I, too, would prefer it if we dispensed with formality. Please call me Charles.'

He took my hand, and to my surprise, raised it to his lips. So, the impression of his Mediterranean origins did not stop with his appearance, I thought. It extended to his charm too. But the position of estate manager seemed an odd choice of career for such a man.

'Have you worked long for Sir Harry?' I asked, anxious to acquaint myself as far as possible with the situation in which I found myself.

He smiled again, his teeth gleaming like ivory in his swarthy face, but still he gave nothing away.

'Long enough!'

'I can say without fear of contradiction that the estate would be in a pretty mess if it weren't for Charles,' Brad said. 'Now, shall we sit down? I think Dolly is ready to serve. Imogen, if you would like to sit here . . .'

He pulled out a chair for me. I slipped into it, and as Charles Winters took the seat opposite me I felt his eyes once again scrutinizing me with a depth that was slightly disconcerting.

I wondered again just how much he knew about me – and was struck by another thought. If he really was in Miles's confidence, surely he would have been the best person to discover what had become of Rosalie? He must be party to all kinds of information that I had yet to learn. A new wave of misgiving washed over me.

How on earth could I, a stranger, hope to discover something that he could not? My only advantage was that I would have free access to the house, since I was living under its roof, whilst he did not. Though he worked for Brad and was a guest for dinner, tonight at least, he would not have the run of the place in the same way. It might well be that there were silent clues within these walls, for surely silent clues were the only ones that would yield information. Brad would never knowingly proffer any information that would incriminate him.

But there were others who might . . .

For all his seeming forgetfulness, there was always the possibility that Sir Harry knew something of what had occurred, and so, for all her innocent years, might Janine. Some seemingly unimportant fact that I could winkle out of one or the other of them might set me on a trail that would lead to Rosalie – or to her fate. Charles would never have the opportunity to talk to them as I would without Brad being present.

For the moment, though, I must be patient. I must play my part as well as I knew how, and do nothing to arouse Brad's suspicion. It was the only course of action open to me at present – and not only the hope of a solution to the mystery, but also my own safety depended upon it.

Five

I had thought I would find it difficult to sleep that night with so much on my mind and my nerves taut as a bowstring. But surprisingly I fell asleep almost as soon as my head touched the pillow. The day must, I suppose, have tired me out, the glass of wine I took with my dinner induced drowsiness, and the little bed under the eaves was every bit as comfortable as my own at home. There was something truly cosy about being tucked in there under the low, sloping ceiling – like being in a nest, I thought, as I pulled the covers up to my chin.

I must remember not to leap up too suddenly in the morning, I thought, for if I did I would surely crack my head and give myself a nasty shock.

Once during the night I woke and lay listening to the sounds of an unfamiliar house as it sleeps – a soft pattering that might have been birds in the roof-space above the low ceiling, the creak of boards settling like ghostly footsteps in the corridor outside my door, a wind that had sprung up rattling the window panes and moaning a little in the eaves. But I was too drowsy to feel afraid, and in any case, what was there to fear – for the moment, at any rate. I had been accepted as Imogen Black, the new governess, and as yet I had done nothing to arouse the slightest suspicion. I needed my sleep so as to be fresh and sharp for tomorrow – and sleep I did, until dawn light crept in at the high-up little windows and woke me.

Though it was still early, I got up then, for I did not want to drift off again, oversleep myself, and be thought a lazy good-for-nothing on my very first full day. I poured some water from the jug into the basin on the washing stand and washed my face and the sleep from my eyes, and the cold water refreshed me as a jug of hot water would never have done. Then I brushed my hair and fastened it up into the neat fashion that I thought suitable for a governess, buttoned myself into my plainest gown – grey calico with neat white collar and cuffs – and surveyed myself in the mirror.

Yes, that would do nicely! At least this morning Sir Harry would be unlikely to mistake me for Alexandra – unless he was half-blind as well as confused, for I could not believe that Brad's wife, the lady of the house, could ever have looked so stern and forbidding.

I opened the door and peeked out. All was quiet and deserted. There were two other doors on this little branching corridor, and I wondered what the rooms beyond them were used for. Certainly the family would have their own rooms on the floor below, where there was more light and space, and the servants' quarters were, I imagined, in the attics of the wing that housed the kitchens. Curious as I was to learn everything I could about the house and its occupants, I was almost tempted to try those closed doors, but I resisted the impulse. I must be sure of my ground before doing anything so reckless – supposing I was wrong about the family's sleeping arrangement, and opened a door only to find the room occupied!

I made my way down to the main landing, from both ends of which stairs led down – the main staircase to the hall, and a narrow, dog-legged one with bare boards, to the kitchens.

I would take the one to the kitchens, I decided. The household staff would certainly be at work by now – indeed, I could hear sounds of life wafting up – and in any case, it seemed more fitting to my position.

Then, quite suddenly, I changed my mind. I was fairly certain none of the members of the family were up and about yet and it occurred to me that early in the morning might be the best chance I would have of taking another peek at the escritoire in the drawing room.

Moving decisively, so that if I was observed no one could accuse me of creeping about, I made my way to the main staircase and down to the drawing room.

The door was ajar, and to my dismay a maid was there,

busily flicking dust from the ornaments with a feather duster. She was quite young and slightly built, and she glanced at me shyly.

'Good morning, Miss.'

'Good morning.' I decided to behave as if I had every right to be here – which I suppose I did, since I was now a member of the household. 'I am Imogen Black, Janine's new governess. What is your name?'

'Margaret,' she said, still busying herself with her work.

'It looks as if it will be another beautiful day,' I ventured.

'Yes.' She was casting me sidelong glances. 'I've almost finished in here, Miss. Then I'll leave you in peace.'

'Oh, don't mind me.' This girl was certainly not a chatterbox like Dolly, I thought, and decided upon a bold plan of action. 'I need some paper and pens to prepare some lessons for Janine. I thought I might find some here.'

I crossed to the escritoire and pulled open, not the first drawer, which I already knew contained nothing but writing paper and envelopes, but the second. Margaret was plumping cushions now and straightening drapes, taking no notice of me at all.

I slid the drawer open wide – and felt breath catch in my throat.

An envelope lay there on the top of another stack of paper – and the bold script upon it leapt up, shocking me, for I could scarcely believe my eyes. The envelope was addressed to Miles – and the hand that had written it was, I felt certain, Rosalie's! I had always admired her flowing style – she had been quite an artist, always drawing and painting, and whilst I had struggled to make my childish writing neat and even in size, hers had been like another work of art. I had been reminded of it every year when she wrote to send good wishes on my birthday, and thought that for all my efforts I would never be able to make an envelope look as distinguished and beautiful as Rosalie could.

Now I looked at the envelope lying there in the drawer and was in no doubt whatever that it was her handiwork. She must have been writing to Miles shortly before her disappearance, and the letter had never been despatched – perhaps because something terrible had happened to her. But that I should have happened on it so soon after my arrival was almost beyond belief. It was almost as if fate was on my side and had guided me to the escritoire.

All these thoughts rushed through my brain in a hazy flood as I stared mesmerized at the envelope. Could it be that the contents would give me some clue to explain her disappearance? But I could not read it here, with the maid in the room, and the risk of someone else walking in at any moment.

Holding my breath, I pulled a sheaf of paper from the bottom of the pile, placed it on top of the envelope, and then lifted the whole lot out with the envelope concealed in the middle.

'This should do nicely,' I said, striving to keep my voice level.

I closed the drawer, and clutching the bundle of paper to my chest, started across the room. Margaret took no notice of me whatsoever.

A sense of urgency was prickling my skin, making me want to run for the sanctuary of my little room under the eaves. I thought it unlikely that anyone would suspect me of having the letter – or even of being aware of its existence. After all, if Brad had known it was there he would surely have either despatched it to Miles or destroyed it. But I was anxious all the same to conceal it somewhere safe until such time as I could open it and investigate its contents without fear of interruption.

To my dismay, however, as I reached the staircase I saw Brad coming down. My guilty heart was beating so hard I felt sure I would give myself away, but somehow I managed to smile a greeting.

'Good morning.'

'Good morning, Imogen.' He returned my smile, and I was surprised at the way it transformed his face. Yesterday he had looked so dour and stern; now, though the creases between nose and mouth deepened and crinkles formed around his eyes, he looked not only approachable, but very attractive, and I had a glimpse of what had drawn Rosalie into his clutches.

'You're up and about early,' he said. 'I thought after the tiring day you endured yesterday you might have slept late.'

'I'm always an early riser,' I said, my voice surprisingly steady. I was horribly aware of the letter concealed in the stack of paper clutched to my chest. There was no way he could fail to see the stack, and would almost certainly be able to guess where it had come from, so it seemed to me the best course of action was to mention it, casually and openly, as if I had nothing to hide, and hope against hope that he had indeed been unaware of the existence and location of the letter.

'I wanted to begin preparing some lessons for Janine,' I said. 'I found some paper in the escritoire in the drawing room and helped myself to it. I hope you have no objection.'

I held my breath waiting for his reply, but to my intense relief I saw no flicker of adverse reaction cross his face.

'Of course not,' he said. 'Your industry is most commendable, Imogen. I only hope you will find Janine as eager to do her work, but somehow I doubt it. She's more interested in playing in the garden than she is in her books, I'm afraid.'

'Most children are.' Had I not been so nervous I might have been amused at my own impudence, for all the world as if I were quite used to the ways of children. 'I shall do my best to make her lessons interesting.'

'I'm sure you will.' He descended the last couple of stairs and I moved towards the staircase, anxious to get to my room and hide the letter I had purloined.

But just as I was on the point of making my escape, he stopped and turned back to me.

'Perhaps this would be a good opportunity to discuss your duties. We can talk over a cup of coffee – or chocolate, if you would prefer.'

My heart sank, but I did not have so much as the beginnings of an excuse as to why I should not do as he asked.

'Yes, of course,' I said faintly.

'We'll go to the breakfast room,' he said. 'It's pleasant there in the mornings – it catches the early sun.'

He led the way along the hall towards the rear of the house, opened a door, and stood aside for me to enter.

The room I found myself in was pleasant indeed, smaller and more intimate by far than the vast dining room, and comfortably furnished. It must face east, I realized, for the sun was streaming in at the windows and filling the room with golden light.

'I'll arrange for our drinks,' he said. 'What would you like?'

'Oh, chocolate would be very nice.'

Whilst he went to the kitchen to order it, I sat myself down in a chintz-covered easy chair, one of a pair arranged on either side of the window. Perhaps it would have appeared more businesslike to sit up to the table, but I was still uncomfortably aware of what was hidden in my bundle of paper. To set the paper down on the table as I would be forced to would be to expose it unnecessarily; at least in the easy chair I could keep it safely in my lap.

Thankfully, when he returned, Brad took the chair opposite me without comment.

'As I explained to you yesterday, my first concern is that Janine should have some continuity in her life,' he began. 'I want her to learn her lessons, of course – I'm not one of those fathers who think it's only necessary for their daughters to learn how to stitch a sampler or arrange a vase of flowers in order to set them up for life. I happen to believe it's as important for a girl as a boy to be able to read and write and do sums. I want Janine to discover the pleasure that can be found between the covers of a good book, and to be able to write a letter that is not only legible, but a pleasure to receive.'

Rosalie's letter seemed to me to be burning a hole in the paper that concealed it. She had certainly fulfilled those criteria . . .

'But there's plenty of time for that,' he continued, quite unaware of my discomfort and my sly thoughts. 'First and foremost, I should like you to endeavour to achieve some rapport with Janine. She has long lacked a lasting relationship with a woman. Her mother, as I mentioned, died when Janine was so young that she barely remembers her, if at all, and since then there have been a succession of governesses.'

And Rosalie, I added silently, but of course I did not speak the thought aloud. I could not afford to be controversial . . . yet.

'She is probably closer to Dolly than anyone else,' Bart went on. 'Dolly has been nursemaid to her ever since Alexandra died, and she is very fond of Janine. But it's not enough, and good-hearted woman though she is, I don't want Janine to take her as a role model. Besides, she has her household duties to attend to and could not spend time with her even if I thought it suitable. Janine is a solitary child, with no brothers or sisters to play with, nor ever likely to have, no cousins to visit with, and Upton Stowey is quite isolated, particularly in winter. If you can go some way to filling the gap in her life, then I shall be forever in your debt. And I think that the lessons will follow naturally and be more readily acceptable to her.'

'I see,' I said, but his words were burning into my brain. *She has no brothers or sisters, nor likely to have . . .* That did not sound as if he expected Rosalie to return, for she was a young woman still, with many childbearing years ahead of her. Surely when he wed her it would have been in the expectation of increasing the size of his family, and heaven only knew, children almost certainly came along in any marriage, whether they were wanted or not.

But of course his words were not in themselves an admission of guilt, that he knew for a fact that Rosalie had passed beyond ever being able to bear a child. It could simply be that even if she did return he would refuse to take her back as his wife. Certainly yesterday he had referred to the marriage as 'a bad mistake'.

'So you would prefer it if we took some time to get to know one another before beginning formal lessons,' I said.

'Precisely.'

The chocolate arrived, dark and steaming and tempting. Somehow I juggled it on to the stack of paper on my lap, hoping Brad would not expect me to return it to the drawer if we were not to have any lessons today. But if such a thought crossed his mind, he made no mention of it.

'It will give you the opportunity to acquaint yourself with your surroundings, too,' he said, sipping his own chocolate. 'The house and the grounds are quite extensive and can be a little daunting if you do not know your way around. Take time to explore – let Janine show you her favourite places, and I think you'll like what you see.' He smiled, that same smile that had so transformed his face when we had first met on the staircase, and again I was struck by how attractive it made him. 'At least, I hope you'll like it,' he said. 'I very much hope you will like it enough to stay for a good long while.'

I bit my lip and for the first time felt a prickle of guilt at the deception I was practising on him – and on Janine. None of this was her fault, she was just an innocent child, and a lonely one too, who had no mother and no siblings to comfort her. It may well be that I would bring more wretchedness into her life, not only betraying her myself but also depriving her of the her one stable influence – her father – if what I was able to uncover revealed him as the murderer Miles believed him to be. What would it do to her if he was tried, found guilty and hanged, not for the killing of a stranger, but her own mother?

The sweet hot chocolate suddenly tasted bitter on my tongue. But with an effort, I pushed my misgivings aside. I was here to try to learn what had happened to my sister and I must not allow myself to be sidetracked from my quest. Rosalie's life might be at stake, and if I was too late to save her, then I must obtain justice for her so that her soul could rest in peace.

If things turned out badly it was not my fault, but Brad's. That was the reasoning I must cling to.

And cling to it I would.

All that long day I had no chance to examine the letter I had found in the escritoire. When we had finished our chocolate I did excuse myself and take it surreptitiously to my room, where I hid it in beneath the underwear I had stacked in a drawer. And I told myself I must put it out of my mind for the time being and concentrate on playing the part I had assumed. The letter might tell me nothing. It was vital I became accepted as a member of the household and did not behave in any way that might arouse suspicion.

I spent the time as Brad had suggested, getting to know Janine and exploring my surroundings. Janine proved a willing guide, showing me around the gardens and the park – or at least a little of it.

The gardens were extensive and beautifully laid out – a wide lawn to one side of the house, a rose garden where late blooms still hung heavy on the burgeoning bushes and filled the air with their haunting perfume, a vegetable garden where a man and a boy were hard at work, a lily pond full of darting fish. She led me through an orchard of apple, pear and plum trees, and begged me to pick some ripe plums, for she was not tall enough to reach them herself. I stretched up, and as soon as I touched the bough fruit cascaded about our ears, making her scream with delight. We retrieved two or three each and sat in the sun to eat them, though we had to beat a hasty retreat when the wasps began bothering us.

'You have to be careful,' Janine told me solemnly. 'You mustn't bite into a plum that's been lying on the ground, for there might be a wasp inside and it would sting your mouth.'

'That wouldn't be very nice,' I said.

'No, it would not!' She pulled the same face as she had done on my arrival yesterday to express her disgust with her last governess. 'I was stung last year on my arm and it really hurt. I had to run to the kitchen and ask Dolly to put the blue-bag on it.'

She paused, her eyes wide. 'Miss Carstairs was stung too – just here.' She pointed to her neck, just below her ear. 'She screamed and screamed. And her face swelled up like a bladder.' Then her solemn expression disintegrated and she began to giggle helplessly. 'She looked so funny!'

'You shouldn't laugh, Janine,' I told her sternly. 'You know how much it must have hurt if you were stung yourself.'

'Yes, but *I* didn't look funny!'

'Perhaps we'd better get right away from the plum trees,' I suggested. 'I don't want to be stung and have you laugh at *me*.'

'Oh, I wouldn't laugh at you,' she said, and I felt a warm glow of pleasure. I might have no experience of dealing with children, but Janine and I were getting along very well.

We left the orchard and walked along the drive to the edge of the park. The peacocks strutted, squawking at our approach, but there were no deer in evidence this morning. There were, however, two fine horses and a pony grazing in a paddock.

'That's Bracken,' Janine said, pointing. 'She's my pony.'

'You ride?' I asked.

'Oh yes, when Jem has time to teach me. Jem's the stable boy. Papa said that he would ride with me too, but he's always too busy, so it has to be Jem.'

'You are very lucky to be able to ride at all,' I said.

'Don't you ride?' she asked me, looking surprised.

'I'm afraid not. I never had the chance to learn,' I told her.

'Miss Carstairs didn't ride either,' Janine said. 'Rosalie did though.'

A nerve jumped in my throat at the mention of Rosalie's name.

'Did she?'

'Oh yes. Papa said she was a wonderful horsewoman – almost as good as my Mama. She could drive the carriage too, just like Mama. Sometimes she took me out in it. Rosalie could do *everything*.'

Yes, I almost said. *She could*. But of course I bit back the words. I was not supposed to be acquainted with Rosalie.

'Who was Rosalie?' I asked instead.

'She was my stepmama – but only for a little while. She went away. Papa said he expected it was too dull for her here. But I wish she hadn't gone. She was fun. Not like a stepmama at all. They're supposed to be wicked, aren't they? At least, they are in all my fairy stories. I was really sad when she went away.'

A lump formed in my throat. Janine, at least, had liked Rosalie. Janine, at least, missed her . . .

Through the trees I could see what looked like a cottage.

'Is that where Mr Winters lives?' I asked, for it suddenly seemed very important to me that I should know where to find him if the need arose. He was, after all, the one person who Miles had said I could rely on for help.

Janine, however, had little interest in Charles Winters.

'Yes . . .' But already her attention was elsewhere. 'There's a deer! It's just a baby – look!'

'So it is!' I said. Clearly I would gain no more information from Janine at the moment.

Brad must have gone out. We took luncheon with Sir Harry, who seemed a little less confused today – at least he managed not to call me Alexandra – though he did embark on a long and repetitive account of some long-ago event concerning her which he recounted as if it had occurred just this morning.

'She was just a little girl at the time, but pretty – oh, so pretty!' he said, smiling vaguely and indulgently. 'She had come to visit with her Papa. He was a good friend of mine, you know, very good. Whilst we were talking, Alex ran outside to play and lost herself in the grounds. We looked for her everywhere. Her Papa was frantic, naturally. We feared she might fall into the river, down in the dell. We searched high and low, all the estate workers we could muster, riding and walking and calling her name. And when we found her, do you know where she was? Why, in the spinney, fast asleep under a tree! Her Papa scolded her, of course, but he couldn't be cross with her for long. No one could be cross with her for long.' He paused, his eyes narrowing. 'You don't think she could be there now, do you? Should we look, do you think?'

'I don't think she's there now,' I said gently.

'No. Perhaps not. Oh dear, oh dear. Where can she have gone this time?'

Sir Harry was certainly obsessed with Alexandra, I thought. And it seemed he had known her since she was a little girl. Unless of course he was confused again and relating the story of something that had happened to Janine, thinking it had been Alexandra.

Confused or not, however, he ate a good lunch. When we had finished eating, Dolly, ever solicitous, bundled Sir Harry off for his afternoon nap, and Janine asked me to go with her to her room so that she could introduce me to her dolls.

As we crossed the hall, she pointed to a large portrait, framed in gilt.

'That's my Mama,' she explained. 'She was beautiful, wasn't she?'

'She was indeed,' I said, and it was no lie. Indeed, I could not begin to imagine why Harry should have mistaken me for her.

I was, I supposed, about the same age as she had been when the portrait was painted – perhaps on the occasion of her betrothal to Brad, or their marriage, and like mine, her skin and hair were fair. But there any similarity ended. Where her hair shone like burnished gold, I always considered mine to be more the colour of straw. And her features were the most perfect I had ever seen. Her chin and cheekbones were clearly defined, sculpted almost, her mouth a perfect bow, her nose small and straight, her eyes so dark a brown that they looked like polished mahogany. Beneath that perfect face her neck was swan-like and her shoulders creamy and beautifully shaped. The suggestion of a voluptuous décolletage was just visible above the sweeping neckline of a rich brown gown which, far from making her look dowdy, only served to enhance her fairness and the colour of her eyes, and lent her an air of sophistication.

'When I grow up I am going to be beautiful, just as she was,' Janine said, and somehow I did not doubt it.

She had her mother's looks, certainly; young as she was, I could already see the likeness. I only hoped that fate would treat her more kindly and she would not die so young, a tragic and mysterious death.

My opportunity to look at the letter I had purloined came when Dolly came to take Janine to have her tea.

'She always has it in the kitchen where I can keep an eye on her,' she said firmly when I offered to accompany Janine. 'Always has, and always will – leastways, until she's grown up enough to stay up and have dinner with her father. I'll bring you a dish of tea and some little fairy cakes, though, if you fancy a bite yourself.'

'No, it's quite all right, thank you,' I said.

For one thing, I still felt more than satisfied from luncheon, but more importantly, I thought that this was very likely the best chance I would have to peruse the letter.

Nervousness already prickling my skin, I climbed the stairs to my room and shut the door firmly behind me. Then

I retrieved the envelope from my underwear drawer and sat down upon the edge of the bed to open it.

The envelope was not sealed, but merely tucked in, as if Rosalie had not yet prepared it for despatch. I drew out two sheets of folded vellum and could see at once that the letter was, indeed, unfinished. The second sheet had but a few lines written upon it, and there was no signature beneath. But I needed no signature to know it was Rosalie who had been writing it and, for some reason, never completed her task. As if the beautifully-formed script was not autograph enough, the opening words left me in no doubt whatsoever.

'My dearest brother Miles.'

For just a moment I felt a pang of misgiving. The letter was, after all, meant for Miles and not for me. Perhaps I should seal the envelope with the letter unread and ask Charles Winters to deliver it to my brother. But in spite of Miles's assurances that Charles would help me if I needed it, I was still unsure as to just how much he knew. And besides . . .

I was the one in the house where some evil had surely been perpetrated. I needed to be in possession of any facts that might enlighten me as to Rosalie's fate. Taking a deep breath, I began to read.

My dearest brother Miles, *Rosalie had written.* Though it pains my heart and offends my pride, I cannot leave this letter unwritten. I must share with you the terrible secrets I have learned, or go mad with bearing them alone. And I admit to you now, most humbly, that you were right in warning me against marrying Bradley Palmer. Would that I had heeded your good counsel! But I was deluded, blinded by love, and I chose to ignore your advice, deny to myself that the man I loved hides a heart as black as Hades beneath his handsome exterior – if he has a heart at all!

Now, too late, I have learned the truth of how Alexandra died, and the misery she suffered for many years before, and I cannot help but feel that in the end that untimely and terrible demise might have come to her as a blessed release, an end to her torment.

There is so much I have learned, dear Miles, since becoming Brad's wife, things that have been kept from us and which you should know. I beg you to talk to Papa and ask him about his relationship with Sir Harry – the relationship that was terminated so abruptly when Bradley wormed his way into the household. What he may decide, at long last, to share with you, could be of vital importance to you. But it is for Papa, not me, to enlighten you.

To return to Alexandra. There is no doubt in my mind that Bradley was indeed responsible for her death. I intend to do everything in my power to obtain the evidence that will bring him to justice, and release me from my own torment.

I must stop now, for Brad has just ridden up the drive. But the moment I can safely do so, I will complete this letter and send it to you by way of our trusted friend Charles Winters.

There the letter ended. Clearly Rosalie had not felt it safe to continue just then. But the ink of the last words had smudged a little as if she had been crying and a tear had fallen on to them. And the sight of that smudge tore at my heart.

Six

I gazed at the letter. In spite of the warmth of the afternoon I was cold, and trembling from head to foot. What did it all mean? What had Rosalie learned that had turned her against Brad and convinced her that he was indeed responsible for his first wife's death? Why had she never completed the letter and sent it to Miles? What had happened to prevent her? Had it been that Brad had discovered she knew his secrets and made away with her before she could incriminate him? Clearly she had known she was taking a desperate risk in committing her knowledge to paper, but equally clearly Brad had not discovered it, or he would surely have destroyed it. Had she perhaps confronted him? That would be very like the bold, fearless Rosalie I knew. Or had she left of her own accord, either in fear of her life, or in pursuit of evidence to support what she had learned? Yet in either case, surely she would have made contact with Miles or with her father.

Thinking of Raymond reminded me of the other assertion contained in her letter – that there was something Miles should know concerning Raymond's relationship with Sir Harry and what had occurred to cause the rift between them.

'*I beg you to talk to Papa . . . What he may decide, at long last, to share with you, could be of vital importance to you . . .*'

What could she have meant – and did it have any bearing on what had happened to Alexandra – and Rosalie? *Relationship . . .* Did that imply a direct family connection, or simply refer to the friendship between the two men? Certainly, as I remembered it, they had once been very close.

I reread the letter, committing every word of it to memory, then replaced it in my underwear drawer, concealing it as thoroughly as I was able. The last thing I wanted was for anyone to discover it in my possession. Then I stood, nibbling on a fingernail and trying to decide upon my best course of action.

In itself the letter told us nothing new. If only Rosalie had spelled out what she had learned without preamble! And yet, at the same time, it told us everything – that Brad was indeed a man who was capable of wickedness. I was in no doubt that I must get the letter to Miles, or at least inform him of its contents, at the very earliest opportunity.

It seemed to me there were two choices open to me. The first was to take it to him myself, and hope he would know how best to proceed. But the only way I could do that was to announce that I was leaving Upton Stowey, and if I did that there would be no way back, no further opportunity to learn what it was that Rosalie had discovered, and I was not ready to give up so quickly. The answer to the puzzle was to be found here, within these walls, I felt certain.

The second option was to ask Charles Winters to act as a courier. Miles had told me he was trustworthy, Rosalie had referred to him as 'our dear friend' – why, then, was I reluctant to take him into my confidence? It was, I told myself, natural caution, since I barely knew him, and he had seemed so at ease with Brad. I must take Miles's word for it that he would assist me, and in all probability he already knew that I was no genuine governess but a spy in the camp. But all the same, I could not help feeling apprehensive at the thought of approaching him with proof of it. And a little anxious as to how I could do so without arousing suspicion.

I must wait my chance, I decided. An opportunity would present itself and when it did I must take it. In the meantime, I must hide my turmoil and continue to act in a way that would do nothing to arouse Brad's suspicion.

It was not going to be easy, but my own life might depend upon it.

The days passed uneventfully enough, and had it not been for the black cloud hanging over me and pervading my every thought, I might well have enjoyed them. Life here at Upton Stowey was so different to the dull existence that had been mine previously. Instead of the solitude I had grown used to whilst working on Grandpapa's manuscript, I was surrounded by others – Sir Harry, unsettling in his confusion, but rather sweet in spite of – or because of – it, a houseful of servants headed by the chatterbox Dolly, and Brad, who was unfailingly, deceptively pleasant. Most of all, there was Janine.

She was a delight – a little naughty, it was true, but mostly mischievous and great fun. From the time she came skipping downstairs in the mornings to the time she went to bed at night, she was a small ray of sunshine in an uncertain world.

On the second day we began working on some lessons, reading from some simple books which her previous governess had obtained for her, and which I suspected she knew off by heart. I encouraged her to start a journal as a way of practising her writing, and set her some sums, which she completed with ease. 'Old and dull' Miss Carstairs might have been, but I did not think she had been a bad teacher.

But without doubt, Janine's especial talent was artistic. She loved nothing better than to draw, pictures which I thought were very good indeed for a child of her age – or any age, come to that.

'That is far better than I could do!' I told her, looking in admiration of a picture of a deer skipping across a tree-dotted expanse of grass. Artistic ability was certainly not an attribute of mine – everything I tried to draw ended up looking the same, and quite unrecognizable. Janine lowered her eyes, intent on adding a lake to her drawing, but I saw that her cheeks were flushed pink with pride.

I did know something about nature, however, and when the sun shone and we went outside, I took the opportunity to begin teaching her about plants and flowers, insects and birds.

Once I caught sight of Charles Winters striding through the copse and my skin prickled with anticipation, wondering if my chance to speak to him had come. But I was not alone and neither was he – a young lad, one of the estate workers, was at his side, and I wondered despairingly how I could ever hope to even be able to tell him of my discovery, let alone pass him the letter for delivery to Miles. As for looking to him for assistance, should the need arise, I thought that the worst could happen and be well over and done with and he would be none the wiser. All very well for Miles to say he was close by; for all the contact I had with him, he might as well have been a million miles away. And his loyalty seemed to have been little use to Rosalie either.

On my fourth day at Upton Stowey it was arranged that Janine should have a riding lesson.

'Jem will be ready for you at eleven,' Brad told her at breakfast, adding, with a glance in my direction: 'If that will not disrupt your plans for her work today, Imogen?'

'No, of course not.'

It was not for me to object – and in any case, Janine was so clearly delighted it would have been churlish in the extreme to do so.

'Oh Papa, yes, yes!' she cried, hurling herself at him in a frenzy of excitement. 'Bracken's been missing me so – I know she has! I haven't been riding for ages.'

'Jem has had work to do,' Brad said, 'but he can be spared for an hour today.'

'Oh thank you, thank you! I love you, Papa!'

'And I have work to do too,' Brad said, disentangling himself from the plump little arms that were wound around his neck. 'Now just be sure you do as Jem tells you. I don't want to hear that you've gone galloping off like Dick Turpin.'

'I can't gallop, Papa!' she objected. 'Jem won't let me.'

'I should hope not. But I know how wilful you can be, Madam. You have to learn to walk before you can run.'

'Oh, I can *walk*. And trot.' She turned to me. 'You should see how well I rise, Imogen. I don't bump at all any more, do I, Papa?'

'No, you don't bump, and I expect Bracken is very grateful for it.' Brad got up. 'And no doubt you will be grateful for an hour's leisure, Imogen.'

'I think I shall go and watch Janine's lesson,' I said.

'Oh, we shan't be staying in the paddock.' Janine's tone was scathing. 'We shall go for a proper ride.'

'Well, I shall come and watch you set out, in that case,' I said. 'And maybe I shall catch a glimpse of this famous trot of yours.'

'Miss Carstairs didn't like me riding,' Janine confided when Brad had left the room. 'She said it was a waste of time, and not suitable for a young lady. But I expect she was just jealous because she couldn't ride.'

'Not like Rosalie.' I could not resist bringing my sister's name into the conversation. But this morning Janine refused to be drawn.

'No.' She grabbed my hand. 'Come with me – I'll show you my riding habit. It's blue velvet – and it's beautiful.'

Forced to concede defeat, I followed her to her room.

At a quarter to eleven the two of us went down to the paddock. Janine had been wearing her riding habit for the last two hours – after putting it on to show me, she had refused to take it off again.

The sun was high and I thought that velvet would be uncomfortably hot and sticky, but Janine was so proud of her outfit that I believe she would have roasted rather than admit it. Jem, a cheery, freckle-faced lad, had Bracken saddled and ready, and as he hoisted her up she sat tall and straight before giving me a little wave.

'Watch me, Imogen!'

'I'm watching,' I said.

Jem trotted her round the paddock and her rise was indeed most impressive. Then he mounted his own horse, a stocky piebald, and they set out into the park. I turned to go back to the house, and saw Charles Winters crossing the yard – alone.

Instantly a nerve leaped in my throat. This was the chance I had been waiting for! If I did not take it, who knew when it would come again? Taking my courage in both hands, I went towards him, and when I was near enough, called his name.

'Imogen!' He smiled pleasantly enough, but his demeanour gave me no hint as to whether he knew my secret or not. Oh, surely he must! And if not, he soon would . . .

'I need to speak to you,' I said, a small tremble creeping into my voice.

'Concerning what?' He was not making this easy for me. Perhaps, I thought, he was endeavouring to safeguard his own position.

'With regard to Rosalie,' I said.

'Ah.' His eyes narrowed, revealing a crack in his smooth veneer. Yet still he said nothing to help me.

'I have discovered a letter that she wrote to Miles,' I said, deciding against revealing that I was aware of its contents. 'I understand that you are a friend of his, and I wondered if you might deliver it to him for me.'

Charles expressed no surprise that I knew Miles – or Rosalie, come to that.

'A letter,' he echoed, looking at me intently. 'Rosalie wrote a letter to Miles before she disappeared.'

'Yes. Clearly she never had the chance to finish and despatch it . . .' I broke off, biting my lip as I realized I had inadvertently disclosed that I had indeed read it. 'But Miles should see it at the earliest opportunity,' I went on.

Charles hesitated for a moment, then: 'Where is the letter now?' he asked.

'I have concealed it in a drawer in my room, hidden by my clothing.' I felt my cheeks flush a little as I wondered if he would know I was referring to my undergarments. 'I could go and get it now – Janine is out riding with Jem.'

Again Charles hesitated. Then he said: 'It will be two or three days before I can get away to go to Bristol. Perhaps it would be best if you left it where it is until then.'

I was dismayed. 'Oh – I had been hoping . . . Couldn't you at least take it from me so that it will be in your possession when you are free to go to Bristol?'

'I'm out and about on estate business and I have nowhere to put it. If it should be lost . . .'

I bit my lip. True enough, Charles was wearing no jacket with convenient pockets. And there was always the danger that someone would see me pass it to him here in the open courtyard, too.

'The letter gives no clue as to Rosalie's whereabouts, I suppose?' he said.

I shook my head. 'None. But it says—'

'Yes.' His tone was grim. 'I can well imagine what it says. It confirms, no doubt, what Miles suspected all along.' His hands clenched. 'Oh, the silly, headstrong girl! I warned her, as Miles did, but she would heed no advice. She thought she could outsmart him, no doubt. But if this letter contains evidence of Brad's wickedness, it's vital it's kept in a safe place. I will get it from you and deliver it as soon as I can, then Miles can do with it what he thinks best. In the meantime . . . take care, Imogen.'

'I will,' I promised. 'But there is something else in the letter he should know. Something . . .' I broke off. A horse was coming across the park at full gallop. A chill of foreboding whispered across my skin as I recognized Jem on his piebald. As he reached us, he reined in, shouting to us.

'Where is Mr Brad?'

'In his office – or he was a moment ago,' Charles replied. 'What has happened?'

'It's Janine.' The stable lad's face was white and shocked, though a sheen of sweat shimmered over his skin. 'She's had a fall – a bad one. I must get Mr Brad! She must have help!'

Oh dear God! My blood seemed to turn to ice in my veins.

'Where is she?' I asked urgently.

'Over by the copse. She tried a jump. I shouted at her to stop, but she took no notice!'

I scarcely heard his garbled words, yet all too clearly I could picture headstrong, defiant little Janine ignoring his warning because she thought she knew better. And now . . .

Without waiting for anything, I picked up my skirts and began to run down the drive towards the copse, running and running until each breath was a sharp pain in my chest. As I flew on to the parkland my ankle turned on a rough sod and I stumbled, but I recovered myself and ran on, not knowing what I would find, but with only one thought in my mind – to reach the little girl who was my charge and whom, in such a short time, I had grown to care about so much.

She was lying motionless beside a fallen tree. I saw the flash of blue velvet against the green of the grass and headed towards it. Bracken, the pony, was standing nearby, cropping grass as if nothing untoward had happened at all.

I reached Janine and dropped to my knees beside her. Her eyes were closed, her face chalky pale, and for a terrible moment I thought she was dead.

'Oh Janine!' I leaned close and felt the faint flutter of breath on my cheek. She was alive then, thanks be to God, but utterly senseless. I could see no mark on her, and guessed she must have struck her head when she fell. I took her hand in mine, stroking it and whispering soothingly to her, though I did not think she could hear me.

'It will be all right, Janine. Your papa is coming. Everything will be all right.'

Running footsteps. I glanced up. Brad and Jem were running towards us across the parkland, Jem, young and fleet of foot, easily outstripping Brad. Jem, anxious and guilty, bent over Janine, but a moment later Brad reached us, caught Jem by the neck and thrust him aside with a violence that quite shocked me.

'Get away from my daughter! Haven't you done enough? I'll deal with you later!' His voice resonated with barely controlled fury and his face was contorted into an almost feral snarl. Then, as he dropped to his knees beside Janine, his expression changed to one of loving concern and his voice softened, ragged but tender. 'Oh, my little sweetheart, what have you done?'

'She's alive,' I whispered. 'I think she must have hit her head when she fell.'

Brad was running his hands over her now, checking first arms and legs, then shoulders, for any signs of injury.

'Come on, my brave girl,' he said softly. 'I think you can hear your papa, can you not, and you are just pretending to be asleep so as to frighten me. You've taken a nasty tumble, but we shall soon have you back at the house and everything will be perfectly fine.' He turned to me. 'Can you support her neck for me, Imogen?'

I slipped my arms beneath her head and very gently Brad lifted her so that she was cradled against him. Her arm flopped limply and I took it, holding her hand and keeping pace with Brad as he started back towards the house with slow, measured steps so as not to jolt her any more than he could help.

'Charles is riding for the doctor,' he said. 'We'll get her into the drawing room. Can you fetch a blanket to cover her? We must keep her warm.'

He laid Janine gently on the chaise and I hurried to do

his bidding. In the hallway I met Dolly, emerging from the kitchen and looking flustered.

'A blanket, Dolly, quickly,' I instructed. 'Miss Janine has taken a bad fall from her pony.'

'Oh my Lord!' Dolly's plump hands flew to her mouth. 'Oh, the lamb! Is she hurt bad?'

'I don't know,' I said tersely. 'Quickly now, Dolly.'

I waited whilst she fetched a blanket and pillows from the linen store, then took them from her and headed back to the drawing room, Dolly following and clucking like an anxious chicken. I handed a pillow to Brad and he eased it beneath her head, then took the blanket from me and tucked it tenderly around her small, still form.

'There, my darling, is that better?'

I hovered, not wanting to leave Janine, but feeling utterly useless. There was nothing I could do to help; Janine had her father beside her, and the bond between them was clear and complete.

As I stood there, looking on anxiously, I saw Janine's eyelids flicker. Just a tiny movement, so tiny I wondered if my desperate wishing for it had made me imagine it, but Brad had seen it too.

'Sweetheart!' he said, softly but urgently. 'Janine – can you hear me? It's Papa, my darling. I'm here, right beside you.'

'Papa . . .' It was just a whisper, muffled and thick, but it was the most welcome of sounds. Her eyelids flickered again, and her eyes opened.

'Oh, thank God!' I murmured.

'Just lie still now, sweetheart. Don't try to move.' Brad glanced up at me. 'A glass of water, perhaps, Imogen.'

I turned to go and fetch it but Dolly, fluttering in the doorway, intercepted me.

'I'll fetch it, Miss.' And she was gone, moving faster than I had ever seen her move before, a surprising rate considering her rotund shape.

She was back within moments, it seemed, and Brad moistened Janine's lips, then raised her enough for her to be able to take a little sip.

'That's my good girl. Oh Janine, fancy frightening your poor Papa so!'

'It was Bracken's fault.' Still her voice was thick, as if coming from between lips that refused to work properly.

'I don't believe that for one moment,' Brad said, but there was no censoriousness in his tone. 'If I did . . .' He broke off, and judging by the way he had turned on poor Jem, I was in no doubt as to what he had been going to say. If he believed Bracken to be an unsafe mount, he would have dealt with her in the most severe manner. I believe Janine knew it too, for with an effort she spoke again.

'No – it wasn't Bracken's fault, it was mine. I thought she could do it. I made her. I was in a hurry – I saw Rosalie and I wanted to get to her.'

My heart sank. Clearly she was confused and rambling.

'Sweetheart, you know that cannot be so,' Brad said.

'Well, I thought it was her . . . and I jumped . . . and . . . oh, Papa, don't be cross with Bracken. And don't be cross with me . . .'

'I'm not cross, sweetheart. Well, I am – with Jem – but mostly I am only relieved that you are talking to me and making your excuses. No more of them now! You must rest. The doctor will be here soon, and I'll be the one in trouble if I let you upset yourself. Do you want another sip of water?'

Janine closed her eyes briefly and screwed up her face, indicating that she did not.

'Lie down, then, sweetheart.'

'Don't go away, Papa.'

He took her hand. 'Don't worry. I am not going anywhere.'

The doctor came, examined Janine, and declared that she was most fortunate not to be more badly injured.

'She must be kept quiet, though,' he instructed. 'And watched for any signs of deterioration. She's been knocked senseless, and that can be dangerous.'

I bit my lip. Though he had taken Brad out into the hall to speak to him whilst I remained with Janine, I could hear quite clearly every word he was saying, and I thought Janine must be able to hear too.

When he had left, Brad re-entered the room looking serious.

'If you would like to take some time for yourself, Imogen,

you may as well do so,' he said. 'Janine will not be having lessons today.'

'No.' I smiled a little at the very idea. 'I could sit with her, though, if you would like me to.'

'Stay by all means,' Brad said, 'but I shall be sitting with her myself. Work, I am afraid, must go hang for today. My daughter comes first.'

Especially when I thought I had lost her . . . He did not say the words, but somehow I knew he was thinking them.

I took a seat in one of the armchairs, and as I sat there, watching them, it occurred to me that it was hard to believe that this loving father, caring so tenderly for his daughter, was the same monster who was responsible for the death of his first wife and the disappearance of his second. And with a shock, I realized that I did not want to believe it. This Brad, calm, strong, gentle, was a man I could so easily have fallen in love with . . .

With an effort I pulled myself together. What I was seeing now was the side of Brad that had deceived the shrewd Rosalie. But there was another side, a dark side, that he kept hidden from the world – a side I thought I might have glimpsed when he had turned on poor Jem. Though of course, he had been beside himself with anxiety, yet still there had been something terrifying in the display of barely controlled fury – the tone of his voice, the vicious curl of his lip, the violent manner in which he had pulled Jem away from Janine. It showed a man whose mood could turn ugly when his blood was roused – and heaven only knew what other dreadful traits were kept hidden beneath that cool exterior?

Even monsters could love – and show tenderness – towards their own, I reminded myself. That was what Brad was. A monster – a fiend in human form. And I must not forget it.

Seven

But for all my efforts, and in spite of everything, I could not forget the strange surge of emotion I had experienced as I watched Brad's tenderness towards Janine, nor the man I had glimpsed, caring, gentle and strong. It was something I had never expected to see and it coloured my image of him, pervasively yet so strongly that I could not look at him and be unaware of it.

I looked at him and was utterly confused by the way I was feeling. I could not find such an evil man attractive – I must not! It was madness! And yet I did. Whilst my head was telling me that I was allowing myself to be deluded and deceived just as Rosalie had been deluded and deceived, my foolish heart was trying to persuade me otherwise.

Was there some other explanation for Alexandra's death and Rosalie's disappearance that exonerated Brad? Was it possible that he was entirely innocent and the blame that attached to him was all a mistake? No – given the contents of Rosalie's letter to Miles, which still lay concealed beneath my undergarments, she had been in no doubt as to his guilt. To her horror she had learned something which had convinced her of that. But could she have been wrong? Had someone told her untruths concerning Alexandra's death – either deliberately or because they themselves believed it? Oh, I wanted so much for that to be the case! I could scarcely credit how much I wanted it.

The turmoil would not leave me, waking or sleeping. I simply could not get Brad out of my mind – or my senses. I cursed myself for a fool, and it made no difference. No difference at all. Somehow his very existence had become imprinted upon me at every level, so that the way I was feeling, somehow, unbelievably, occupied me even more than my mission.

And yet I knew I must persevere. I must not let go for an instant of my determination to learn the truth. In some ways it seemed to me to be more important than ever, and added a new impetus. One way or another I had to know the truth – either to clear Brad of the evil deeds which we believed he had perpetrated, or to know him beyond doubt for what he was, and scotch forever these treacherous emotions that were making me long to find him innocent.

It was important that Janine should rest and not exert herself in any way for a few days at the very least, the doctor had said, and naturally I was charged with ensuring she followed his instructions and keeping her amused. This was not an easy task, for the moment she felt better she could not understand why she should be required to lie on the chaise, and as is the case with most children of her age, I suppose, she became easily bored and frustrated by her enforced inactivity.

I read to her, and sang songs, but for all my efforts she was in a peevish ill-humour, which I supposed was a good sign, since if she had suffered any serious damage when she hit her head she would not have had the energy to be difficult. But I was unable to leave her side for more than a few minutes for fear she would get up to some mischief, and the hours passed slowly indeed.

Sometimes Sir Harry came and sat with us. He did not care for listening to me read, but when I sang he would join in in a dry tuneless cackle, and though he frequently forgot the words, the old songs set him off on his long rambling excursions into the past, reminiscing about his mother, who had sung this ditty to him, or a family party when they had gathered around the piano to join in with that one. It was strange indeed, I thought, that whilst he was so confused about the present, he seemed to have such perfect recall of events that had happened so many years ago.

Janine's accident set him off on more stories of Alex, too. As a child, she had come here to Upton Stowey to learn to ride, he said, because there was no suitable paddock at her own family home in the Leigh Woods in Bristol. When he said this, I thought he must be getting muddled again.

'It was the Voiseys who lived in the Leigh Woods,' I said, without even thinking about the fact that I was not supposed to be acquainted with the Voiseys. The moment the words were out, I froze in horror at what I had said, but mercifully Sir Harry did not appear to have noticed anything amiss.

'And the Suttons, too,' he said testily. 'You think I don't know where the Suttons lived? You think I'd muddle them up with the Voiseys? Pshaw! I know I'm getting old and forgetful, but I'd never make a mistake like that. I'm not quite in my dotage yet, however much you might like to think I am.'

'Of course I think no such thing,' I said hastily.

'Everybody that was anybody in Bristol lived in the Leigh Woods in those days,' he went on, his annoyance forgotten. 'It was quite the place – very fashionable. And near enough to the city to be convenient for business. Wouldn't like it myself. Rather be out here in the country, but then that's what I've always been used to. Alex loved it, too. She kept her pony here and came whenever she could. She had a fall once, too – gave us all a terrible scare. Knocked herself silly, just like Janine. Raymond was all for shooting the pony, but I told him, it wasn't the pony's fault, dammit.'

I was uncomfortably reminded of Brad's reaction to Janine's fall, and Janine herself grew very upset and agitated.

'He didn't shoot the poor pony, surely?' she exclaimed in horror.

''Twasn't his pony to shoot,' Sir Charles pointed out. 'Anyway, senseless she was – senseless! Had to lay up for days, just resting here on the chaise.'

I had begun to wonder if he was confused again and attributing Janine's accident to her mother, obsessed as he seemed to be with Alexandra, but given his reaction to my earlier comment I had no intention of saying so. Then, to my surprise, he went on:

'Twisted her ankle, too – and hurt her shoulder. We thought it was broken, but Raymond rode for the doctor and he put it right. Just pushed it back in, and poor little Alex too stunned to cry – only whimpered. She wasn't well enough to go home to Bristol for a week or more. Spent the whole time there on the chaise, looking for all the world like a china doll. Beautiful. So beautiful . . .'

So it seemed the accident really had happened, I thought. And Raymond had been here. My skin prickled a little as I remembered the passage in Rosalie's letter which had referred to the relationship between Raymond and Sir Harry, and wondered if I might be able to learn what she had meant from Sir Harry himself. Though the two men had fallen out and not had any contact for years, Sir Harry had spoken Raymond's name without rancour. Perhaps he had forgotten what had gone wrong, and remembered only the friendship they had once shared.

'Raymond was here, then, when Alexandra had her accident,' I said, leading him gently and hoping he would not notice that by rights I should have had no idea who Raymond was.

'Yes . . . yes. He brought her over, as often as not.' Sir Harry sounded tetchy again, as if, contrary to my fears, he thought that I should already be in possession of the facts. 'They were neighbours, as near as dammit, and her father was always too busy with his banking business. As for her mother . . . well, she was a sickly soul, always taking to her bed and complaining of being poorly. She outlived Roger, her husband, though, and dear Alex too – but then these creaking gates often do.' He paused, reflecting, then went on: 'Alex was an only child. She didn't have companions – or a lot of fun, except when she came here. That was the root of the trouble, I think. She was lonely, and looking for excitement. Oh dear, dear. Dearie, dearie me.'

'The root of the trouble?' I repeated. 'What trouble?'

'With poor Alex of course! None of it would ever have happened if she hadn't been lonely. And then again, maybe it would. He was too fond of her. Too fond by far . . .'

I leaned forward, all my senses prickling. There was some story here, and I was on the point of learning it. And somehow, it seemed, Raymond, my stepfather – no, my *father*, I reminded myself – had a part in it. Was this what Rosalie had referred to in her letter? I had to know!

'Tell me what happened,' I urged.

'Oh, it was such a terrible thing . . .' Sir Harry's face crumpled suddenly, and at that very moment, Janine decided she had had enough.

81

'I want a story,' she demanded petulantly. 'Read me a story, Imogen.'

'In a minute.'

'No, now. I want a story *now*.' She thrust the book into my hand. 'This one. Read to me, Imogen, or I'll ...' She made an attempt to swing her legs off the chaise.

'You will stay where you are, Miss,' I said, but I knew that whatever Sir Harry had been on the point of saying, I would not learn it now.

And perhaps that was just as well. Perhaps it was not something Janine should hear. But all the same I burned with frustration as I began to read and Sir Harry shuffled out of the room. All I could hope for was that another opportunity would soon present itself when I could try to winkle the story out of the old man. Confused as he might be where the present was concerned, his recall of the past seemed unimpaired. If only I could choose my moment carefully and lead him along, I might well learn a great deal of the truth from him. In the meantime ... I would keep my eyes and ears open, and my mind too.

And still my treacherous heart hoped desperately that what I learned would, by some miracle, exonerate Brad from blame for the terrible things which had happened in this house.

With my new-found confidence in the habits of the household, I dared to explore the other rooms that were situated on the same floor as mine. But they yielded nothing that I could see at the cursory glance I was able to give them. One of the doors opened into a box room that was clearly used for storage – travelling trunks, riding boots that had seen better days but had been kept anyway, an unwieldy old camera and tripod, and a pile of hat boxes. All were covered with a thick layer of dust and had clearly not been disturbed for months, if not years. It was really much as I had expected, but I decided that if the opportunity presented itself, I would investigate the contents of the trunks and boxes a little more closely. It was yet possible I might find memorabilia stored there that might add to my so-far scant knowledge.

The other door was locked. That did puzzle me a little, for in my experience doors within a house were rarely locked, except on the inside if the occupant wanted a little privacy. I tried it two or three times, wondering if the catch had merely grown stiff and rusty from disuse, but made no impression on it. The knob turned but the door remained firmly shut. There was no more to be learned here for the moment. I must look for other ways to further my investigation.

It had occurred to me that Dolly, the maid, might well prove a good source of information. She had, it seemed, been employed here for years, and I rather thought there was little that escaped the attention of servants. The best of them liked nothing more than a tasty morsel of gossip, the worst were prone to snooping. And Dolly was nothing if not a chatterbox – pumping her should not be too difficult.

I was not often alone in her company, however. Most of my waking hours were spent with Janine, and I had already decided the revelations I might elicit might not be fit for her ears, even if Dolly, garrulous as she was, could be persuaded to speak in her company. Besides this, I did not want her to relay to her father the fact that I had been asking questions.

My chance came at last, however, when I went to the kitchen to fetch a cup of beef tea for Janine. Cook was in the scullery, washing vegetables, and Dolly was alone, busying herself with polishing silver. It was, I thought, quite a menial task for a servant as senior as Dolly, but she was attacking it with vigour and I thought that perhaps she considered keeping it nice her special responsibility.

'It's so sad for Janine that she has no mother, especially when something like this happens,' I said by way of tentative introduction. 'No matter how much the rest of us might care for her and do our best, there's no substitute for a mother's love.'

'That's true enough,' Dolly agreed, rubbing vigorously on a miniature picture frame. 'I remember as clear as yesterday when I had the whooping cough, though I was only a mite. Nobody but my ma would do – if she so much as left my side, I couldn't be consoled. All I wanted was to have her there beside my bed day and night.'

This was not the turn I had intended the conversation to take.

'I suppose Rosalie was the closest Janine has come to

having a mother since Alexandra died,' I said, steering it back again.

'That's what Mr Brad hoped for when he married her, no doubt. And they got along well enough, she and Janine. But truth to tell, I'm not sure how much good she'd have been at a time like this. She wasn't the one to have the patience to sit beside a sick bed. She wanted to be up and doing, did Mistress Rosalie. Always on the go, she was, lively as if she'd sat herself down on a nest of ants.'

Under other circumstances I might have been amused by Dolly's way of describing Rosalie's demeanour, which matched all too well with my own memories of her. Now, however, I was anxious only to elicit as much information as possible in the short time available to me.

'It was no shock, then, when she went away,' I said, using Dolly's own comment to help me probe further. 'She couldn't settle here in the country, I suppose.'

'Indeed it was a shock!' Dolly retorted. 'She'd settled in very well – too well, in some ways.' Her lips tightened, and I suspected Rosalie had upset the apple cart in some way, interfering with a routine Dolly had become set in over the years. 'None of us thought for a minute ... well, she was here one minute and gone the next. Fair moonstruck we were over it. And to go off in the middle of the night, too!'

'She left in the middle of the night?' I repeated, stunned by this.

'In the middle of the night. Dark as Hades, it must have been. She was still here at ten o'clock – I saw her with my own eyes. She and Mr Brad were in the drawing room together. He rang for some water to go with his whisky – he always has a whisky before retiring – and they were both there together, just as usual. I went to bed then – I have to be up first thing, and I need my sleep. When we came down in the morning the kitchen door was off the latch. I had words with Margaret about it – I thought she'd forgot to lock it, and I told her – anybody could have got in and ransacked the house or murdered us in our beds. Then when Mistress Rosalie didn't come down for breakfast I went up to see if she'd overslept, or been taken poorly, and there was no hide nor hair of her. Her bed hadn't been slept in and she was gone. Well, I didn't know what to make of it, I can tell you.'

'Did she and Brad not share a bed then?' I asked before I could stop myself, and promptly blushed at my indelicacy.

Dolly, however, seemed unperturbed. 'Oh no, no. They had their own rooms, right from the day they wed.' She set down the picture frame and reached for a salt cellar. ''Twas different with Mistress Alex, of course. They were never parted for a night. Though gentlefolk often do sleep apart, they never did. And his bed was Mistress Alex's place, if you ask me. He wouldn't have felt right taking another wife into it.' She sniffed, wiping her nose on the back of her hand.

'So nobody heard her go,' I said.

'Nothing we thought anything of at the time. Margaret said afterwards she thought she'd heard a horse on the drive, but she couldn't swear to it. Busy as we are in the day, we sleep like the dead at night. But somebody must have come for her. She couldn't have just walked out on her own. We're too much out in the wilds for that. Somebody must have come for her.'

Or taken her from the house, dead or alive, and returned the carriage under cover of darkness . . . The thought was a chill on my skin, a knot in my stomach. Just so, it seemed, had Alexandra disappeared.

'And you heard nothing?' I asked again. 'No sounds of an argument, or . . . ?'

Dolly drew herself up, stopping her polishing abruptly.

'Whatever are you suggesting?'

I hesitated, unsure how to put my suspicions into words, and even wondering if I dared voice them at all, and Dolly, a bundle of indignation now, answered her own question.

'Not that Mr Brad did her a mischief, I hope! Because if you are, let me tell you he'd never do such a thing – never! He's a gentleman, Mr Brad. Oh, I know he was known for being a bit on the wild side in his younger days, but he left all that behind him when he became Sir Harry's heir. And I know there was talk when Mistress Alex died that he'd played a part in it. Anyone who could near kill a man could just as easy kill his wife, that's what they said. But—'

'Kill a man?' I interjected, shocked. 'Brad killed a man?'

'Oh, 'twas long ago, when he was young and hot-headed,'
Dolly said dismissively. ''Twas just a brawl, the sort young
bloods do have all the time, and the other man was a ne'er-
do-well, and more to blame than Mr Brad, as like as not.
He didn't die, just spent a few weeks laid on his back, that's
all, and 'twas no bad thing, in my opinion, for he did no
good to man nor beast when he was up and around, for all
I ever heard of him. But you know how tongues wag and
stories grow in the telling of them. Oh, Mr Brad's got a
temper when he's roused, that much I will admit, but he
would never have harmed a hair of Mistress Alex's head.
He worshipped the ground she walked on. And he'd never
have hurt Mistress Rosalie neither.' She glanced at the pot
steaming on the hob. 'The beef tea's hot. More than hot.
You'd better take it before it all boils away to nothing.' Her
tone was tight and she returned to polishing the silver with
renewed vigour, her message to me as clear as day.

I had outraged her, aroused her fierce loyalty to Brad and
I was not welcome in her kitchen any longer.

'Really, I didn't mean . . .' Desperately I tried to appease
her. The last thing I wanted was to make an enemy of Dolly.

'Well, I should hope not!' Dolly responded sharply. Her
face was still set, and I decided that for the sake of future
relations the best thing I could do was to make myself scarce.
But as I returned to the drawing room with Janine's beef tea
I could not forget what Dolly had said. Not only had she
admitted that he was possessed of a temper, but . . .

Brad had nearly killed a man. Dolly did not seem to think
he had been to blame, but it was further evidence of that
vicious streak I had witnessed when he had dragged Jem
away from Janine. Why, if he had not been so concerned to
tend to his daughter, I could well imagine that the assault
would have gone much further. And the man Brad half-killed
was a 'young blood', Dolly said, a man well able to defend
himself; who knew whether he would have survived Brad's
attack if he hadn't been a match for Brad's strength? If he
hadn't been able to fight for his life against Brad, as a young
woman could never do? Was it possible, then, that that same
tendency had something to do with Alex's death and Rosalie's
disappearance? All very well for Dolly to maintain he would

not have harmed either of them ... it might be that when his blood was up, he was not responsible for his actions.

The thought nagged at me like a splinter in my flesh. And it would not go away.

Several days passed and I had seen nothing more of Charles Winters. How could I have, confined to the house nursing Janine and trying to keep her occupied? At least she was making a good recovery, thank goodness, with no apparent ill effects, though the doctor insisted she must still rest and not over-excite herself, and I told myself I must be patient. But still I was anxious to get Rosalie's letter to Miles at the very earliest opportunity, and I was very aware that it was still there in my underwear drawer, incriminating evidence, should anyone come across it, that I was a far more interested party in the happenings at Upton Stowey than anyone had so far guessed. It was reasonably safe there, I reassured myself – unless someone chose to go snooping amongst my things. But still it was on my mind, a nagging disquiet.

One morning, almost a week after Janine's accident, Brad announced that he intended taking her for a carriage drive.

'I have some calls to make, but if you would like to come with me, Janine, the fresh air will do you good,' he said.

Janine, understandably, was excited at the prospect of getting out of the house – so excited we had to warn her to calm down. I helped her to dress, and when they had left, trotting off down the drive, and I was left alone, I decided I would go in search of Charles. For I could not imagine when such an opportunity would arise again.

I went to my room, retrieved the letter from its hiding place, and tucked it into the bodice of my gown. The paper felt scratchy and uncomfortable against my tender skin, but it was the safest hiding place I could conceive of. As I went back downstairs, I met Sir Harry, ambling along the hall.

'Time to yourself, eh?' he said. 'Perhaps you can spare a little of it for me.'

I hesitated, torn. This could be a good opportunity to try to elicit some more information from him. But the letter seemed to be burning a hole in my gown, and I thought that Brad and Janine would be out for most of the day.

'I'll sit with you later, gladly,' I said, 'but first I must take a little constitutional. I'm fading away for the lack of fresh air.'

'What a good idea!' he enthused, and for a moment I feared he might suggest accompanying me.

'I'll be back very soon,' I said gaily – and made for the door as fast as my legs would carry me.

I really had not the first idea where to begin looking for Charles Winters. The estate was vast and he could be anywhere – even visiting one of the tenant farms, for all I knew. If so, I had no hope whatever of finding him. All I could do was go out and about and hope that fortune smiled on me and our paths, by some miracle, crossed.

I walked first to the copse and to the pheasant pens, but there was no sign of him. I stood for a moment listening for any sounds of activity deeper in the woodland but could hear nothing but the chatter of the birds. Wherever Charles was, he was not working in the immediate vicinity, and I began to realize just how hopeless was my task in finding him.

Perhaps, I thought, he was not out and about at all, but at home, working on the records I felt sure he must keep. It was, I knew, a long shot, but it was the only one I had. And even if he was not there, perhaps I would find the door open. If I did I would be able to leave the letter somewhere he would be sure to find it, and at least it would be on its way to being delivered to Miles.

I cut through the copse, following a well-worn path through the undergrowth, which had burgeoned thickly through the summer months, and the piles of decaying leaves which must have fallen a year or more ago. It was cool here, sheltered as it was from the sun by the trees, and the air was heavy with the pungent smell of wild garlic. I walked briskly, full of intent, and before long I reached the cottage – a small square stone building flanked by a number of outbuildings.

They were deserted, I could tell, but I looked in them all the same. A wood-store, a workshop with a bench and tools, the floor covered thickly with sawdust, a shed full of implements – scythes and spades and hoes. But no Charles.

I went to the front door of the cottage then and knocked on the door, but there was no reply. Tentatively I tried the latch, but it did not give. My heart sank. I looked around for some safe place where I could deposit the letter, but I could see none, and in any case I did not think I dared leave it outside the house. Who knew how long it would be before I would see Charles and be able to tell him what I had done? If we should get a storm of rain or even a heavy dew it could be damaged, and however I secured it, a fitful wind might blow it away. I could not risk such a thing happening; the letter was too important – the only evidence I had so far managed to acquire.

Despairing, I started away from the cottage, my only hope now that I might yet encounter Charles before I had to return to the house. Just before entering the thicket once more I turned back, as if still harbouring the hope that he might by some miracle appear, or the locked door be standing open. And in that moment I saw – or thought I saw – a figure at the upstairs window, blurred by the reflection of the trees in the glass. It was only for a fleeting second and then it was gone. But I stood stock still, eyes wide, breath catching in my throat.

There was someone in the cottage – I was sure of it. But it was not Charles Winters. The figure I had glimpsed so briefly had, without doubt, been a woman, for no man that I had ever seen wore his hair flowing loosely to his shoulders, nor that startling shade of emerald green attire.

A woman – in Charles Winters' cottage when he was not there! Could it be – could it possibly be – that it was Rosalie?

Eight

I ran back along the path – I could not help myself. I hammered on the door again and rattled the latch. But the door did not give and there was only silence from inside the cottage. Again I moved far enough back into the copse to gain a view of the upper windows, but now there was nothing to be seen but the half-drawn drapes and the reflection of the trees in the pane.

My thoughts were racing. Had I imagined it? Surely I must have done! Yet at the same time, I was sure I had not. I had seen a woman at the window, I was certain of it. But why had she not answered my knocking? She could not have failed to hear it. And surely she had seen me too?

A madness took hold of me then. 'Rosalie!' I shouted, staring up at the window. 'Rosalie!' My voice was shrill in the silence of the woods, echoing, then fading. 'Rosalie – are you there? It's me – Imogen!'

But the figure did not reappear.

I was frantic now, convinced without reason that my sister was there in an upstairs room, being held prisoner against her will. But why did she not make her presence known? Why did she not rap on the window pane when she saw help at hand? Had she fainted, perhaps, the shock of seeing me too much for her? Was she at this very moment lying senseless on the floor of that upper room? But she would not have known who I was, I realized – she had not seen me since I was ten years old.

Could it be, then, that there was someone there with her, who had dragged her away from the window and was preventing her from calling out to me? Had Charles Winters been there all the time? Perhaps he was not the ally she had thought him, but in league with Brad and allowing his cottage to be used as a prison. If so, then I had no ally in this place of dark secrets either, no contact I could trust to assist me if I were in danger or to take a message to the one person I knew would come to my rescue – my brother Miles. But the letter scratching at my breast reminded me that it made no sense for Charles to be Brad's accomplice in whatever wickedness he was perpetrating. If he had been, he would surely have taken the letter from me when I had offered it to him, and destroyed it, for he had known it contained incriminating accusations against Brad – and had said as much. But he had not taken it from me, and neither had he warned Brad of its existence. Though I had told him where it was concealed, it had remained there, undisturbed.

He had not told Brad that I was suspicious, either, or that I was connected in some way to Miles and Rosalie – at least, I supposed he had not, for I could not believe that I would have been left to continue in my position as governess to Janine if he had. No, Charles could not be in league with Brad. There must be some other explanation for the presence in the cottage of the woman I had seen – or thought I had seen.

I was calming down a little now, my normal good sense beginning to reassert itself. Desperately worried as I was for Rosalie, I had let my imagination run riot. If there was a woman there at all, then the most likely explanation was that she was a secret lover. That would explain why she had not answered the door and drawn back from view when she realized I could see her. Perhaps she was a woman of easy virtue, or even some other man's wife, and both she and Charles were anxious that no one should know she was there. When I had first knocked, she had slipped up the stairs for fear I might peer inside, then, when she had thought I had given up and was leaving, she had risked a look to see who it was who had been hammering at the door, only to see me staring back at the windows.

Colour flooded my face as I thought of it – how I had blundered into a delicate situation and made a dreadful scene. And deepened as yet another thought occurred to me.

Was it possible that Charles's secret lover was, in fact, Rosalie herself? Had she run from a disastrous marriage to the arms of a man who promised her sanctuary? Had they discovered that they were not just friends, but in love – and was she in hiding because she and Charles both knew that Charles would lose his employment and his home with it if Brad discovered that Charles had stolen his wife?

A sudden surge of foolish hope lifted my spirits. If Rosalie had run off to be with Charles, that would clear Brad of causing her any harm! It would make him innocent, and with the treacherous feelings I had been entertaining for him, I so desperately wanted him to be innocent.

But that explanation did not hold water either. I could not believe Rosalie would willingly cause her family such anxiety, for she would be well aware that her disappearance would make them fear for her safety, given the fate of Brad's first wife and the rumours surrounding it. And surely, if he was hiding her, Charles would have taken the letter from me when I offered it. He would have wanted to return it to her so that she could either finish it or destroy it as she thought fit. And besides, it would be too dangerous for them by far to live together right under Brad's nose, and no life at all. If they had fallen in love, then surely they would have eloped. Charles would have sought employment somewhere far away where they were not known and neither the scandal nor Brad could touch them. But though Rosalie had disappeared, Charles seemed as entrenched here as ever he had been. In addition, Charles had seemed genuinely worried about Rosalie – and concerned for my safety too.

No, if the woman I had seen had been a secret lover, I could not see that it could be Rosalie. If I had seen her at all . . .

I looked again at the window, reflecting the copse it faced. It had seemed to me that the woman had long dark hair and a green dress – there, dancing against the pane were brown branches and green leaves. Thinking about it logically now, it seemed to me that it had, most likely, been an illusion I had been all too ready to believe was reality, nothing more than a trick of the light and my own fevered imagination. Nothing else made any sense at all.

The letter still scratching at my skin beneath my bodice, I turned and walked away from the cottage.

* * *

I went back to the house. Though I had managed to rationalize my strange experience and the madness that had overtaken me, it had left me shaken. And I was no longer sure I wanted to encounter Charles Winters this morning either. I still felt ashamed of my behaviour at his cottage and did not think I could face him without cringing, even if there had, in reality, been no one there to witness it.

And strangely, I now felt reluctant to hand the letter over to him in any case. Though I had told myself it was ridiculous to imagine he might be in league with Brad, and holding Rosalie at the cottage against her will, yet the fact that I had thought it at all had somehow left an indelible imprint on my unconscious, a misgiving that coloured my senses and undermined my determined rationale.

Badly as I needed to know I had an ally in the camp, much as I told myself that Miles would never have told me I could trust Charles unless he was quite sure of his unswerving loyalty, yet for the moment, my nerves in tatters and my thinking totally confused, I preferred to rely only upon myself.

I walked around the house and went in by the kitchen door. Cook was there, and Dolly too, collecting plates from the china pantry ready to lay up luncheon. She smiled a greeting, then her eyes went to the floor and she bristled with indignation.

'Oh Miss, just look at the mess you're making! Mud and leaves all over my clean floor!'

I glanced down. I had not given a thought to the fact that I had been walking in the woods, which even after a spell of dry weather were always damp. Now I saw that my boots were caked with dirt and I had indeed left a trail of muddy footprints on the pristine flags which were scrubbed meticulously each morning.

'Oh – I'm sorry!' I exclaimed.

'Best take those boots off and clean them before you track muck right through the house!' Dolly said sternly. 'They'll need scraping as well as polishing, and you should've done that before you came in. That's what the scraper's for, you know. My, if you'd got that on the carpets . . . !'

'I'm sorry,' I said again, making to go back to the door – and the boot-scraper outside.

'No – don't track it all back again!' Dolly set the pile of plates down on the table. 'Dear, dear, and I thought you were a country girl, used to this sort of thing. Take them off and give them to me before you make things worse.'

Obediently I unlaced my boots and handed them to her. Carrying them by the ankle cuffs at arms' length as if she might be contaminated by them, Dolly dumped my offending footwear outside the back door.

'Now go and put some slippers on, then you can come back and clean up the mess,' she instructed me as if I were a naughty child.

Her sternness, I must confess, took me quite by surprise. Dolly was usually such an amiable soul. But I was in no mood to argue, and in any case I knew that she was in the right and I was in the wrong.

Shoeless, I headed for the stairs – and my clean slippers. Did Dolly expect me to wash the floor as well as cleaning my boots? I wondered. What was the etiquette for a governess in such circumstances? Given the seriousness of all my other concerns, it seemed quite incongruous that I should be worrying about something so trivial. But the success of my mission to find Rosalie, or what had happened to her, not to mention my own safety, depended on me maintaining my pretence. I did not want anyone, even Dolly, to suspect that I had never worked as a governess before and knew nothing of the workings of a household such as this one.

I reached the upper landing and started along the narrow corridor to my room. Then I stopped, eyes widening.

One of the doors on the opposite side to my room stood ajar – and I did not think it was the one I had found to be a box room. No – I was certain it was not. It was the other door – the one I had tried and found securely locked.

My skin prickled a little with curiosity. I walked straight past my own room and went to the open door.

What I should have done, I suppose, was merely peep in. But it would look suspicious in the extreme if anyone should see me creeping about with no shoes on and prying. Better by far to act boldly, as if I had every right to be there. Taking

94

the handle, I swung the door wide – then caught my breath with surprise.

The room, much bigger than I had imagined, was full of photographic equipment, along with some sealed chests, all of which was covered in a thick layer of dust. Half the room seemed to have been set out as a studio, the other half as a dark room for the development of photographic plates. I recognized it immediately, since Raymond had had a similar room which I had once visited, though he had been very angry with me and forbidden me to go there again, saying that I could have ruined everything and wasted hours of his work. But it was not the contents of the room that took me most by surprise – it was who was there, a sheaf of prints in his hand.

It was Sir Harry.

'Oh!' I was so startled the exclamation escaped my lips before I could stop it.

He looked up, as startled as I had been, and guilty, almost, like a little boy who has been caught stealing the biscuits hot from the oven. The sheaf of prints fell from his hand, scattering on to the floor. Then he smiled, that same smile with which he had greeted me on my first day, and spoke the same name.

'Alexandra!'

'No,' I reminded him gently. 'Not Alexandra – Imogen.'

This time, however, he seemed not to hear me.

'Oh Alexandra, you shouldn't be here! You know that, don't you? Only trouble will come of it.' He sounded agitated.

'I think that *you* are the one who shouldn't be here,' I said, trying to inject a little levity into my tone. 'Climbing all those stairs! What were you thinking of?'

'Why, you, of course. I think about you all the time. Oh Alexandra, I am so sorry. So sorry!' He was becoming more and more distressed, and making no sense at all. 'I only wish I could make things right, but it's too late – too late. And it's my fault – all my fault . . .'

Never before had I seen him quite so confused. At a loss to know what else to do, I took his arm.

'Let's go downstairs,' I said gently. 'I promised to sit with you, did I not? Well, here I am.'

'But the pictures . . .' He gesticulated helplessly towards the sheaf of prints that had scattered over the floor. 'We can't leave them here.'

I did not spare them so much as a glance. I was much too concerned about the state Sir Harry was in.

'Never mind the pictures,' I said. 'Let's get you to the drawing room.'

I urged him towards the door and somewhat reluctantly he allowed me to do so. But outside in the corridor he became agitated again.

'The door must be locked. I must secure it.' He broke away from me, pushing the door shut and trying to turn the heavy old key. But his hands were shaking so much that he somehow managed to wriggle it out of the lock and it fell with a clatter to the floor.

'Oh my, my, whatever is the matter with me? Help me, Alex, quickly now!' he gibbered. 'I must lock the door. Brad mustn't know . . .'

A small chill whispered over my skin as I realized that Sir Harry's agitation was due in part to having been discovered in the room that was usually kept locked. It was his house, and yet he was concerned that Brad should not know he had been there. But why – why? I could not begin to understand and for the moment, could not even try.

'I'll do it.' I bent and retrieved the key, fitted it into the lock and turned. Metal grated on metal – the lock was surprisingly stiff, as if it was not used very frequently, and had not been oiled in a long time. But turn it did. I tested the knob, turning it and pushing at the door, which rattled slightly but held, and withdrew the key.

'There we are.' I said. 'It's securely locked, you see?'

'Yes . . . oh, you are a good girl, Alex . . .' He broke off, looking at me intently, his eyes puzzled. 'No – it's not Alex, is it? It's Janine's governess. You told me that, didn't you? Oh, I am so sorry, my dear. I am a foolish old man. Janine's governess, yes. And not a bit like Alex at all. I don't know what gets into me sometimes . . .'

'Don't worry your head about it,' I said, relieved that he seemed to be coming out of his fog of confusion, like a man waking from a dream. 'Let's go downstairs and get you something nice to drink – a hot toddy, perhaps? Would you like that?'

'Yes, that would be very nice . . .'

He let me lead him along the passage and down the stairs. The key was still in my hand – Sir Harry seemed to have forgotten all about it. Surreptitiously I slipped it into the pocket of my gown. If there was one single place in this house where I might learn some of the answers I was seeking, it was that room, I thought. For some reason it was kept locked. For some reason Sir Harry had looked guilty when I surprised him there. For some reason it had made him hark back once again to Alexandra and upset his fragile hold on reality, and for some reason he was anxious Brad should not know he had been there. I could not for the life of me imagine what there could be amidst that dusty old para-phernalia that would help me solve the mystery, but I intended to investigate it all the same if I could.

What an adventuress I was becoming! I thought wryly. A stolen letter tucked into my bodice and a misappropriated key in the pocket of my gown. But my voice was steady as I called for a good strong toddy for Sir Harry, and I was careful not to mention to Dolly where I had found her master. It might, of course, have no connection to what had happened to two women in this house, but then again it might. And I was anxious indeed that I should not do anything to precip-itate the same thing happening to me.

When I had settled Sir Harry in the drawing room I managed to slip upstairs to my room. There I extracted the key from my pocket and the letter from inside my bodice, and was about to conceal them again in my underwear drawer when a thought struck me. An underwear drawer was such an obvious hiding place, and I had more or less told Charles Winters that it was the one I was using. If by some chance Miles was wrong about his loyalty to Rosalie, and he was, in fact, in league with Brad, then the letter would not be safe there.

I scanned the room looking for another place of conceal-ment, and my eyes lit upon the little fireplace. I doubted a fire was ever lit in it, even in winter, for such an extravagance would be unlikely to be afforded to a humble employee who spent little time in her room except tucked up asleep under the covers, and in any case, winter was still some way off. Though every instinct in my body was clamouring against hiding a letter in a grate where, in theory at least, a fire could be lit, I told myself its implicit danger made it the safest place of all. Surely no one would ever dream I would do such a thing.

Fighting against the misgivings I felt sure were groundless, I removed the newspaper which had been crumpled into the fire basket, laid both the letter and the key on the bars, and covered them again so that the grate looked exactly as it had before. Then I put on a pair of slippers and went back downstairs.

Though Sir Harry was still a little distant and preoccupied, he seemed to have found himself again, and he made no further mention of Alexandra. But as we chatted of inconsequential matters, my mind kept returning to the strange things he had said. Rambling he might have been, but to him they had made some sort of sense. Not only was he obsessed with Alexandra, it seemed he also harboured some deep-seated guilt where she was concerned. But what could it be? Had he had a hand in her disappearance and death? Why had he been so insistent that she should not be in that little room? And why was he so anxious that Brad should not know that he himself had been there?

As for the photographic paraphernalia I had seen there, that in itself was something of a puzzle. It must be quite valuable, I guessed, for I could remember my mama berating Raymond for the money he had spent on his own equipment and which she had said we could ill afford. Clearly it had been put together by someone with an overwhelming interest in the hobby which had become increasingly popular as new and simpler ways of making photographs were discovered. Yet the thick layer of dust and the stiffness of the door lock suggested it had not been used in a long while. Had it been Sir Harry himself who had once dabbled in the new art and been forced to give it up because of his failing health – or Brad, who had simply lost interest? Brad did not seem to me to be at all the artistic type, but if the equipment was Sir

Harry's own, why should he want to hide from Brad the fact that he had decided to take a look at it again? Surely Brad did not share my grandpapa's view that photography was the work of the devil, like some old crone who thought that having your picture taken was akin to having your soul stolen!

My head ached with wondering. The more I learned, it seemed, the more unanswerable questions I encountered. But I would find out the truth – I would! That much I was determined upon. Impatience burned in me – impatience that was all too soon to make me behave in a very foolish and reckless manner . . .

The drink I had fetched Sir Harry seemed to be making him drowsy, and perhaps too he had exhausted himself with his earlier outburst and emotional state, for before long he was nodding and a few minutes later fell fast asleep, his head tucked into the corner of his big wing chair, snuffling and snoring gently.

I sat for a moment watching him sleep, relieved not to have to try to carry on a conversation any longer. And then the madness took hold of me, though it did not seem like madness at the time, but an inspired opportunity.

Sir Harry was fast asleep, Brad and Janine were out, the servants were all busy in the kitchen. And upstairs was a locked room of secrets, and the key in my possession.

Scarcely daring to breathe, I stood up, waited a moment to be sure Sir Harry did not stir, then crept from the room and made my way up the main staircase, for I could not risk going by way of the back one where the servants might see me. I went to my room and retrieved the key, ensuring the letter remained well hidden. Then I went along the corridor and inserted the key in the door I had locked under Sir Harry's instruction such a short time ago.

Again I was struck by the stiffness of the lock; when the key turned, the noise it made sounded loud enough to alert the whole house. Carefully I eased the door open and went inside. Then I looked around, wondering where to begin my search.

Once again, too, I was struck by the quality of the equipment I saw there – despite its obvious neglect. Yet strangely, the way it was all set out looked as if it had been used just yesterday – a shrine to a once much-loved pastime now simply abandoned.

And scattered across the floor, the sheaf of prints Sir Harry had dropped when I had surprised him.

I took a step into the room, intending to retrieve the prints and see what – or who – they depicted. Then started in shock and dismay at a piping, incredulous voice from the doorway behind me.

'Imogen! What are you doing?'

Janine! I spun round, looking, I feel sure, every bit as guilty as Sir Harry had done when I had found *him* there.

'Janine – you're back! I didn't expect you yet awhile . . .' I gabbled foolishly. 'I didn't hear the carriage . . .'

She was staring around the room, wide-eyed. 'How did you get in here? It's always locked. I've tried and tried to get in and I never could. Not to play hide and seek – or anything. I thought there must be something really dreadful in here. I mean, really dreadful, like skeletons or a monster. But it's just a lot of dusty old stuff . . . Really boring!'

'Janine!' Brad's voice. My heart sank like a stone. 'Janine – where are you?'

'Here, Papa. I came to look for Imogen. We're in the secret room.' Her voice was bubbling with excitement.

Brad appeared, his face like thunder.

'You know you are not supposed to run about yet . . .' His voice tailed off as he saw the open door.

'I'm perfectly fine, Papa!' Janine cried, unabashed. 'And I want to go into the secret room like Imogen.'

Brad reached us in just a few quick strides. He took hold of the door knob, slamming the door behind us.

'You know that room is out of bounds.' He glanced at me. 'How did you come to open the door, Imogen?'

I was at a loss to know what to say. Considering Sir Harry's anxiety that Brad should not know that he had been there I was reluctant to tell the truth, but I could not see that I had any option but to give at least an approximation of it.

'Sir Harry was there,' I said. 'He was confused and distressed. I've taken him downstairs and come back to lock the door again as he wished.'

Brad swore. 'The devil he was! And I suppose you have been in there too, poking about.'

'No,' I protested. 'No, I haven't.'

But Brad was in no mood to listen to me. He turned the key in the lock, pulled it out and palmed it.

'I'll take care of this.' His voice was harsh. 'Now, downstairs, Janine, at once – but steadily. I don't want you running about contrary to doctor's orders.'

He turned on his heel and followed her back down the stairs and I was left to trail behind them, trembling from the shock of being caught red-handed, frightened as to what the consequences might be, and deeply frustrated.

Without a doubt there was something in that room that Brad did not want me – or anyone – to see. But with the key now back in his possession, I could not imagine how I could possibly find out what it was.

Nine

After the flurry of disturbing events of the morning, the afternoon passed quietly enough. Brad was insistent Janine should rest in case the trip out had tired her, and I sat reading to her in the drawing room. At first she pestered me with questions about the 'secret room' upstairs, but I assured her I knew nothing and suggested she forget about the incident if she did not want to annoy her father. He had made no mention of it, and to my knowledge – and relief – had not spoken to Sir Harry about it either, and the old man had gone off for his afternoon nap in a much calmer mood. I was still as jumpy as a kitten, however, and my head was spinning as I went over and over all that had happened and tried to make sense of it.

To discomfit me further, Charles Winters had come to the house to discuss estate business with Brad. They were closeted in his study and I thought it likely he would be invited to stay for the evening meal.

How ironic it was, I thought, given that I had not seen him for days when I had been most anxious to do so, that on the very same day that I had gone to his cottage and made an exhibition of myself, the very same day that I had decided I was not sure whether or not I could trust him with the incriminating letter, he should be here, under the same roof. A little worm of discomfort squirmed deep inside me as I wondered if it were indeed the coincidence it appeared to be – had he come to tell Brad I had been at the cottage this morning shrieking Rosalie's name? I tried to dismiss the thought, telling myself I had been mistaken about the woman at the upper window, that I had seen no one and no one had seen me, but still it niggled at me.

I was right about Charles being invited to stay for the

evening meal; when I went into the dining room I saw an extra place had been set, and again the niggle of unease surfaced. For a humble estate manager Charles was very welcome within the household, with Brad treating him more like an equal than an employee, if not actually a friend. The realization fuelled my misgivings.

When he greeted me, his hooded eyes gave nothing away, not the slightest indication whether he knew I had been to the cottage or not. Brad, on the other hand, was quiet, and when he spoke at all it was in short, terse sentences, as if he was brooding upon something. As for Sir Harry, he seemed to have quite forgotten his upset of the morning, rambling as usual about old times, repeating himself and things others had just said as if he had just thought of them himself, and being, though I hate to say it, generally trying. So far I had striven to make allowances for him and treat him with the gentleness a man in his state of health deserved, but tonight, with my nerves jangling, I found myself driven half to distraction by his ramblings.

All in all it was, for me, a tense meal and something of an ordeal, and when at last it was over and the men were on the point of retiring to the drawing room, I decided that what I needed most was a breath of fresh air. I said as much, excused myself, and went to my room to fetch a wrapper, for though the day had been warm, the nights were drawing in and I thought it might be a little chilly outside.

It was as I came back down the stairs that I saw Charles in the hall, lurking almost, and it occurred to me to wonder if he had been waiting to waylay me, for I could hear Brad and Sir Harry's voices coming from the drawing room and there seemed no good reason why he should be there in the hall alone.

At first, however, he said nothing, but as I reached the door he was there behind me, touching my arm. I stopped and turned to face him.

'Imogen.' His dark, Mediterranean-looking gaze was intent, his voice low, so low that no one but I would hear it. 'Imogen – take care, I beg you.'

That was all, no more, but the urgency of his tone was enough to fill me with alarm. Then, before I could ask him what he meant, why he had felt the need to engineer this moment to warn me, he was gone, crossing the hall and disappearing into the drawing room where the other men – and his glass of port, no doubt – were waiting for him.

More disconcerted than ever, I went outside. The night air felt cool on my burning cheeks and the light had faded so that the park was shrouded in an ethereal silver haze. As I followed the gravel path around the house I could smell the haunting perfume of honeysuckle and stocks on the still air. I walked a circuit of the lawn at the side of the house, pausing at a little open-fronted summer house on the far side and considering sitting there for a while. But there was a slight mustiness about the place that dissuaded me, and instead I completed my circuit of the lawn and the rose garden beyond, and returned to a stone bench set against the wall of the house, facing back across the lawn.

In many ways, this side of the house was even more impressive than the frontage. Above the four tall windows of the dining room, a sort of ledge that was almost a balcony was decorated with urns of the same stone as the house, and behind it were more tall floor-to-ceiling windows which I now knew gave on to a well-stocked library. The whole effect was gracious in the extreme, though of course sitting on that stone bench I was not in a position to admire it, even if I had been of a mind to do so tonight.

The light was fading fast now, so the garden was mostly illuminated by the light spilling out from the dining room windows. Dolly and Margaret were there, bustling in and out as they cleared the table, but they had not drawn the drapes, presumably because the room would soon be shut up for the night. In the still evening air a flight of swifts – or possibly martins, I never had known the difference – swooped and soared, catching the last of the flies for their supper. Somewhere over the parkland an owl hooted, an eerie, almost human cry. There were sounds from the house too – the clatter of china as Dolly and Margaret stacked it for carrying to the kitchen, the slam of a door, the creak of a window. I took little heed of any of it – it might have been in another world, isolated as I was with my thoughts.

But I could not remain there forever. At long last I stood

up, smoothing my skirts and trying to make the moment last before I had to go back inside, go to bed, and try to sleep. Reluctantly I took a step and then . . .

At the time I simply did not know what was happening. All I was aware of was a sort of whooshing noise that made me start and lurch involuntarily to one side so sharply that I stumbled over the little step between paving and grass, turning my ankle and falling headlong. As I fell, crashing to the ground, there came an explosive thud that made me scream aloud in shock, for it was close beside me and the very ground seemed to shake with it.

For a long moment I lay motionless where I had fallen, my leg twisted awkwardly beneath me, wondering confusedly how I had come to be there on the grass and what in the world had happened. Then, as I struggled to sit up, I saw a solid object on the path that had not been there before. In the half-light it looked almost sinister – a boulder fallen from the sky. But its curves and planes had not been shaped by nature – they were man-made. This was no rough uncut rock, but one of the stone urns that graced the balcony above the dining room windows. It had come crashing down, missing me by inches. In fact, had it not been for that involuntary movement which had sent me sprawling, it would not have missed me at all!

A shudder of horror ran through me as I realized how narrowly I had escaped serious injury. I had fallen, yes, and not only was my ankle throbbing but my wrist was paining sharply and the palm of my hand smarting. But if the urn had struck me, it would have caved in my skull. I could at this moment have been dead instead of lying ignominiously in the grass, hurting, it seemed, all over.

Trembling now from the shock of it, I tried to rise from the grass that was already damp with the rising dew. But as I tried to put the weight on to my ankle, the pain shot through it like red hot knives and it gave way beneath me again, so that I was forced to subside once more to the ground, gasping.

There was nothing for it – I was going to have to crawl. Hitching up my gown, I got on to my hands and knees, but my hand and wrist were hurting almost as much as my ankle and my skirts kept flopping down and impeding my progress.

There was a stone sundial set at the edge of the lawn. I grasped it and managed to pull myself up, wondering how I was going to negotiate the width of the path to reach the support of the wall. And then, to my intense relief, two figures rounded the corner of the house. Brad and Charles.

'Help me, please!' I called.

Brad reached me first.

'Imogen! What has happened? What's wrong?'

I must have made a strange sight there in the half-light, clinging for dear life to the sundial, yet incongruously I was only glad I was not still on my hands and knees. I would have hated for him to find me so!

'The urn,' I said. 'It fell and I . . .'

'The urn?' he repeated, sounding puzzled. 'What urn?'

I nodded in the direction of where it lay on the path.

'Sweet Lord!' Brad exclaimed. 'How in the name of heaven . . . ?' He turned back to me. 'Did it strike you, Imogen? Are you hurt?'

'It missed me – just.' My voice was shaky. 'But I fell and twisted my ankle and I can't walk.'

'Don't worry,' he reassured me. 'I'll get you inside and we'll send for the doctor.'

'Oh, there's no need for a doctor.' I felt guilty suddenly, as if this whole thing had been my fault. 'I'm sure if we bind it with a cold compress that's all that is necessary. We can't call the doctor at this time of night.'

'We'll see.' Brad's tone was firm. 'Now . . .'

I had expected him to support me back to the house, but to my surprise he leaned towards me, placing one hand behind my knees and the other around my waist. Then he lifted me into his arms as easily as he had lifted Janine, and just as tenderly. Automatically I put my own arm around his shoulders. The taut muscles were hard and strong beneath my touch, and as my cheek inadvertently brushed his, something sharp and sweet quivered deep inside me, shocking me almost as much as the events of a few minutes ago.

A little gasp escaped my lips.

'Am I hurting you?' There was concern in his voice now.

'No . . . no.' Colour was flooding my cheeks; suddenly the pain in my ankle and hand were as nothing compared to the awareness prickling over my skin and the turmoil within me.

He carried me into the house, Charles following, and shouted for Dolly.

'Oh lawks!' Dolly appeared in the doorway, her hand flying to her mouth when she saw the little procession. 'Oh, whatever in the world has happened now?'

'Imogen has met with an accident,' Brad said tersely. 'A cold compress, if you please, Dolly. And quickly about it.'

'Oh my Lord . . . we heard a crash. I said to Margaret, whatever in the world was that? Scared us clean out of our wits, it did—'

'A cold compress *now!*' Brad reiterated sternly.

Dolly retreated, still twittering, and he carried me into the drawing room and set me down on the chaise, plumping a cushion behind my back. Then he knelt beside me, raising my skirt to reveal my injured ankle.

At the best of times I would have been mortified that a man should do such a thing; now, with my heightened awareness, I was utterly overcome with confusion. But I could do nothing but lie there as his fingers ran lightly over my skin.

I had lost my slipper, I realized, and my ankle was already badly swollen. But I was able to move my toes when he asked me to.

'No bones are broken, then,' he said, straightening. 'But it will be a day or two before you are able to put weight on it.' He turned to Charles, who was hovering in the background. 'Pour Imogen a brandy, my friend. She's had a nasty shock. And it will help to dull the pain too.'

A decanter of cognac and a tray of glasses stood on one of the small console tables; Charles poured me a measure and brought it to me. As he placed it into my hand his fingers squeezed mine, surreptitiously but urgently, and when I looked up his eyes were on me, deep and intent, as if he were trying to convey some unspoken message. Then he straightened, turning to Brad.

'How in heaven's name did that urn come to fall?'

I remembered, then, his earlier warning, and knew that he was insinuating that this was no accident. Into my mind flashed the fact that this morning Brad had discovered me in the room upstairs that was kept locked, his anger, and his assumption that I had been poking about in there. I had not, of course – Janine had surprised me before I had the chance – but Brad had been in no mood to listen to my denial. Did he think I had found something incriminating to him there? Had he tried to get rid of me before I could tell anyone else what I had discovered?

Oh, surely not! It was too ridiculous. For one thing, he and Charles had been in the house together when the urn fell; for another it would be – as the outcome had proved – a very hit-and-miss way of trying to dispose of me. And he was treating me with such gentle concern, such kindness, I did not want to think for a moment that my mishap was anything other than an accident. I did not want to think it – and yet . . . and yet the nagging doubt was there all the same. What *had* caused the urn to fall just when I was directly beneath it?

'The ledge must be crumbling,' Brad said as if to answer me as much as Charles. 'It's been giving way, no doubt, for some while, little by little, in the same way that the threads of a cord fray until the weight of the picture it supports proves too much and it suddenly gives altogether. It's just unfortunate Imogen was nearby – and at the same time fortunate that it did not hit her when it fell.'

'She could easily have been killed,' Charles said grimly.

'She could indeed. We must have a look at the condition of that ledge – ensure the same thing does not happen again. I'll have one of the men get up there first thing tomorrow to carry out a thorough inspection.'

I had sipped the brandy whilst they were talking; the golden liquid was pungent in my throat and already trickling a warm path to my stomach. I did not care for the smell or the taste but it was certainly calming my nerves.

Dolly came in with a bowl of cold water and bandages and an old newspaper to stand the bowl on so as not to mark the Indian carpet, which covered almost the whole of the room.

'Now then, Miss, we'll have you seen to in no time . . .'

She kneeled beside the chaise, taking charge of the operation, and I felt ridiculously disappointed that it would be her and not Brad who was tending my injured ankle. And not just because her handling of it was a great deal rougher than his, either, I thought, gritting my teeth as she pulled my foot this way and that. And cursed myself for a fool.

'You might as well go home now, Charles,' Brad was saying. 'I'm sorry this has delayed you. I know you have an early start in the morning.'

'If you're sure . . .' But it was at me that Charles was looking, his expression still concerned and serious.

Dolly completed the bandaging of my ankle most efficiently, then fetched warm water and cleaned the grazes to my hand, chattering all the time.

'What a thing to happen! When you think of it – to be nearly brained by a lump of stone! Oh, lawks, it fair makes my blood run cold thinking of it. You must make sure, Mr Brad, that the rest of it is safe.'

'Yes, thank you, Dolly. You may rest assured I shall,' Brad said shortly.

When she had finished and we were alone he took my brandy glass and refilled it.

'Are you feeling a little better now?' he asked anxiously.

I nodded. 'Yes. And my foot feels more comfortable, too. Though I'm not sure how I am going to walk on it.'

'I don't think you will for a few days.' Brad handed me the brandy and sat down beside me.

'I really shouldn't drink any more of this,' I said, a little anxiously. 'I'm not at all used to strong spirits.'

'Nonsense. It will do you good.'

I raised the glass. The brandy did not smell as repulsive to me now; in fact it tickled my nostrils quite invitingly, and when I sipped it I thought I was getting used to the taste, too, a great deal too readily.

'My grandfather would have a fit if he knew about this,' I said without thinking. 'He doesn't approve of liquor at all. He thinks it's a device of the devil. My grandmother was only permitted to wave the bottle under my nose if I was sickly – and a very little bottle too.'

'You lived with your grandparents?' Brad said questioningly. 'Where were your mother and father then?'

Confusion flooded me as I realized I had unwittingly

strayed into forbidden territory. Clearly the shock of what had happened – and the brandy too – had addled my brain and loosened my tongue. And it was blurring my wits too.

'My parents are both dead,' I said, struggling to avoid blundering into yet another blind alley and reveal more than I should about my background. 'My grandfather was a schoolmaster, though he's long since retired from his calling.'

'And he taught in South Somerset?'

'Yes,' I lied, knowing I was now on dangerous ground indeed.

'It's no wonder then that you became a governess – and a good one,' Brad said. 'I had wondered . . . I know so little about you. And I would like to know.'

There was nothing in the least threatening in the way he said it, but his words panicked me none the less. So far he had indeed asked me nothing about myself. He had seemed content to take me at face value and where, when I had first arrived, I had been half prepared to face awkward questions, as the days had gone by I had ceased to rehearse the answers I could give. Now, unexpectedly, they were confronting me – and I was in no state to be able to reply convincingly.

'Please don't think me rude, but I really don't feel like talking now,' I said shakily. 'I think perhaps it would be best if I were to go to bed.'

'Of course it would. How thoughtless of me. I am going to have to carry you, I expect.'

My heart lurched, remembering how good it had felt in his arms.

'I'm sure that won't be necessary,' I said. 'If I could just lean on you . . .'

'With pleasure.' There was a wicked gleam in his eye suddenly, a little half-smile lifting one corner of his mouth. His tone was not in the least lecherous, yet I felt hot colour flooding my cheeks. 'Do you want to finish your brandy?'

'I think I've had more than enough,' I said.

His smile broadened. 'If you say so.' He took the glass from me, setting it down on one of the small tables. 'Come along then, Miss Black. Let's see how much help you need.'

I swung my legs on to the floor and pushed myself up a trifle unsteadily, wincing as the weight went on to my injured ankle. As I lurched, he put an arm around me, supporting me. And somehow, without the faintest idea of how it had happened, I was in his arms.

I was in his arms, my head spinning a little from the brandy, sensations I had never before experienced coursing through my veins. I was in his arms, my body resting against his, my heart pounding and singing both at the same time, my flesh drawn to his like iron filings to a magnet. For a moment we stood there close together, still as a statue. I was no longer aware of the throbbing of my ankle or the stinging in my palm. I was aware of nothing but Brad, the feel of his hard, muscular body, the masculine scent of him, his breath on my cheek, even the beat of his heart. Time stood as still as we two, a moment elongated into a lifetime; though not a single word was spoken it was as if we were alone together in a private world where words were quite unnecessary to know that we were sharing something extraordinary and special. There was no kiss – our lips did not so much as touch – but it was as if our hearts and souls and spirits had met.

It would not be enough for long – the sensitizing of my flesh and the yearning deep within me told me that. But for the moment it was an experience so profound that I did not want it to be marred by the urgent fumblings of physical desire. And besides . . .

All too soon reality was creeping in, reminding me that this man was my sister's husband and perhaps her murderer too. And here was I, longing for him helplessly and hopelessly, wanting only to remain this close to him forever.

Brad must have felt it too because quite suddenly his body stiffened and he moved away. His arm still supported me but our bodies were no longer in close contact and I felt he had wrenched himself away from me emotionally too.

'Let's get you to your room,' he said and there was an edge to his voice. 'Lean on me and if necessary we will call Dolly to help.'

No more mention of carrying me, then! My heart longed for him to sweep me up off my feet and hold me like a child in his arms; my imagination raced as I pictured him carrying me into the bedroom, laying me down upon my bed and lying down beside me. And my head told me I was wicked – crazy – or just plain inebriated. But for the moment I could not care.

Somehow we managed to climb the stairs and when he opened my bedroom door it was all I could do not to clutch at his shirt and beg him to stay with me. Not just for a few moments, but all night. Not just all night, but forever.

But of course I did nothing of the sort. He deposited me on the bed but I was still sitting there, on the edge, when he left me, not lying against the cool sheets in blissful abandon as I had been in my imagination. I slipped out of my gown where I sat, dropped it on to the floor beside the bed and wriggled between the covers. Then I lay with my muzzy head singing, my ankle throbbing dully, and the room spinning round me, thinking that nothing mattered, nothing at all, except the way I was feeling at this moment.

I was in love. And in spite of everything it was the most wonderful thing that had ever happened to me.

Ten

Next morning I woke with a dull thudding headache but also a rosy glow of happiness seasoned with excitement. Then, as full consciousness returned, the confusion began. What was I thinking of? How could I feel this way about a man my brother suspected of being a murderer? It was madness, utter madness. I knew it, and yet I could not help myself. Everything in me was crying out that he could not be the monster Miles thought him – he must not be! I wanted him desperately, as I had never wanted anyone in all my life before. I wanted him, and at the same time knew that it was terribly wrong, that even if he was innocent, he was Rosalie's husband. I longed to see him, hear his voice, be in his presence, and yet a part of me shrank even from that.

How could I face him after the shameless way I had behaved? He could scarcely have failed to notice how I had responded when I was in his arms, the eagerness with which I had pressed my body against his. He must have known that in those few crazy moments I was his to do as he wanted with. Hot colour suffused not only my face but the whole of my body, and I thought that perhaps I would take the coward's way out and stay here in my bed, feigning sickness, until he had left the house on his day's business. Not that I would be feigning exactly. My ankle had begun to throb again, and when I raised myself on my pillows my stomach churned nauseously.

This whole mission of mine had turned into a disaster, I thought. Not only had I learned nothing as to Rosalie's fate, I had jeopardized everything by falling in love with the very man we suspected of doing her harm. Perhaps it would be for the best if I were to abandon my efforts and leave Upton Stowey, taking myself out of the way of temptation.

113

And danger. So preoccupied had I been with my tumultuous emotions I had almost forgotten that I had come very close last night to meeting a horrible death. It might have been an accident – and then again, it might not. The look on Charles's face had suggested that, however impossible it seemed, he thought the falling urn had been an attempt on my life. Because I had come too close, perhaps, to discovering the truth. I was becoming a danger to someone at Upton Stowey.

The realization, far from making me more anxious than ever to leave, somehow fired me up again. I could not run away like a lily-livered coward. I must try, for my own sake now as well as Rosalie's, to get to the bottom of the dark secrets I felt sure were buried here. If I did not, the wondering would haunt me all my life.

With an effort I pushed aside the covers, got out of bed, and, hopping and hobbling, got myself ready to face the day.

It was Dolly who heard me struggling down the stairs and came to assist me.

'You shouldn't be coming down on your own!' she scolded me. 'You could have taken another fall and done yourself a mischief. I'd have come up if I'd known you was even thinking of trying, but we thought as how you'd have a nice lie-in.'

All this was delivered with much puffing and blowing; Dolly was far too plump, and too old, to help me with ease.

Brad and Janine were already in the breakfast room. The moment I saw him the colour rose again in my cheeks, but Brad gave not the slightest sign that anything had changed between us. His manner was as contained as ever, pleasant enough though perhaps a little more distant, and he enquired after my ankle in much the way he would of any acquaintance.

'It's still painful, but I'm sure it will soon heal,' I said, and added: 'I think, though, that I took a little too much medicinal brandy. My head is rather sore and my memory of events none too clear. I hope I did nothing to disgrace myself.'

His mouth twisted up then into that half-smile which had

the power to make my heart turn over. 'You, Miss Black? Never!'

It was the only hint of playful teasing he allowed himself, however, and as I toyed with some griddled kidneys I wondered why he had addressed me as 'Miss Black'. He had called me that last night, too, in much the same teasing tone. But it occurred to me to wonder if perhaps this morning he was calling me that in order to establish a little more formality in our relationship.

'I think it might be best if I took Janine out with me again today,' he said, laying down his knife and fork. His plate was quite empty – clearly what had passed between us had done nothing to affect *his* appetite. 'I think you might find it difficult to cope with Madam's naughty ways in your present condition.'

'I don't find her naughty at all,' I protested honestly.

'But a handful, none the less. No, Janine can accompany me and you can rest your ankle and give your aching head a chance to right itself.'

'If you are sure . . .' Fond as I had become of Janine, I was grateful for the opportunity to have a little peace and quiet – and time alone to try to sort out my racing thoughts and churning emotions.

'That's settled then. Go and wash your face and hands, Janine. I don't want you disgracing me with egg all over your chin.'

Her hands flew to her face. 'Papa – I haven't . . . ?'

'You have indeed. Do as I say now.'

I thought that when we were alone he might make some reference to the events of the previous evening, but he did not, and his apparent dismissal of it was more disturbing to me than anything he might have said.

Sir Harry, who had retired soon after the evening meal was over, apparently, and knew nothing of the accident, joined us soon afterwards.

'Why is there a stone urn in the middle of the path?' he asked, puzzled for once with good reason and not simply as a result of the confusion inside his own head.

'Because it has fallen down,' Brad replied shortly.

'Fallen down? But they've been there for years! Why

should it have fallen down now?' Sir Harry muttered in his croaking voice. 'Why, it's a good thing there was no one on the path beneath when it fell.'

'Imogen was,' Brad said. 'She jumped out of the way and injured her ankle. You'll have her company today, Uncle – a captive audience, I should think.'

'Good, good.' He smiled at me benignly. 'We'd better get it seen to, though. Don't want any of the others coming down on top of you again. Or me. Or little Janine.'

'One of the men will be seeing to it shortly – if he's not already up there.' Brad pushed back his chair and stood up. 'I must go. It's my day for visiting Chewton Pit, seeing the manager there and showing my face to the men. Too long between visits and they're ready to cast me as an uncaring and distant coal-owner.'

'And that hothead Fred Dawkins doesn't take much excuse to stir things up with the men,' Sir Harry said bitterly. 'We should have got rid of him years ago – he's nothing but a troublemaker. Chewton would run a lot more smoothly without him.'

He seemed remarkably lucid this morning, I thought. But it was the fact that Brad was taking Janine to a coal mine where a troublemaker was at work that worried me. Coal miners could be a violent crowd if roused, I had always heard.

'Are you sure it's wise for Janine to go with you?' I asked anxiously.

'She'll be perfectly safe with me,' Brad replied. 'I don't stand for any nonsense and the men – even varmints like Dawkins – know that.'

That hard tone was there in his voice, an echo of the tone he had used to Jem on the day Janine had fallen from her pony, and I found myself remembering that Dolly had told me he had once half-killed a man when his temper had got the better of him. The miners would very likely know about that – and the rumours concerning Alexandra's death would have no doubt confirmed their opinion that he was not a man to cross. I was still not sure that a coal mine was a place to take Janine, though –but it was not for me to object. Brad was her father, and where he took her was up to him.

116

When they had left I settled myself on the chaise in the drawing room, glancing through some periodicals. I would have liked to take the opportunity to read a book, for the library, I knew, was well stocked with interesting volumes, but I did not want to attempt the stairs again, and in any case I doubted I would be able to concentrate on anything but the lightest reading matter. Before long Sir Harry joined me, and remembering how lucid he had been on the subject of the coal miners, I thought it might be a good opportunity to pump him a little with regard to the past.

The subject of Alexandra was, I felt, best avoided, since any mention of her name seemed to set him raving, and in any case I rather doubted that he knew any more than was common knowledge concerning her death. If Brad had had a hand in it and Sir Harry knew it, he would certainly not be on such friendly terms with him, I felt sure. Given Sir Harry's obsession with Alexandra, I could not see him allowing a man he knew to be her murderer to remain under his roof, let alone continue as his heir. But Rosalie . . . Rosalie was a different kettle of fish. He had no love for Rosalie, and he might well be drawn on the subject of her relationship with Brad.

As we chatted, my mind was busy trying to think of a way that I might turn the conversation to my advantage, though the connivance of it made me feel guilty, as if I were plotting to take a sweetmeat from a baby. And then, to my surprise, Sir Harry himself offered me the opening I had been unsuccessfully searching for.

'I'm very glad it's you that has care of Janine, you know,' he mused. 'And Alex would be glad too if she knew, God rest her soul. You are a nice young woman.'

His words made me feel more guilty than ever. His good opinion of me would soon evaporate if he knew the deception I was perpetrating, I felt sure.

'Yes, you'll be good for Janine,' he went on. 'Much better than that mealy-mouthed Carstairs woman – and certainly better than Rosalie Voisey.'

'Rosalie *Palmer*,' I reminded him. 'She was Brad's wife, wasn't she?'

'Yes, dammit, she was – the scheming little minx. But

117

first and foremost she's a Voisey. And the Voiseys . . . well, they're a bad lot, I'm afraid. They can't be trusted, any of them.'

This was such a close approximation of what Grandmama had said that I was quite startled. It was a little like hearing an echo of her voice – and her sentiments.

'Why do you say that?' I asked.

'Phwah!' Sir Harry shook his head. 'All that one wanted was to worm her way in here like her father before her. Well, she took Brad for a fool right enough. Persuaded him she'd be a good mother to Janine. That was the only reason he wed her, you know. There's never been anyone for him but Alexandra, and I doubt there ever will be.'

I could not help the way my heart lurched miserably when he said that, but I did not dwell on it.

'Raymond put her up to it, I don't doubt,' Sir Harry went on. 'Saw another chance of getting a foot in the door and getting his hands on what he sees as rightfully his. And damned close he came to it, too.'

I leaned forward, puzzled by his words, yet with every nerve ending in my body tingling suddenly.

'What do you mean? Why should Raymond feel he has a right to Upton Stowey estate?'

Sir Harry huffed angrily. And said something that surprised me so much it quite took my breath away.

'Why? Because the bounder claims to be my son. That's why.'

For a moment I was too startled to say a single word. I could only stare at him, dumbfounded by his revelation.

Raymond – Sir Harry's son? I could not believe it! And yet it explained the passage in Rosalie's letter to Miles that had puzzled me so. I had read and reread it so often that I could recall it word for word.

'There is so much I have learned . . . things which have been kept from us and which you should know . . . Talk to Papa and ask him about his relationship with Sir Harry . . . what he may decide, at long last, to share with you, could be of vital importance to you . . .'

If Raymond was indeed Sir Harry's son, then it was he

and not Brad who should inherit the Upton Stowey estate, and perhaps the title too, though I did not know if it was hereditary. And by the same token, the next in line would be Miles. But he did not know it, and neither, it seemed, had Rosalie, until she had come here, and perhaps Sir Harry had told her, just as he was telling me now.

No – not just as he was telling me. He would have railed at her, no doubt, accused her of being her father's puppet . . .

Her father. *My* father. Yet more shock waves ran through my body as the realization dawned on me. If Raymond was Sir Harry's son, and I was Raymond's daughter, then Sir Harry was my grandfather! Oh dear God, the twists and turns, the secrets, the deceits. It was all quite beyond belief.

'Raymond is your son?' I asked.

Sir Harry humphed again. 'So his mother said – and I've no reason to doubt her, though I wish I had. The thought that I spawned that devil is repulsive to me.'

'His mother,' I repeated stupidly. 'But you never married . . .'

'She was not my wife, no. But she was pretty and had a way with her, and I was young and foolish. When she came to me and told me she was having my child, I did the right thing by her. I bought a house for her and set her up in it, made an allowance to keep her and her child in comfort.'

'But you did not wed her.'

A look of astonishment came over Sir Harry's face.

'Of course not. She was not of the class . . . she did not expect me to wed her. But I saw that she and her son wanted for nothing. She found a husband in time, a cobbler, a decent enough fellow. But still I supported Raymond, saw to it that he had a good education. I barely saw the lad, of course, in those days. But when he was old enough he came here and made himself known to me. I took quite a liking to him, fool that I was. Should have seen his dark side even then, but I suppose I did not want to. I had no other close kin that I knew of, and no one to inherit all I'd worked for. And there he was – my son.'

He broke off and in his face I could see all the hopes he had entertained. They were written there as clear as day, and no doubt he was reliving them, for he was always more at home in the past than in the present. Then, quite suddenly, his expression darkened.

'Damn him!' he exclaimed. 'If I had known the evil that pleasant manner of his concealed! If I had known what he was capable of, he would never have set so much as a foot over my threshold, never mind me promising to make him my heir. It was what he wanted, of course. Thought he could have it all, thought it was his by right, though he was born on the wrong side of the blanket. And if he had behaved decently it would have been. But when I got to know what he was up to, I sent him packing. He was furious, of course, that I should disinherit him and leave everything instead to Bradley. Even then he had the gall to question my decision. "Bradley is just a distant relative," he said. "I am your son." But I told him: "You are no son of mine. You'll never get so much as a penny piece from me – not after what you have done." But he's determined and he's crafty. First he tried to get to me through Alexandra, and then he sent his daughter to seduce Brad, and he thought I was too old and feeble-minded to know what he was up to.'

This puzzled me. I had been given to understand it was Brad who had turned up out of the blue and somehow caused a rift between Sir Harry and Raymond. But if I understood him correctly, Sir Harry was saying that he had sent for Brad *after* he had fallen out with Raymond, in order to establish a new heir in place of the man who had been his protégé.

But I thought . . . I had to bite my tongue to stop myself from uttering the words that would betray me. But Sir Harry was so lost in his story I am not sure he would have realized what I was saying even if I had come out with something 'Miss Black' could not possibly have known.

'He . . . did something to upset you?' I murmured instead.

'Upset me? That's an understatement if ever I heard one. The man was depraved. The things he was up to – and with a wife and children in the house too. His own – Rosalie and Miles – and the little one, his second wife's daughter. A lovely little thing she was. He used to bring her here sometimes when he visited. Now, what was her name?'

With a shock I realized he was talking about me! I held

120

my breath, praying that he would not recall that the little girl had been called Imogen. Oh, I could not be the only Imogen in the world, of course, but I had never met another – it was not that common a name – and it might prove enough to raise suspicions. What could I say to divert his attention? But as I sought around desperately for some distraction, Sir Harry gave up the struggle to remember, too immersed in his story to be diverted by such details and never guessing for a moment how close he had come to unmasking me.

'Oh, I don't know, and it doesn't matter now. But to expose that sweet innocent to his wickedness . . . Why, it's a good thing her mother died, if you ask me, and her grandparents came and took her away. The mother was in thrall to him, and if she'd stayed under his roof Raymond would no doubt have used her as he used Alexandra. She'd have been broken and ruined just as my dear Alexandra was. Oh dear Lord, when I think of it! When I think of what he did . . .'

He was becoming distressed now and I wondered about the wisdom of pursuing this. Perhaps I should endeavour to change the subject and return to it another day. But I was so close to learning something of the truth – if truth it was, for I could not help but wonder if Sir Harry's mental frailty was making him confuse people and events in his rambling tale. Miles and Rosalie had both believed it was Brad who had caused the ruination and death of Alexandra. Now Sir Harry seemed to be saying the villain of the piece was in fact Raymond – my father! I had to persuade him to continue so that I could piece the story together and draw my own conclusions.

'What happened to Alexandra?' I asked urgently. 'Are you saying that Raymond killed her?'

He shook his head impatiently. 'No – no. It wasn't Raymond who killed her. But he might as well have. He destroyed her – her health, her happiness, her very sanity. And in the end it cost her her life.'

'But what did he do?' I persisted, intrigued.

'I'll show you.' He got up from his chair. 'Wait here.'

He fumbled in the pocket of his smoking jacket and pulled

out a key that I recognized at once as the one that had briefly been in my possession yesterday.

'Is that the key to the little room upstairs?' I asked. 'But I thought Brad . . .'

Sir Harry grinned at me conspiratorially.

'You think I don't know where the spare keys are kept in my own house?' he said. 'Bradley might be my heir but he's not master here yet. The pictures should have been destroyed long ago, of course. I thought Bradley had destroyed them when . . . but he didn't. They're still there under lock and key, kept away from prying eyes.'

Pictures. I remembered the sheaf of prints in Sir Harry's hand when I had surprised him yesterday, the prints that had fallen, scattering, to the floor. I had guessed there was something in that room that was the key to the story, but I had not realized it was those prints. They had been there, within my reach, if I had just stooped and picked them up, but I had not. It had not occurred to me that a sheaf of old pictures were of such importance.

'What are they?' I asked.

Sir Harry faltered, then his hand went to his mouth and he crumpled, tears filling his rheumy old eyes.

'No – what am I thinking of? You mustn't see them. No one should. And especially not an innocent young lady such as yourself. Why, I'm as bad as him! I don't know what I'm doing sometimes. Forgive me, my dear.'

He replaced the key in his pocket, extracted a handkerchief and sat down again, mopping at his face. Clearly he no longer had any intention of showing me the prints, and I have to say I was not sorry. Whatever they depicted, if they had the power to upset Sir Harry so, I was not at all sure I wanted to see them. Besides . . . what if Brad should return unexpectedly and find me looking at them? Heaven only knew how he would react – perhaps it was this self-same transgression that had sealed Rosalie's fate. She had found these pictures and looked at them and Brad had . . . my blood ran cold.

But I had to know what he was talking about, however distressing it might be. I had gone this far and I could not give up now.

'Sir Harry,' I said urgently. 'Please tell me what happened to Alexandra. For her sake – tell me, please.'

He mopped his face again so the tears were gone, but the agony remained. His eyes were very distant, as if he were seeing only the past, and that, I think, is what made him so lucid.

'Between us we killed her,' he said. 'Dear Alex. She was the most beautiful girl who ever lived. And between us we ruined her and sent her to a cold grave, buried for months beneath the snow and ice, with not a prayer said over her for her soul. May God forgive us, for I never shall. We destroyed her. The most beautiful girl in the world. Everyone said so.'

Book Two

Alexandra

Eleven

Alexandra Sutton was beautiful – everyone said so, and they had been saying it from the time she was just a little girl. With her golden curls, dark brown eyes and perfect features, she was ethereal. But it was not only her physical appearance that made people love her – though it was without doubt what drew them to her in the first place. But Alex's nature was beautiful too. She was kind-hearted and sweet-tempered, and if she was possessed of a stubborn streak, it was easy to forgive as a foible that made her human.

Alex was born into a family of wealthy Bristol bankers who lived in a grand house with extensive grounds in the exclusive Leigh Woods, which overlooked the city from the far side of the Avon Gorge. She wanted for nothing, except perhaps companionship, for she was an only child. Though Nell, her mother, had borne four other children – all of them sons – none had survived infancy.

Alex was happy enough alone. In summer she had the run of the grounds with all their exciting hidden places amongst the trees; in winter the vast attic room which ran the length of the house was her special domain. Her doll's house was there, and a trunk full of pretty clothes for dressing up, and a swing had been hung from a rafter so that she could swing herself, petticoats flying. And for company, there was always her imaginary friend, Barbara, to whom she chattered incessantly as she played. But the best times of all for Alex were when her father, Roger, took her with him on visits to his friend, Sir Harry Palmer.

Alex loved everything about Upton Stowey. She loved exploring the house and the grounds, loved to watch for the deer that ran and skipped in the park, loved playing with Maude Cunningham, the daughter of the manager of one of

Sir Harry's coal mines. She was an only child, too, and Sir Harry encouraged the two girls to be friends. Best of all, Alex loved to ride. Sir Harry had seen her staring longingly at the horses in the paddock and he suggested to Roger that he should buy a pony for her and stable it at Upton Stowey.

As Alex became a proficient rider she began to forget 'Barbara' and her dolls. Her only passion was Folly, her pony, and when she could go to see him again. But Roger was a busy man. He could not always spare the time to drive her. And there was someone else who lived in the Leigh Woods and went frequently to Upton Stowey. Raymond Voisey had a house not far from the Sutton mansion and he had a close relationship with Sir Harry. Soon, he became Alex's salvation, for each time he made the journey – generally two or three times a week – he took Alex with him

Nell, her mother, complained that Alex spent more time in the depths of the country than she did at home, but in reality she did not mind at all. She was not a strong woman – she spent a good deal of her time confined to her bed – and Alex's trips to Upton Stowey relieved her of the responsibility of worrying about her daughter. It never crossed Nell's mind that Raymond was a little too generous with his time and patience where Alex was concerned, and if it had she would no doubt have dismissed it. The arrangement was altogether too convenient to allow anything to spoil it.

Contrary to all appearances, Raymond Voisey was not a pleasant man. His smooth and charming exterior concealed a deep-seated resentment of his humble upbringing.

The disapproval honest folk had shown to his mother when he was a small boy and she still a single woman had left its scars – he could well remember her distress when neighbours cut her as she passed, then turned to stare and whisper, and the taunts of his peers, who were forbidden to play with him. He despised his stepfather, who eked a humble living as a cobbler, feeling nothing but scorn for the man who had been prepared to give him a name, and from his earliest years harboured a fierce ambition to better himself. When Sir Harry began to take an interest in him, the way of life he saw at Upton Stowey House only served to fuel that ambition, and he was determined that somehow he would himself aspire to the finer things that money could buy.

With Sir Harry's patronage, he set himself up in business, dealing in art and curios, but it was not long before he discovered a most profitable sideline – one that appealed greatly to the darker side of his nature and was a far cry from the artworks that respectable folk purchased from him to display in their drawing rooms. Raymond began dealing in erotica. His business took him far and wide, but it was conducted in such secrecy that no whisper of it reached the ears of Sir Harry and his circle, and even if it had, they would no doubt have discounted it as malicious gossip, for Raymond was both plausible and charismatic and, to all intents and purposes, an upright art dealer.

From the moment Sir Harry made him his first loan – a loan he felt sure he would never be called upon to repay – Raymond suspected that the great man might actually be his father. He asked his mother, but she was reticent on the subject, afraid, no doubt, that the applecart might be upset if the truth were to come out and Sir Harry decided to publicly disown him. But the more Sir Harry indulged him, the more certain he became. And when he was twenty-five years old, not long married, and with his first child expected shortly, his suspicions were confirmed.

Sir Harry called him to Upton Stowey – Raymond was, by now, living in a house in the Leigh Woods area of Bristol, bought with yet another generous loan from his benefactor – and told him it was time they had a serious talk.

'You are a grown man now, Raymond, and I'm getting older. I want you to know that I have made a will naming you as my heir. I expect you might have your own ideas as to why I should do such a thing, and there will be others, too, who will speculate when I'm gone and they learn what I have done. But I have to warn you that if so much as a whisper gets out about it while I'm still drawing breath, then I shall disinherit you. Do I make myself clear?'

Raymond's heart was pounding, exhilaration making him light-headed, but somehow he contained himself. 'Yes sir.'

'Good. Now, I think it would be best if you were to give

up playing about with your arty bits and pieces and come here to learn something about the estate. If it's to be yours one day you need to be *au fait* with how it should be run. Agents are all very well, but if you don't have your finger on the pulse they could be doing a bad job for you or even fleecing you and you would be none the wiser.'

At this, Raymond's heart sank. Whilst the prospect of inheriting Upton Stowey – the house, the grounds, the fortune – was a seductive one, the thought of running the estate was less appealing by far. Riding from farm to farm or coal mine to coal mine on a fine horse, with tenants and labourers tipping their hat to him, he would rather enjoy, it was true, but he suspected that 'learning how the estate was run' would involve a good deal of book work, checking entries in dusty ledgers, making projections, and balancing profits against expenditure. Raymond disliked book work, keeping his own to a bare minimum, and not only because of the secretive nature of many of his transactions.

He was not ready to leave the city, either, and bury himself in the countryside. He enjoyed the opportunities for both leisure and his dubious trade that it offered. He enjoyed his business! Why, it could well be another twenty years or more before he inherited and could do as he pleased with Upton Stowey – Sir Harry was, after all, still in his prime, whatever he might say to the contrary – and Raymond had no desire to waste those twenty years kicking his heels as heir apparent.

'Well, my lad, what d'you say?' Sir Harry pressed him. 'There's plenty of room here for you and your family. Goodness knows, I rattle around in the place!'

Raymond hesitated. 'It's an uncommonly generous offer, sir,' he said, feeling about for a way out of this unexpected and unwelcome development. 'But I'm not sure how Amelia would feel about leaving Bristol just at present. This pregnancy has affected her very badly and I'm not sure I should take her away from her family and friends when she needs them most.' He paused, his expression studiedly anxious. 'Truly, I would like nothing better for myself. But I must put Amelia's happiness and well-being first. That has to be the most important consideration.'

'A most commendable sentiment!' Sir Harry applauded him. 'A woman who is carrying a child can be easily upset, I've heard – though I've no experience of it myself, of course. And I can understand she might very well want her mother close by when her time comes. Once the young pup is born, however, I expect she'll feel differently. Upton Stowey would be a marvellous place for a child to grow up – and one day it will be his, too, remember.'

Raymond hid a smile. Sir Harry was no doubt thinking that this boy – if boy it was – would be his own grandson.

'I'd like to continue with my own business for the time being, too,' Raymond went on. 'I wouldn't wish to be entirely dependent on your good offices. But perhaps I could divide my time and spend a few days here each week working with you and learning all you have to teach me.'

'That would be a possibility, I dare say.' Sir Harry looked a trifle disappointed. 'Let's go along that road for the present then and once the baby is born and Amelia more settled, we'll review the situation.'

'We shall indeed!' Raymond exclaimed, well satisfied.

But of course they never did. Raymond ensured he did enough on the days he spent at Upton Stowey to satisfy Sir Harry that he would be capable of taking on the estate when the time came, and continued with his own life, enjoying the pleasures the city had to offer and the business that was not only lucrative but satisfying to his hedonistic nature.

The arrangement continued in much the same way for the next ten years, though Raymond managed to subtly alter the balance of how his time at Upton Stowey was occupied so that less and less was spent on estate business and more on the social aspects of life as a country gentleman. He hunted with Sir Harry and shot pheasant in the season. Alexandra rode with the hunt too, as did his own daughter, Rosalie, but his son, Miles, was away at school, and to Sir Harry's disappointment showed little interest in joining them even when he was at home for the holidays. Raymond, however, was not sorry. Miles was rather overweight and awkward in the saddle. Raymond thought he would not acquit himself very well chasing the fox over hedges and ditches, and was glad Sir Harry would not witness his shortcomings.

When Raymond's wife, Amelia, sadly died, and Raymond married again – a Devon woman with a daughter of her own – Sir Harry was glad he had never persuaded Raymond to move into Upton Stowey House. The little girl, Imogen, was charming and well-enough behaved whenever Raymond brought her to visit, but Sir Harry did not care for the idea of children galloping around his house and disturbing his peace. With the passing of the years he was becoming a little crusty and set in his ways.

A new hobby was consuming him too. Photography – the new art form – was becoming all the rage, and Sir Harry indulged himself with a camera and all the equipment required to produce prints of the pictures he could capture through the lens. He designated one of the small rooms on the upper floor of the house his 'studio and dark room' and spent many happy hours there trying out new techniques. Very soon he was sharing his enthusiasm with his protégé.

Raymond was a willing pupil, for he had been quick to see the possibilities – possibilities he could use to his own advantage. As society had become more repressed, the market for the explicit pictures, books and sculpture had grown, and the tastes of his customers became ever more depraved, so that finding items which would satisfy them grew more difficult and expensive. A photograph, Raymond realized, could be produced in a fraction of the time it took to complete a drawing, and needed no special artistic skill or training beyond mastering the basic techniques. What was more, by using the new 'Cullodian' process, any number of prints could be made from just one exposure. The detail in the pictures was seductive, and an extra frisson was added by the fact that the subjects were real people and not the figment of some artist's imagination.

With Sir Harry in thrall to his new hobby, Raymond had plenty of opportunity to practise and perfect his skills, using the equipment Sir Harry had purchased. Sir Harry was enthusiastically making a series of pictures of workers on his estate – the oldest tenant farmer, clutching a hazel cane between his gnarled hands; a miner, fresh up from the bowels of the earth, his face blackened so that his teeth showed very white in the set smile he held patiently for Sir Harry's camera; the village washerwoman with her basket of clean linen. Raymond pretended admiration – and thought of how different his own subjects would be.

In preparation, he set up a studio of his own at his home and when he was ready, began procuring women of easy virtue to pose for him. But after his initial excitement he quickly became dissatisfied with the results. The women might be willing enough to do as he asked – though one had flounced out in a huff of indignation at what he suggested – but however he tried to disguise it, there was no mistaking they were professional whores. They were either too bold or too jaded, the life they had led written too clearly into their faces to be hidden from the pitiless camera. There were those amongst his clientele, of course, who liked that sort of thing, those whose blood was raised by the earthiness of the backstreet hussy, but most preferred wholesome innocence and youth, and Raymond counted himself amongst them. Vulnerability was what would lend his pictures the greatest appeal – innocence and vulnerability and perhaps even a little modesty; the contrast with the poses he planned would render such pictures irresistible, and make him a fortune.

Raymond needed a fortune badly – or an extra income, at least. Recently he had been living way beyond his means and gambling heavily – and losing. His creditors were not ones he could expect Sir Harry to pay off, and if he asked for a loan of the enormity he needed, the old man would demand an explanation as to how Raymond had run up such debts and be shrewd enough to see through any story he might concoct. No, he needed to make more money quickly to ensure no whisper of his troubles reached Sir Harry's ears.

It was when the old man made a portrait of Alexandra that Raymond realized the answer to his problems had been staring him in the face all the time. Alexandra would be the perfect model. She had grown now into a beautiful young woman, with sweet clear features the camera loved and a body that had developed the curves of womanhood whilst retaining the slender perfection of youth. Alexandra could without doubt make that fortune for him – if he could persuade her into posing for him. Raymond was determined to find a way.

He cultivated her gently, careful to do nothing to alarm her, and found it so much easier than he had dared to hope. For unknown to him, Alexandra was already infatuated by the handsome, charismatic man who was heir to her beloved Upton Stowey estate.

It had begun, that infatuation, when she was just a little girl. Across the years she could clearly remember the excitement that had bubbled in her as she waited at the window for him to collect her and take her to Upton Stowey, an excitement that stemmed partly from the lovely prospect of the day's riding ahead of her, but also from her anticipation of seeing Raymond and riding alongside him in the carriage, alone. Raymond made a great fuss of her as her own father never did, and he was so handsome and dashing too! Alex thought that when she grew up she would like to marry Raymond, though she could not see how that could be since he already had a wife and two little children.

Her admiration for him had not dimmed with the passing of the years. And she was thrilled and flattered by the attention he was paying her now. Unlike all the other adults in her circle, he treated her not as a child but an equal. His dark hypnotic eyes seemed to share secrets. Alex hugged to herself the way he made her feel – as if she were aglow from the inside out, burning with an unidentifiable anticipation.

He began inviting her to spend time at his home, just a short walk from her own in the Leigh Woods, where she enjoyed the company of his daughter Rosalie and, when he was home from school, the clumsy attentions of his son, Miles. She had not the slightest interest in Miles – besides being two years younger than she was, he was stout and not very tall, and an angry rash sometimes erupted under the sparse growth that was beginning to sprout on his upper lip and chin. But it pleased her, all the same, that he seemed to like her and find her attractive enough to risk the inevitable rebuffs she dealt him.

One day Raymond suggested that Alex might allow him to take a portrait of her as Sir Harry had done.

'I'm getting some new equipment and I am most anxious to try it out.' He smiled. 'How things have improved in such a short time! Do you know that not so long ago you would have had to sit in the blazing sun for minutes on end, your face whitened by flour? Now it's so quick!'

'Why me?' Alex asked, flattered but puzzled. 'Why not Rosalie?'

Raymond's eyes held hers. 'I shouldn't say this, my dear, I know. But you are . . . so much better suited to the camera than Rosalie . . .' He let his voice tail away, leaving Alex in no doubt as to his meaning. 'Now, what do you say?'

Alex hesitated for barely a moment. 'Oh – yes. Why not?'

'Capital! As soon as I've taken delivery of the new camera we'll arrange a suitable time. Only . . .' he lowered his voice conspiratorially, 'let's keep it our secret. I don't want Sir Harry to know I've more up-to-date equipment than he has, and in any case it may not be as good as I hope. But if it is – if I get the result I should – then your portrait will be a wonderful surprise for him – and for your parents. I'll make copies and have them framed and you can give them as presents. But you mustn't breathe a word or the surprise will be spoiled. Do you promise me now?'

Alex glowed with pride. Sharing a secret with Raymond made her feel important indeed.

'Of course I promise.'

He laid a finger on his lips and touched it to her cheek.

'We'll speak again about it very soon,' he said.

A week went by – a busy, exciting week. The annual Sheep Fair was being held in Chewton, the next village to Upton Stowey, and Alex went with her friend Maude Cunningham, the pit manager's daughter. The two girls spent a happy day together, wandering amongst the stalls and booths that had been set out on the village green, listening to the jangling music of a hurdy-gurdy and even taking a ride in the swinging boats, giggling and blushing as a swarthy gypsy lad helped them in. He allowed their turn to last much longer than it should and they both felt quite queasy by the time he helped them down again. They were soon laughing again, however. But a cloud was cast over an otherwise perfect day when an old crone accosted Alex.

There were always gypsies at the fair, of course – tinkers and sly sallow men who looked as though they might well be horse-thieves given the chance, handsome lads like the one at the swinging boats and brown-skinned woman selling pegs and sprigs of lucky heather. Sometimes they tried to persuade girls to have their fortunes told: 'Oh, you've a lucky face, me darlin', and no mistake . . . Come here . . . give me your hand. There's travel for you, across the seas. And romance too. A dark handsome man – and rich besides . . . Cross my palm with silver, me darlin', and it'll all be yours . . .'

But the gypsy who accosted Alex said none of these things. She made no promises of health or wealth, no prediction for a golden future. She did not even ask for money. She simply grasped Alex's arm with bony fingers and uttered a dire warning.

'There's trouble ahead for you – terrible trouble. You must beware or your whole life will be in ruins . . .' The look on her face, urgent and dark as the knell of doom, frightened Alex as much as the stark words. 'There's a man – no, two men. One is handsome, the other rich. But they spell danger for you. Darkness – and danger. Between them they will bring about your ruin.'

Maude, full of spirit as Maude always was, flew at the old woman, telling her to keep her horrid predictions to herself, and pulled Alex away.

'Take no notice of her. She should be put in the stocks on the village green for saying such things! I'd be the first to throw a rotten egg at her, and be blowed to her silly curses.'

For a moment Alex did not answer. But she was thinking: *Two men, one handsome, the other rich.* The old woman might well have been describing Raymond and Sir Harry. But why should they spell darkness and danger? Oh, it made no sense – no sense at all.

'Why did she pick on me?' she asked, a little tremble in her voice. 'Why didn't she say such things to you?'

'Because she could see that you're the gullible one, I

shouldn't wonder,' Maude said shortly. 'Don't let some mad old crone spoil our day now. Look – there are the Morris men – they're going to dance. We'll go and watch and you must forget all about her silly nonsense.'

Alex forced a smile and took her friend's arm.

'You're right, of course. That's all it was – silly nonsense.'

But there was a shadow now across the sun. Nonsense the predictions might be, but shaking off the bad feeling they had given her was not going to be easy.

Twelve

'My new equipment has been delivered,' Raymond told Alexandra a few days later. 'Shall we arrange a day for you to come for your sitting? Next Tuesday, perhaps, at about three?'

Alex nodded. She was much looking forward to it; the little thrill of excitement that ran through her each time she thought of it had helped to dispel the unpleasant feeling of foreboding that had descended on her when the old crone had singled her out for such a dire warning on the day of the fair. And her time was her own. Apart from her trips to Upton Stowey, her days were mostly spent at home, reading or working on her needlepoint, which she had no real aptitude for but which her mother insisted was a necessary accomplishment for a young lady.

'You have told no one?' Raymond asked.

'No, of course not! I promised, did I not?'

Raymond smiled, satisfied. 'You are a good girl, Alex.'

Alexandra glowed with pleasure.

On the following Tuesday Alexandra set out on the short walk along the narrow lane overhung with trees that were heavy with summer leaf. She had chosen her prettiest dress – a fine rose-sprigged lawn – brushed her hair until it shone, and topped it with a flower-decked bonnet. When she knocked at the door Raymond himself answered and she was surprised that none of the other members of the family seemed to be at home. Miles, she knew, was spending a week of the summer holiday with a friend in South Somerset, but she had expected Rosalie to be there, and little Imogen, as well as Raymond's new wife, Sarah.

'They have gone for a picnic on the Downs,' Raymond

explained. 'It's one of the reasons I suggested today for our sitting. We can be undisturbed.'

For the first time Alex felt a twinge of misgiving, but she quickly thrust it aside. She had never before been alone in a house with a man – not even her own father – and especially not one who stirred in her the strange feelings that Raymond did. To feel a little shy was only natural.

Raymond must have sensed her hesitation, for he went on: 'You haven't changed your mind, I hope? The picture will be such a wonderful surprise for your parents – and I did tell you it was to be our secret.'

'No, of course I haven't changed my mind,' Alex said hastily. 'It's just that . . . I didn't realize it was to be a secret from your family too.'

Raymond smiled. 'If my family knew, so would the whole of Bristol. Come on up to my studio, Alex, and we'll begin. Everything is ready for you.'

He led the way upstairs. The studio was at the very top of the house, a converted attic room. Alex had been there before, of course, but not for some time, and when he opened the door she was surprised to see that whereas before it had been relatively uncluttered, with just a stool and a plain white backdrop arrayed along one wall, now a whole collection of properties was assembled.

There was a velvet-covered chaise, a huge aspidistra, several Grecian urns and plaster plinths. How he had got it all up the narrow steps she could not imagine.

'I've been experimenting with something a little different,' he said by way of explanation. 'It's possible now to incorporate a number of pictures into one, so that it tells a story.'

Alex frowned. 'I don't understand.'

'And you do not need to. Today I am simply making a portrait. But we'll do a little experiment first. Sit on the chaise for a moment.'

Alex sat down obediently and Raymond disappeared beneath the cloth that covered camera and tripod. He re-emerged smiling.

'You look quite beautiful. I think I shall photograph you there. Now – if you could remove your bonnet . . . just pretend to do so for the moment. Can you sit quite still with your hands at your throat as though you were untying the strings?'

Alex giggled. 'I expect so.'

'And now . . . take the bonnet off. Tip your head, just so . . .' He touched her chin gently, tilting her head to one side, and a little shiver ran through Alex.

'Are you cold?' he asked solicitously.

'No – no . . .' The shiver had not been a chill; rather it had been pleasurable.

The session progressed and Alex began to enjoy herself, quite forgetting her nervousness. It was fun to look at the camera teasingly and have Raymond praise her, telling her how lovely she looked, and encouraging her to yet another pose. She was startled, however, when he suggested her gown was spoiling the line of her shoulders.

'It's a shame you did not wear something that left them bare,' he said.

'It's my very best dress,' Alex protested.

'And very pretty it is too. The puffed sleeves are most charming. But through the camera lens I fear they make your arms look a strange shape. Deformed, almost.'

'Oh!' Alex was horrified. *Deformed?*

'I've upset you now. I'm sorry. But you are such a beautiful girl – I want to show you at your best.' He hesitated. 'Perhaps it would be best if you were to take it off.'

'Take off my dress?' Alex squeaked.

'It does sound outrageous, I know. But sometimes for the sake of appearances . . . I have a wrapper.' He crossed to a small screen in the corner of the studio and fetched a scarlet silk kimono. 'If you were to put this on we could arrange it so as to leave your shoulders bare and no one but you and I would ever know that you were not wearing an off-the-shoulder gown.'

Alex hesitated, biting her lip, and he went on: 'I want this picture to be perfect – to show you as lovely as you really are, not as some hunchbacked . . .' His voice, sincere in tone, tailed away. 'Don't you want that too?'

'Well yes, of course, but . . .' Still Alex hesitated. The last thing she wanted was to look *deformed* . . . but to take off her dress . . . !

'Wear this and we can achieve perfection.' Raymond held

the kimono out to her. 'You can change into it behind the screen. And I shall turn my back so you can be sure of your privacy.'

He turned around to face the wall, standing arms folded, legs splayed. Alex felt that unfamiliar frisson of excitement dart in her, and a sudden daring took hold of her. What harm could there be in doing what he asked? The kimono would more than cover her modesty. And she did so want to please him. To be the best model who had ever sat for him. To facilitate a portrait that would be stunning in its perfection. She threw caution to the winds.

'Very well. Just as long as you promise that no one will ever know . . .'

'How could they?'

Behind the screen she unfastened her gown with fingers that trembled a little and laid it carefully across a chair she found there. Then she slipped into the kimono, tied the sash firmly around her waist and smoothed the silk around her hips.

'You can look now,' she said a trifle flirtatiously as she emerged.

His eyes moved over her, admiring and approving. Curiously, she felt less awkward than she had before; it was as if she had become a different person, an actress playing a part. She was no longer a little girl in a lawn gown but a seductive woman. The silk caressed her bare skin and whispered against her legs and she experienced a heady abandon.

'Perfect,' Raymond said softly.

He posed her on the chaise, viewed her through the camera lens, returned to loosen the sash to enable him to ease the kimono from her shoulders. Alex allowed him to do so without protest. The sense of abandon was pervading her senses now, Raymond's fingers on the base of her throat were seductive yet curiously unthreatening.

'You are a very beautiful girl,' he murmured, and she glowed, a warmth that might have been a blush suffusing her body.

She was almost unaware of the kimono slipping away, for she was in a dreamlike trance, merely moving in accordance with his softly spoken instructions, lifting an arm, tilting her head, leaning forward on to the chaise, lying back. It was only when he asked her to cup her bare breasts with her hands that the spell was broken and she looked down at herself, horrified. What was she doing? What had possessed her? Colour flaming in her cheeks, she scrabbled at the scarlet silk, holding it up to cover herself.

'Alexandra!' He emerged from behind the camera. She stood up, startled like a fawn, wanting only to run for the cover of the screen yet afraid the kimono would fall away still more and leave her completely naked. And suddenly she was a child again.

'I want to go home!' she wailed.

'And so you shall,' he said soothingly. 'You have given me everything I could wish for. I have more than enough.'

The meaning behind his words was quite lost on her. She was beyond comprehending that she had, in the last few careless minutes, given him a hold over her from which she would never break free. She ran to the screen, scrambled, trembling, into her gown. Shame washed over her in waves; she could not believe she could have behaved so. Her teeth were chattering now in spite of the warmth of the attic room, her stomach churning so that she was afraid she would be physically sick. She did not want to leave the sanctuary the screen provided, did not want to have to face Raymond again.

When she gathered the courage to emerge he was already busy with the camera plates and scarcely spared her a glance as she stood there, clutching her bonnet by its strings as if her life depended on it. The corners of his mouth, however, were twisted into a satisfied smirk.

'I'll be in touch, Alexandra.'

She did not know that it was more of a threat than a promise.

For days Alex hid in her room, feigning a sickness that was not so far from being the truth. She could scarcely believe what she had done, yet the memory of it was all too vivid. What madness had possessed her? Shame made her cringe, even though she was alone. What a wicked girl she must be! How could she ever face Raymond – or anyone – again?

And supposing Raymond were to show someone the results of the sitting? Terror washed over her; she wished she could die.

On the day she normally visited Upton Stowey her mother became very concerned when she said she did not feel up to going.

'Miss your ride?' she said anxiously. 'You must be poorly indeed. I think it's high time the doctor took a look at you.'

Alex experienced a fresh wave of panic. She did not want the doctor to examine her. She didn't want anyone seeing her undressed ever again. And though there were no physical signs that she could see when she washed herself, she thought irrationally that a doctor would somehow know that she was sullied forever.

When she heard Raymond at the door, calling for her, she crouched on her bed, hugging her knees to her chest, hot with shame and very afraid he would tell her mother how disgracefully she had behaved. Long after he had gone she remained there, seeming to hear again the old gypsy's dire warning. *There are two men, one handsome, the other rich. Between them they will bring about your ruin . . .*

Oh, if only she had paid heed! And what would she do next week when she was due at Upton Stowey – and the week after that? She couldn't skulk in her room pretending illness forever. Mortified, frightened and lost, Alex buried her face in the pillows and wept.

The following week as the day for her ride approached, Alex was no closer to knowing how she could avoid Raymond. But to her surprise, salvation came in a most unexpected way.

'If you want to go to Upton Stowey I shall have to take you myself,' her father informed her. 'Raymond tells me he is not going.'

Alex felt a flood of relief, but she was also puzzled.

'Why not? Is he ill?' she asked, surprised that after all that had happened she should still feel concern for him.

'No.' Roger's tone was short – he was annoyed, no doubt, that he had to make the journey himself for once. 'It seems he and Sir Harry have had some kind of disagreement. It will all blow over and be forgotten in a day or two, I expect. These things usually do.'

At once Alex was overcome with the fear that the disagreement might be over what had happened at the sitting, and her stomach churned relentlessly as her father drove her to Upton Stowey. But Sir Harry greeted her as warmly and affectionately as he always did; there were no accusations nor even any veiled questions that might indicate he was aware of what had happened. Alex breathed a little more easily. Whatever he and Raymond had fallen out about, it did not seem that it could be her shameful behaviour.

Several weeks passed and still Raymond did not resume his visits, and it was left to Roger to drive her whilst Sir Harry charged a groom with driving her home again. One day she dared to ask Sir Harry why Raymond no longer came to Upton Stowey, but received no satisfactory answer.

'Because I don't want him here,' Sir Harry replied shortly. 'And I have to tell you I don't even want to hear his name. I intended to leave the estate to him, you know – fool that I was. Well, he won't get a penny from me now. I've a nephew – a great-nephew to be precise – and I've asked him here so I can take a look at him. If I like what I see, he'll be my heir. If I don't . . . well, the good Lord alone knows what I'll do with it. Perhaps I'll leave it to you.'

'And what would I do with an estate?' Alex said, smiling, but all she could think was that fortune seemed to have smiled on her. If Sir Harry had fallen out so badly with Raymond that he had disinherited him, she was not going to have to face Raymond ever again, and there was no risk of him telling Sir Harry of her shame either. Perhaps the nightmare was over.

Little did she know it had only just begun.

It was some weeks later and summer was fading into autumn. Alex had taken a walk into the Leigh Woods to look at the blaze of colour the trees were making as the leaves changed from vibrant green to glowing red and gold, and she was making her way home when she heard the sound of a horse and carriage in the lane behind her. She stepped to one side, looked over her shoulder, and, to her horror, saw that it was Raymond Voisey.

As he came alongside he reined in the horses. Colour flooded her cheeks; she hurried on. But there was no escaping him. He drew alongside her again calling her name.

'Alexandra – what a pleasant surprise.' She did not reply, simply staring at her boots and avoiding his eyes. 'It's been so long since I saw you,' he said. 'I do so miss our visits to Upton Stowey.'

'Then you shouldn't have quarrelled with Sir Harry,' she said, surprised by her own words – and that she should have the courage to say such a thing.

'Oh – that,' he said carelessly, as if the quarrel was of no importance at all, when in fact it had been utterly disastrous for him. Not only had he lost the prospect of inheriting the estate and all that went with it; with the removal of Sir Harry's financial support, he was finding it impossible to maintain the lifestyle to which he had become accustomed, and he was desperate to find a way of increasing his income.

Now here was the solution in the shape of Alexandra.

'Let's not talk of Sir Harry,' he said smoothly. 'Let's talk of more pleasant things. The pictures I took of you turned out very well. I'd like you to see them. And I'd like you to sit for me again.'

Alex could feel tears beginning to prick her eyes. 'I don't want to see them. And I certainly don't want to sit for you again.'

'But why ever not?' he asked slyly.

'You know why not,' Alex whispered.

'Oh Alex, I can't believe you are suffering from a sudden fit of shyness! You were not shy that day.' She was silent and he went on: 'And I have so many ideas for the pictures we could make! Call tomorrow afternoon at around three. My family will be out visiting, I know, and we'll be undisturbed. Yes, tomorrow afternoon would be perfect.'

'No!' Alex said. 'No, I shan't come. I must go home now.'

'Oh dear.' Raymond's voice was silky. 'I can see you are in need of a little persuasion. I had hoped to keep the pictures we took just between ourselves – for our own pleasure. But if you do not do as I ask, then I shall have no alternative but to share them with others . . . your parents, perhaps.'

The colour drained from Alex's face. 'You wouldn't!'

'Oh yes, Alex, I would.'

'But I have no clothes on!'

'And very lovely you look without them too. Others should have the opportunity to appreciate your charms.'

'Please!' she begged. 'You can't! Oh, please . . . !'

Raymond smiled, flicked the reins. 'Tomorrow, Alex. At three o'clock. Don't be late.'

As the carriage moved away down the lane Alex stood rooted to the spot. She was numb with horror. The thought of going to his house again filled her with revulsion and dread. But what choice had he left her? If he showed the pictures to her parents it would break their hearts. And if he made them public it would not only be her reputation that was destroyed, but her whole life. Just as the old gypsy woman had predicted.

In a bleak daze, Alex stumbled home.

It was a nightmare which could grow only darker, for the photographs which Alex had so foolishly allowed Raymond to take gave him a hold over her which she was powerless to break. With the threat of the involvement of her family, Raymond forced her into posing for him in ways that defiled her body and broke her spirit. With every picture he took, the web held her more firmly. Sometimes Alex tried to summon the courage to confess to her parents the awful thing she had done, for at least it would mean she no longer had to endure the humiliation of the sittings which Raymond continued to demand from her, but she simply could not bring herself to do it. If only she had been brave enough to admit in the beginning to that first, almost accidental lapse! They would have been shocked and horrified, of course, but they might eventually have forgiven her. Now . . . When Alex thought of the brazen ways in which she had allowed herself to be captured, she knew she would die of shame if anyone should see them. And she had no idea that Raymond was selling them to his clientele at a fat profit.

The photographic sessions were only part of Alex's torture, for Raymond began to molest her too, touching her and making her touch him in intimate ways. It sickened her, and she could not believe she had ever found him exciting and attractive. Now her whole body recoiled from his touch, but she was too frightened to do anything but remain there, compliant, complicit.

And then one day in the summer that Alex was seventeen the most terrible thing of all occurred.

The photographic session was over and as always Alex was left feeling used and sullied, yet strangely lethargic, for the only way she could survive the degradation was to distance herself from it, so that whilst her body adopted the poses that Raymond demanded, her mind and spirit were elsewhere, mere spectators of a scene of debauchery such as she could never have envisaged before the nightmare had begun. Then, smiling the smile which had once hypnotized but now repelled, he took off his jacket, sat down on the chaise and instructed her to sit upon his knee.

Alex knew what was coming and the familiar fear and revulsion rose like bile in her throat, yet obediently she did as he bid.

'My beautiful girl,' he murmured, stroking first her breasts, then her stomach, before burrowing between her thighs.

For a few minutes he prodded and kneaded her, his breath hot against her cheek, then he shifted her slightly, unbuttoning his trousers so that the hot hardness of him rose between her legs.

This was usually the extent of what she had to endure and she prayed that it would soon be over. But today Raymond was in no mood to stop. He lifted her, turning her to face him. 'Sit upon me, Alex.'

A sob broke in her throat. 'No! No, please!'

'Come along now, I won't hurt you.'

'No!'

'Very well. Have it your way.' Suddenly he was no longer cajoling, pretending concern for her. An almost feral look came over his face, eyes narrowed, lips drawn back in something close to a snarl. 'You are mine,' he grated, 'and you will do as I say.'

She began to struggle then, sobbing and crying out. She no longer had any thought for his threats of exposure – all

147

that mattered was that he was about to ravish her. But her protestations were useless; he was too strong for her by far. He lifted her bodily and forced her to the ground, her arms twisted painfully above her head. And then he was on her and in her. She screamed as he thrust into her again and again, her body writhing uselessly, her mind an abyss of black horror.

She did not hear the door of the attic open; the first sound that penetrated the swirling darkness was the sound of a woman's voice.

'Raymond? I heard screaming . . .'

He paused in his disgusting pumping, shifted a little. Over his shoulder she saw his wife, Sarah, standing there. Her body was swollen and heavy with the unborn child she carried, her face carved into a mask of disbelief.

'Raymond,' she said again, her voice far off and faltering. 'What . . . ?' and then, as if she had only just realized what she was witnessing: 'Oh Holy Mary! Oh sweet Jesus!'

'Get out of here!' Raymond roared.

But Sarah stood there motionless in the doorway, white as a ghost. Still pinned to the floor by Raymond's heavy frame, Alex sobbed, soundlessly now. Then he moved, and Sarah's stunned glance fell full on Alex. She gasped.

'Alexandra – oh no!'

'Go, I told you!' Raymond was on his feet, fastening his trousers. 'And you . . .' He glowered down at Alex. 'Cover yourself, you brazen hussy.'

In a daze Alex scrambled up. Her legs were shaking so they would scarcely support her as she ran, trying to cover her body with her hands, for the sanctuary of the screen. Sarah gasped again, this time, it seemed to Alex, from a sudden wracking pain in her stomach, and doubled up in agony.

'Sarah?' There was anxiety in Raymond's voice now where before there had been only anger. 'Sarah? Oh dear God!'

'My baby!' she groaned.

'Alexandra – help me get her to her bed!' Raymond ordered.

Terrified, her fingers too clumsy to manage the fastenings of her gown, Alexandra peeped around the edge of the screen.

148

There was no way on earth she could have done as he bid, but in any case he was not waiting for her assistance. Already he was supporting the stumbling, bent figure of his wife towards the door. Alex heard Sarah gasp again, saw her falter, yet try to push her husband away and grasp instead the door jamb for support.

'Don't be a fool,' Raymond said impatiently, retaining his hold on her. And then they were gone.

Alex crept across the attic to the top of the little staircase and saw them stumbling along the landing. When they disappeared into a bedroom she edged down the stairs, still trembling, and as the door closed after them she began to run. Her shoulder was throbbing painfully and there was a terrible burning pain between her legs. But she scarcely noticed. All she could think of was getting out of this terrible house.

She encountered no one. She never did – Raymond always made sure the family would be out when he arranged for their photographic sessions. Why Sarah had returned this afternoon she neither knew nor cared.

Perhaps, she thought afterwards, the baby had already begun to come and Sarah had felt unwell. Alex hoped with all her heart that it was so, for she could not bear the burden of guilt for what was to follow. But at the time there was no thought in her head but escape. And to hide herself away like a wounded animal.

Her home was mercifully as deserted as the Voisey house should have been. She washed herself and changed her dress in a frenzy that was at the same time almost trancelike. Coherent thought was beyond her. And yet, for all her shame, Alex experienced a strange feeling of relief – of freedom.

Sarah Voisey would undoubtedly tell her parents what had occurred. And then there would be no more need for secrecy, no more humiliating visits to Raymond's studio. At long last his hold over her would be broken without her having to take that impossible step of telling someone herself.

It would be a dreadful time, she had no doubt. But at last she would be out of his clutches. It was the only comfort she could cling to.

But it was not to be.

Alex heard the terrible news next day. Her father came into the drawing room where she was helping her mother sew new drapes for her bedroom, oblivious, it seemed, to the fact that Alex was silent and preoccupied. Nell had never been observant of her daughter's moods – or anyone else's for that matter – but not even she could fail to notice that Roger was visibly upset.

Alex's blood ran cold when she saw his face.

'What ever is the matter?' Nell asked.

And the words her father spoke shocked Alex to the core.

'Sarah Voisey. She's dead.'

'Dead? Sarah? But how . . . ?' Nell's needle was poised above the fabric, her task forgotten.

Roger shook his head. 'It's terrible. She went into premature labour, it seems, and died whilst trying to deliver her child. The baby is dead too, of course. Never even got to draw breath, poor mite.'

Alex's hands flew to her mouth and her stomach heaved. Somehow she forced herself up on to trembling legs and ran from the room. But before she had gone more than a few yards she was violently sick.

Sarah – dead – and it was all her fault! Oh dear God, how could she ever live with such a terrible thing upon her conscience?

Thirteen

She would kill herself. It was the only way out that remained to her. The blackness that had enveloped her swirled around and around and she knew she could not bear to go on living. She had been the cause of Sarah's terrible death and of little Imogen being orphaned. The child's grandparents had come and taken her away, and Alex thought it was a good thing, for Raymond was not fit to have the care of a child. But the mite had lost her mother and her stepbrother and sister, and Alex knew she was to blame.

The fact that her secret was still her own was no consolation now. She was certain it was only a matter of time before Raymond's demands upon her began again and the thought was quite unbearable.

However she pondered it, Alex could think of only one way in which she could take her own life. From the Leigh Woods and from the Clifton Heights the cliffs dropped steeply away into the Avon Gorge where the river flowed from the sea into the Bristol docks. If she jumped when the tide was high she would certainly drown, and if the tide was low she would be smashed to pieces on the mud flats.

The nights were drawing in now for autumn and the dark evenings only served to tighten the jaws of the trap of her depression. One evening at dinner she decided she could bear it no longer.

'Are you unwell, Alexandra?' Nell asked, noticing she had not eaten so much as a mouthful.

Alex pushed a piece of meat around her plate with her fork. 'I'm not hungry.'

'You must eat,' Nell admonished her. 'I know you want to have the smallest waist in Bristol, but if you don't take some nourishment you will faint in church.'

Alex felt a bubble of hysteria. To faint in church was the worst catastrophe her mother could imagine, a matter for humiliation, the height of bad manners. What in the world would she say if she knew the dreadful truth? Why, having her daughter jump from the top of the gorge would be nothing compared to the shame of being faced with the evidence of the things Alex had done.

When the meal was over the family retired to the drawing room, but Alex excused herself and went to her room. There she spent a little while setting all her belongings in order and saying a private farewell to them. She felt strangely calm now. The decision had been made, and now was the time to implement it. If she delayed, her courage might fail her.

She put on her new velvet coat trimmed with astrakhan, for strangely it seemed important to her that she should look her best when her body was discovered, and went down the stairs. In the drawing room her mother was playing the piano and singing, as she sometimes did. The hauntingly sweet notes brought a lump to Alex's throat. But like a sleepwalker she crossed the hall, opened the door and went out.

It was but a short walk to the place where the gorge dropped steeply to the river below. Alex made her way to the very edge. In the bright moonlight she could see the port and the city away to her right; on the other side of the gorge lights burned in the windows of the great houses on the Clifton heights. She could see the dark silhouette, too, of Brunel's Suspension Bridge, which was in process of construction and would one day link the two sides of the gorge. And below . . .

The tide was in; boats bobbed at their moorings. Alex glanced down and felt vertigo tighten her stomach. She had thought it would be easy. Just walk and keep walking, or stand for a moment, inhale deeply, and jump to oblivion. Now, suddenly, she realized it was not so easy at all. She began to tremble; her body shrank. And suddenly Alex knew that however deep her shame and guilt, whatever pain she had inflicted and might yet inflict on those closest to her, she was not ready to die.

For a moment she felt that she was drowning in despair

– she was failing even this test. Then a new determination took hold of her. There must be a better way than this, and somehow she would find it. Alex turned and walked away from the cliff edge, not creeping in defeat but striding with taut purpose.

As she went back into the house her mother was still playing the piano and singing.

'Mid pleasures and palaces though we may roam
Be it ever so humble, there's no place like home . . .

Nothing had changed and yet everything had changed. Alex crept up the stairs and no one in her family ever knew how close they had come to losing her that night.

With the passing of the nadir the blackness began to lighten little by little. The guilt and the anxiety remained, and there were days when the blackness encroached again, over-whelming her, but also days that were not so bad. She wasn't entirely to blame for Sarah's death – she wasn't! It was Raymond who bore the heaviest responsibility of guilt. And perhaps he felt it too, for there were no more sly summons to his studio and no threats of exposure either.

Gradually life fell back into an even pattern and Alex dared to begin to feel safe. She resumed her visits to Upton Stowey and Sir Harry, who had missed her badly, was delighted. She saw a change in him, however; he seemed older and more frail suddenly, and he suffered from occasional lapses in memory which could be quite disconcerting. And there was a new member of the household – his great-nephew, Brad, whom he had made his heir. Alex could not help feeling that Sir Harry had ideas for matchmaking between the two of them, and it made her uncomfortable in the extreme.

Brad was pleasant enough, and had she not been so emotionally vulnerable Alex thought she might even have found him attractive. But she was not ready to trust another man – sometimes she doubted she ever would – and she avoided him wherever possible. Better to ride out alone with the wind in her hair and the ground flashing past beneath the galloping hooves of her horse. Her mother might consider

153

it a dangerous sport; Alex had learned the hard way that there were far greater dangers.

Maude Cunningham's eighteenth birthday was approaching fast and her parents were planning a ball to celebrate it. Naturally Alex was invited. She had seen little of Maude in recent months – the terrible secrets in her life had opened a gulf between the two girls and Maude had become impatient with the change in Alex from a happy carefree girl to one who could be withdrawn and moody – and besides this, she had a sweetheart, a young army officer named James Dalley, who occupied a great deal of her time. When he heard of the invitation, Sir Harry suggested that Alex should stay over on the night of the ball at Upton Stowey, since it would be the early hours before the dancing ended and the journey back to Bristol would be a long one.

In spite of herself, Alex found herself looking forward to the occasion. Maude had asked her to come early, and when she arrived she could scarcely believe the transformation the manager's sturdy old house had undergone. The draughty hall had been transformed into a ballroom with banks of flowers, potted ferns and a dais where a quartet would play for the dancing, whilst cold tables groaning with food and a champagne bar had been set up in the dining room.

Maude herself was dizzy with excitement, grabbing Alex by the hand and taking her to her room, ostensibly to show her friend her new ball gown. But she had another motive, Alex soon discovered.

'I shouldn't really be telling you this – it's supposed to be a secret – but there is to be a special announcement tonight,' she said excitedly. 'James has asked me to be his wife and Papa has agreed. I'm going to be married to the most wonderful man in the world! Isn't it marvellous?'

'Oh Maude, yes!' Alex hugged her friend, happy for her, but unable to help a pang of envy. How wonderful it must be to be in love with a sweetheart who was also in love with you; to have a secure future to look forward to. Alex could not imagine such good fortune would ever be hers. She could not so much as look at a man without wondering if he was as debauched as Raymond and hiding it as successfully, and feeling an echo of the revulsion he had evoked in her. And certainly no man would ever want her if he knew how sullied she was.

Surrounded by excited bustle and happy anticipation, Alex felt sadder and lonelier than ever.

As the guests arrived and the music began Alex tried hard to hide the way she was feeling. Her lips felt stiff as she forced herself to smile at the young men who asked if they might claim a dance, her laughter and chatter sounded brittle to her own ears. The music grated on her ears, the heat of the room and the buzz of merriment made her long only to escape. At last, unable to bear it a moment longer, she slipped away and found a corner shielded by a potted palm.

'Alex! What are you doing hiding away here?'

She jumped, startled, and looked up to see Brad Palmer standing there.

'Why shouldn't I be?' she retorted sharply. In his evening dress he looked all too attractive, the cut showing off his lithe but well-muscled frame, the colour flattering his angular, clean-shaven face, mid-brown hair and hazel eyes. Alex did not want to find him attractive; it made her most uncomfortable.

'No reason at all, if that's what you enjoy,' he said easily.

'I'm not enjoying it,' Alex admitted. 'In fact I wish I'd never come at all. But Maude and I have been friends for so long, she'd have been most hurt if I'd turned down the invitation.'

'You're happiest on your horses, aren't you?' Brad said. 'Never mind. It will soon be over. And perhaps it would be more bearable if you were to have a glass of champagne.'

A waiter was passing, bearing a tray of glasses that were filled to the brim and sparkling in the lamplight. Without waiting for her reply he took two, handing one to her. 'We really should drink to something,' he suggested.

'Maude's betrothal, I suppose.' The moment the words were out Alex realized she had broken her friend's confidence. Her fingers flew to her lips. 'Oh – I shouldn't have said that. It's going to be announced later and it's supposed to be a surprise. Can you forget it – please?'

'I didn't hear a word. The music is so loud.' Those hazel

eyes twinkled. 'I think we should drink to both of us finding ourselves here alone tonight – and both hating every moment.'

'I'm not sure that's a proper toast at all,' Alex said.

'Perhaps not, but I'm drinking to it anyway.' He lifted his glass and clinked it with hers.

Alex sipped. The bubbles tickled her nose and throat and seemed almost to tingle in her veins. She began to feel a little light-headed, and the weight around her heart felt lighter too. Ridiculous! How could a few sips of champagne alter her mood so suddenly and so completely?

'Do you think anyone would miss us?' he asked.

Alex looked at him over the rim of her glass, puzzled.

'Miss us?'

'If we were to escape all this racket and take a turn round the garden. I've never had the chance to get you on your own before, Miss Sutton – Sir Harry is very possessive of you – and I don't know when the opportunity will come again. What do you say? The moon is bright and the stars are shining and we can take another glass of champagne with us to keep us warm. And I won't be able to tell a single soul the momentous news you let slip – and which of course I never heard anyway.'

Alex laughed. A few minutes ago she had been in the depths of depression, now, for the first time in months, she was laughing.

'You have a very persuasive way with you, Mr Palmer,' she said.

In Brad's company the evening which had been dragging by with unbearable slowness now sped past. Brad was so easy to be with; she wondered why she had gone out of her way to avoid him previously. There was nothing remotely threatening about him; she felt more at ease with him than she had ever felt with any man before. Yet at the same time she was drawn to him. They walked in the garden, talking as if they had known one another all their lives and when they felt it would be impolite to absent themselves for any longer they returned to share a dance. Brad's hand was about her waist, their bodies close though not quite touching, but Alex felt none of the revulsion she felt with other men. She could not believe it. It was, she thought later, as if she had come home.

They were married on Alex's twentieth birthday. From that first night she had known somehow that it was inevitable, and thought how ironic it was that on the very night she had believed she had no future to look forward to she had fallen in love.

Sir Harry, of course, was delighted by the match, and welcomed Alex into the family with open arms. Her father, though, had been a little more uncertain, hesitating over giving his permission. He had heard from Sir Harry himself that Brad had got himself into a spot of trouble or two in the past, and had been involved in a brawl which had almost claimed a man's life. But in the end Alex's persuasion and the fact that Sir Harry vouched for Brad being a reformed character – ''Twas nothing but youthful folly on the boy's part,' he asserted – won the day.

At last Alex had found real happiness. She adored Brad and he worshipped her. She had, Alex thought, been so much luckier than she deserved. And she prayed God that the nightmare was at long last over for good.

A year after they were married, Alex gave birth to a little daughter whom she named Janine. The confinement had been difficult and the birth long and painful, but holding her baby in her arms Alex thought that she had been worth every moment of it. Brad was delighted with the child too and in no way disappointed, as Alex had feared he might be, that he did not have a son.

'Next time,' he said, smiling. 'And maybe the time after that. We have all our lives to produce a whole string of sons and heirs. For the moment I am more than satisfied with this little one.'

Messages of congratulation arrived from all their friends and relatives and Alex opened and read them, resting against the pillows in the big marital bed with little Janine in a crib at her side. One envelope, however, was addressed to her alone, with no mention of Brad. Alex frowned, thinking it strange, and tore open the envelope. Then she started, the blood leaving her face in a rush, a wave of shock making her tremble.

The note was from Raymond Voisey.

> I was delighted to hear you had been safely delivered of a little girl, *Raymond had written.* I send my heartiest good wishes to you and your husband. However, now that you have a daughter, I am sure you will be most anxious to do whatever is necessary to protect her and ensure her continued well-being. We all wish for our children a charmed life, happy, secure, and free from any hint of scandal. To this end I would be most pleased if you would call upon me so that we can discuss ways in which you can safeguard your future and that of your daughter. And I enclose a memento of the times we shared, in case they may have faded in your memory. I treasure my copy of this picture. Do you think your husband would appreciate seeing it too? Ever your friend and devoted admirer, Raymond Voisey.'

The paper fluttered from Alex's nerveless fingers and she scrabbled inside the envelope to extract the photograph he had mentioned.

Oh dear God, it was appalling – erotica of the most explicit kind. And she was the model degrading herself for the camera. Alex gazed at the picture in utter horror, her skin crawling. She had thought she was free of this terrible man and his evil threats, but there was no mistaking the meaning behind his weasel words. Once again, for some reason she could not fathom, he was tightening the hold he had over her. It was all beginning again.

Trembling, sick to her stomach, Alex stuffed the letter and the disgusting picture back into the envelope. Then, though the doctor had warned her not to so much as set a foot to the ground, she pushed aside the covers and got out of bed. She had to conceal the letter and the picture where no one would find it whilst she thought about what to do.

Somehow she staggered across the room, wrenched open

a drawer where she kept her knick-knacks and thrust the envelope to the very bottom. Though she could no longer see it, the picture still swam before her eyes, and Raymond Voisey's silky, menacing tone seemed to ring in her ears as if he had not written a letter at all, but whispered his threats to her as he used to do.

The blackness was there again, surrounding her, so thick she could almost see it. The room began to swim around her, she no longer had control of herself and her legs were buckling beneath her. She tried desperately to reach the bed and could not. As she slumped down to the floor she seemed to hear Raymond Voisey laughing unpleasantly in the encroaching darkness.

'I am very worried about Alex,' Brad said to Sir Harry one day when Janine was four months old. 'She does not seem to be recovering from the birth as she should.'

'She's certainly not herself,' Sir Harry agreed, evenly enough, though he himself was most concerned about the change in Alex.

Though the doctor could find no physical reason for her continued ill health, Alex had scarcely left her room, let alone the house, and she looked a shadow of her former self, with great dark shadows under her eyes and the weight dropping from her face and shoulders, giving her a sunken, haunted look. She was different in herself, too, tense and jumpy, seemingly unable to take the pleasure she should in her child.

She was still breast-feeding, of course, and Sir Harry had heard that sometimes a woman could suffer severe depression following a confinement. But he could not help remembering the time when she had shut herself away before, eschewing her visits to Upton Stowey, and he wondered if perhaps she was not as strong emotionally as she should be.

'Perhaps the inclement winter weather is not suiting her,' he said now. 'Why don't you take her on an extended trip to Europe, my boy? I've thought for some time it might be useful for you to take a look at the farming methods the French employ and see if they could be implemented here. And the coal mines too. Wider knowledge of other ways is always helpful and you've learned all you can here. Then perhaps you could go on into Italy – simply travel and enjoy the sights – and the sunshine. I think it might do Alex the world of good.'

'Are you sure I can be spared?' Brad asked. He had noticed a slow but steady decline in Sir Harry's own health.

'I'll be good for a while yet,' Sir Harry replied. 'And I've got good managers to rely on. No, Alex's well-being is the most important thing just now. Take her to Europe, my boy, with my blessing.'

And so it was arranged. Brad, Alex and little Janine left the shores of England for a tour which was planned to last six months, and those who cared deeply for her prayed that the Alex who returned would be the girl they knew and loved.

Gradually the bloom returned to Alex's cheeks. Away from England and Raymond's threats she felt more free than ever before. She could not forget completely, of course, but the shadow was more distant. She could not imagine Raymond's motive for sending her the letter and that terrible picture – surely he did not want her to pose for him again? She was no longer young and lithe; her breasts were swollen with milk and her waist still flabby from bearing a child. And she could not imagine he wanted to ravish her again either – dear God, surely he did not? No, it made no sense at all. Perhaps he had simply wanted to disconcert her and let her know he still had power over her. And certainly the thought that the pictures were still in existence was a sickening one. But Alex succeeded in convincing herself that he must eventually cease threatening her, since she could not see that he had anything to gain from exposing her shame.

Alex determined to try and put it all behind her and enjoy the love of her husband and daughter. She must not allow that evil man to blight her future and that of Brad and Janine. Little did she know that Raymond had no intention of letting her escape his clutches so easily.

The next letter was waiting for her on her return to Upton Stowey. It was couched in much the same terms as the first and contained another disgusting picture of her. Another followed a few weeks later – and another. Their tone displayed Raymond's growing impatience. She must come to see him at once, or he would be forced to visit Sir Harry and Brad and show them the rest of his collection. He had numerous prints of each pose, he assured Alex. And he would not hesitate to make them public unless she did as he asked.

Alex was distraught, scarcely able to think straight. She only knew that somehow she had to try to stop him from carrying out his threats; somehow persuade him to promise that the horrible pictures and the negatives he had made them from should be destroyed.

The only opportunity for seeing him without Brad's knowledge, she knew, would be when she was visiting her parents. Raymond still lived in the Leigh Woods, and the next time she was there she steeled herself to make her excuses to her mother.

'I'd love to explore some of my old haunts,' she lied. 'Would you look after Janine for half an hour whilst I go for a little walk?'

'Why don't you take Janine with you?' her mother suggested. Though Janine was a good child, Nell, who was as feeble as ever, shrank from the thought of having sole care of her for even a short while.

Alex's heart sank. 'The lane is thick with leaves,' she improvised in desperation. 'It will clog the wheels of the baby carriage. And Janine is due for her afternoon nap. She'll sleep soundly all the time I'm gone, I'm sure.'

She rose quickly before Nell could protest further and set out, her heart beating a tattoo, a tightness in her chest and a sickness in her stomach.

A maid answered the door of the Voisey house, which relieved Alex somewhat. At least she would not be alone in the house with that terrible man.

'Who should I say it is?' the maid asked.

'Mrs Palmer,' Alex said, trying to keep her voice from trembling. 'Mrs Bradley Palmer.'

She was shown into the drawing room and a few moments later Raymond appeared in the doorway. He looked older than she remembered him; there were streaks of pure white in his hair and his face had become more raddled – from grief? Or from his excesses in his way of life? There was also a worried look about him she had never noticed before.

'Alexandra!' He greeted her, suave as ever. 'At last! And looking very beautiful, too, if perhaps a little pale . . .'

'What do you want from me?' she demanded shortly.

He twirled his moustache. 'You received the photographs, obviously. Did you like them?'

'They are disgusting. You are disgusting.' Marriage and motherhood had given a new confidence. Though she was still afraid of him, she was determined to stand her ground and refuse to be cowed. 'And if you think I have forgotten what you did to me when I was last here you are much mistaken.'

'Given the unfortunate consequences, that is hardly surprising,' he said silkily.

Unfortunate consequences! she thought furiously. What sort of man could refer so casually to the death of his wife? But she knew only too well what kind of man Raymond Voisey was.

'There were plenty of happier times, though, when we both enjoyed ourselves, were there not?' he went on.

'You might have enjoyed them. I most certainly did not!' Alex retorted. 'You don't have it in mind we should repeat them, I hope.'

'No.' He smiled a little and she thought he might be mocking her. 'No, that was not the reason I wanted to see you.'

'Then what?' she demanded.

'I need a favour of a different kind. One which I think you might be readier to agree to. And which would ensure the photographs remain our secret – if you are successful in what I am asking of you. And I see no reason why you should not be. You can be very persuasive where gentlemen are concerned, as I'm sure you know.'

Alex frowned. 'I don't understand.'

'I'm sure you recall that once Sir Harry and I were close. We had a foolish disagreement – I don't need to concern you with the details and I feel sure Sir Harry would not wish you to know them. Suffice it to say that he cut me off and

I have never received any further assistance from him, nor any hope for the future. I want you to intercede with him on my behalf, Alex.'

'If Sir Harry has a quarrel with you, he'd never listen to me,' Alex said, relieved that Raymond was not asking any sexual favours but puzzled and concerned, too, that the favour he was asking, and which would avert the disaster of exposure for her, was beyond her.

'I think he would,' Raymond said. 'He thinks the world of you, Alex. And if he proves difficult then – and only then – you can tell him from me that unless he assists me now out of my present financial difficulties, then I shall undoubtedly make a claim on his estate as his rightful heir. I don't think he is any more eager to have the details of my birth made public than you are for your pictures to be passed from hand to hand and leered over. Do I make myself clear?'

Alex stared at him in disbelief.

'Oh yes, I am his son,' he went on, smirking now. 'A fact he prefers not to acknowledge publicly, though there must be those who have guessed. I'm surprised you have not. I am his rightful heir, not your husband. And I shall make a great deal of trouble for you all if you are unable to persuade Sir Harry to assist me. Is that clear?'

Alex nodded. She was at a loss for words.

'Good. I await with interest some word from Sir Harry.' Raymond rang the bell and when the maid appeared in the doorway he said laconically: 'Please show the lady out, Mary.'

Alex went, dazed and still anxious. She had no doubt that if she was unsuccessful in mending the bridges between them, Raymond would carry out his threat. Either way, it seemed she was a long way from being rid of him.

Alex approached Sir Harry with trepidation. She remembered all too clearly that long-ago day when she had asked him why Raymond no longer came to Upton Stowey and his brusque response that he did not want him there. But years had passed since then. Perhaps Sir Harry would have mellowed somewhat and be prepared to forget their differences.

The moment she mentioned Raymond, however, it was plain that nothing had changed.

'I don't want to even hear that man's name!' he declared. 'I think I told you that once before, Alex. As far as I am concerned, Raymond Voisey does not exist.'

'But . . .' Alex hesitated, unwilling yet to pass on the threat Raymond had made to expose his parentage and challenge the inheritance. 'Why are you so against him?'

'You really want to know?' Sir Harry roared. 'Because he is a bounder, that's why, a man without any morals who deals in degradation.'

Alex blanched, and he went on: 'I shouldn't even mention such things to you, my dear, but I learned that Raymond's art dealership was a cover for pictures and artefacts of the most perverted kind. And he was using *my* money to finance the filthy business. I tell you, there is no way that man will ever see another penny of my money. He claims to be my son – did you know that? He took advantage of the fact that I took him under my wing. But he won't take advantage of me again, not while there's breath in my body.'

He glanced at Alex, who was biting her lip and trying not to cry. The hopelessness of her situation had suddenly overwhelmed her, and the realization that Raymond had very likely been selling the terrible pictures of her all along only made things a thousand times worse.

'What's the matter, m'dear?' he asked, putting his arm around her. 'Taken you in, has he? I know you and he were close once. But he's not worth you worrying about, take my word for it.'

His kind tone, the gentle way he squeezed her shoulders, swept away the last of Alex's defences. All the fear and despair she had suffered not just for weeks, but for years, welled up in her and she burst into tears, sobs that came from deep within her tortured soul. She could not bear it alone any longer. She had to confess. Only then would she be free.

'Whatever is the matter, Alex?' Sir Harry asked again, deeply concerned now as well as puzzled.

She told him.

Book Three

Imogen

Fourteen

'She told me everything,' Sir Harry said. 'She did not show me the pictures – she could not bring herself to. I recovered them after her death – the most shameful pictures imaginable. I should have destroyed them, of course, but I did not. I had some idea they might be used against Raymond, as evidence, if ever we could bring him to justice, but that, of course, has never happened. I locked them away in the room I once used as a studio, safe from prying eyes.'

'But sometimes you go there and look at them,' I said.

I was shaken to the core by the terrible story Sir Harry had told me, scarcely able to believe that Raymond could be such a monster, yet knowing Sir Harry had no reason whatever to lie to me and surely could not have dreamed up anything so dreadful about his beloved Alex.

He looked at me now, his faded eyes misted with tears, yet more lucid than I had ever seen him.

'They are all I have left of her,' he said piteously. 'The poses . . . I do not notice them any more, and in any case I only look at those in which her modesty is preserved. I see only Alex as she was – so young and lovely . . . and innocent. An innocence that was stolen from her little by little by that fiend. And I look at them too to remind myself of my own guilt for the part I played in her demise.'

'But you didn't know what was happening,' I said. 'You were not to blame.'

'It was I who brought them together,' he said. He was becoming agitated again. 'If I had not championed Raymond, decided to make him my heir . . . if I had not introduced him to the art of photography . . . And I failed her, too, at the last, when she confided in me. I should have protected her and I did not. I was too intent on having it out with

167

Raymond. I set out for Bristol in the highest dudgeon, leaving her here alone and in despair. The last words she said to me were: "How can I tell Brad? What will he do when he knows the truth?" "Kill Raymond, no doubt," I retorted, "if I have not done so myself first!" And he would have done, too. Brad can be violent when roused, and he worshipped the ground Alex walked on. Set her on a pedestal. Oh, I expected violence all right if I didn't get to Raymond and sort matters out. But I never thought that it would be dear Alex whose life was in danger.'

A chill whispered over my skin. 'What happened to Alex?' I asked.

Sir Harry was staring into space, reliving the past, and when he did not answer I was afraid I was losing him again to that other world which he seemed so often to occupy.

'What happened to Alex?' I repeated.

'Why, we found her in the spring, buried beneath the snow,' he said sadly.

'Yes, but how did she come to be there?' I persisted.

He shook his head helplessly. 'I don't know.'

So he was becoming confused again, I thought. But I must continue to try to prise the facts from him, guilty as it made me feel to harass him so.

'Did she tell Brad – or did you?' I asked. 'Did he lose his temper and do her a mischief?'

'Brad?' He looked shocked for a moment before the vague expression returned. 'Brad adored her. He was left a broken man. He knew no more than I what had become of her.'

Frustration bubbled in me. 'Someone must know how she came to be in the middle of Exmoor!' I burst out. 'Oh, try to remember, please!'

Sir Harry passed a hand that shook slightly across his face, pulled a kerchief from his pocket and wiped his mouth.

'I went to see Raymond,' he said. 'I told him what I thought of him – that the evil, debauched business of his for which I had disinherited him was as nothing compared to this. I told him he would never see a penny piece of my money now. Moreover, I told him that if a word of this terrible affair should ever get out and sully Alex's good name, I would call in all the loans I had ever made him and see him thrown into debtor's prison. Then I set out for home. I intended to advise Alex that Brad should never know, that I did not expect Raymond to ever bother her again – that I had countered his threats with threats of my own and his hold over her was broken at last. I intended that she should be able to put the whole ghastly business behind her for good. Unfortunately, it was not to be. I had scarcely left Voisey's home when I met with an accident that almost claimed my life.'

'An accident?' I repeated. 'What sort of accident? What happened?'

'My horse bolted and threw me. I don't remember much about it. All I know is the poor beast ran into a delivery wagon and had to be put down, and I was taken, senseless, to the hospital where I was cared for for some days.' His eyes grew puzzled. 'I never did understand it, why Rajah should have taken fright and bolted like that. He was such a gentle creature . . .'

'But Alexandra,' I pressed him gently. 'What of her?'

Tears filled those faded eyes. 'I never saw her alive again. When they brought me home from the hospital she was gone, and Brad beside himself with anxiety for her.'

'And had she confessed to him as she did to you?' I persisted. 'Did he know her terrible story?'

Sir Harry shook his head. 'I don't know.'

'Didn't you ask him?

Sir Harry huffed. 'Of course not. If she had confessed he would tell me in his own good time. If not . . . I didn't want to be the one to enlighten him, and I couldn't see the need for it. We've never talked of it from that day to this.'

'But he knows about the photographs,' I said. 'He won't allow anyone into the room where they were hidden. Not even you. Why is that?'

'Oh, I don't know.' Sir Harry's tone was agitated now, a little aggressive. 'He's aware the place upsets me. He wants to spare me. Why are you asking me so many questions? I'm tired and my throat is hurting from so much talking. Why don't you just go and leave me in peace? And send Alex to me. I should like to see Alex.'

I knew then that his grip on reality, surprisingly strong for a surprisingly long time, had slipped once again. I would learn no more from him today – if indeed there was anything more he could tell me. And already he had given me a great deal to think about.

'I'll go to my room then,' I said.

It would be difficult to manage the stairs without assistance, but if I took my time I would do it, I thought. Even if I had to go up step by step on my sit-me-down I would do it. Just now, more than anything, I needed my own quiet company and nothing else.

Somehow I managed to climb the stairs and reached the sanctuary of my room. There I sat down on the edge of the bed, my mind racing.

The terrible story Sir Harry had told me was going around and around in my head, the details returning to shock me again and again. Poor Alexandra, what torment she had suffered! Foolish Alexandra for behaving so in the first place, and then allowing herself to be blackmailed into becoming ever more tightly enmeshed. But I could not find it in me to blame her. How could anyone say with their hand on their heart that they would not have done the same? Would I have been brave enough to tell my grandparents the truth if it had been I who had been tricked into nakedness and then recorded so for all posterity? Imagining such a thing made me cringe inwardly, even though I had never been in the position myself. To have to find the moment and then begin, knowing that the words, once said, could never be unsaid, would be like launching oneself from a cliff – something else Alex had been unable to bring herself to do. As for that first indiscretion . . . had I not discovered how easy it was to throw caution to the winds when emotions were aroused and the heart ruled the head? And Raymond was a very plausible, very persuasive man. It was not only an impressionable young girl he had taken in – he had taken in my own mother, too. And deceived her. And humiliated her. Broken her heart and caused her death.

My father. My father! It was terrible beyond belief to think that the blood of such an evil man ran in my own veins. And the same curse hung over Miles and Rosalie. Somehow, when this was all over, I would have to break it to them, I supposed. Had Rosalie discovered the truth? She had certainly made no mention of it in the letter I had found. But the letter had not been dated. I had no idea how much time had elapsed between her writing it and her disappearance. Anything could have happened between those two events. And I was still no closer to discovering what had become of her. Or, indeed, what had been the cause of Alex's death.

There was a link. There had to be. But what – what? I ran my fingers through my hair until the pins came loose, desperately trying to formulate a scenario that would make sense of it all.

Had Alex, mortified by her past indiscretions and unable to face the thought of confessing them to Brad as she had to Sir Harry, run away? That was what I most wanted to believe, for it would exonerate Brad from the terrible charges Miles had laid against him. Sir Harry's – and Dolly's – assertion that Brad had loved her far too much to harm her gave weight to that suggestion. But it was possible to love someone too much – to lose sight of reason where they were concerned? Possible that great passion could give rise to its exact opposite if the object of adoration was seen to crumble and fall from its pedestal – the idol with feet of clay? Possible that blind rage and despair might have caused Brad to do her some harm that would otherwise have been unthinkable? And the burning question remained – how had she reached Exmoor and no one any the wiser?

Had she killed herself, then? According to Sir Harry, she had attempted it once before. But that still did not explain how she had come to be on Exmoor. If she had made away with herself, she had almost certainly done so here, close to home. Could it be that Brad had discovered her body and driven her far away to conceal it, hoping that the shame and disgrace of her suicide would never be made public knowledge? It was a possibility I could not ignore. It did not seem to me the action of a man like Brad, but who was to say what he might do, crazed with grief? It was certainly more acceptable to me than that he had killed her himself in a fit of rage – and what did I really know of him in any case?

But if he was blameless in the matter of her death, why

had Rosalie accused him in her letter to Miles – and where was she now? The mysterious disappearance of one wife could possibly be explained away – but *two*? It was too great a coincidence to credit. And I still remained convinced that Rosalie would never run in fear, even if she had believed Brad to be guilty of the death of Alex. It was not the Rosalie I knew. Neither could I believe that she would willingly cause her family so much anxiety, for she must have known how desperately worried they would be under the circumstances.

Something else was bothering me too. If Brad had known about the abuse Alex had suffered at Raymond's hands and he had loved her as much as everyone said he did, how had he become involved with Rosalie in the first place, let alone marry her? She was, after all, Raymond's daughter, and I would have thought he would have wanted nothing to do with any of the Voisey family . . .

A sudden chill ran down my spine as a dreadful thought occurred to me. Brad had worshipped Alex – loved her to distraction. Had he devised a terrible plan in order to wreak his revenge? Had he sought out Rosalie and married her for the simple reason that she *was* Raymond's flesh and blood? An eye for an eye – a life for a life. Could it be that he intended Raymond to pay for the torment and death of Brad's wife with the torment and death of his own daughter?

I pressed my hand to my mouth, scarcely able to breathe. Had I hit upon the truth? Little as I wanted to believe it, yet I could not help but realize it fitted the facts and drew together many loose threads.

It would have been a monstrous thing to do, of course, however deranged by grief Brad was, and I could not help but think that if he was capable of such a thing then it was all the more likely that Alex had died by his hand. Guilt would have compounded his grief – the guilt for a violent temper he could not control – and he might well have tried to ease his conscience by telling himself that Raymond was to blame for that too – that he would never have harmed his beloved Alex if Raymond had not defiled her. Perhaps, in order to gain his revenge, he had wooed and wed Rosalie, and then begun to torture her with the truth, little by little, until . . .

Oh dear God, Rosalie, you did nothing to deserve such treatment! I thought, shivering at the very idea. *You should not have had to pay for what your father did, however terrible that was ...*

And then another thought struck me, sending a fresh chill through my blood.

I, too, was Raymond's daughter. If I was right in my reasoning, that fact alone could put me in danger if Brad learned the truth. As yet, of course, he did not know ... Or did he?

My brain was whirling now with each new leap of reasoning. I thought of the ease with which I had obtained this position, the fact that Brad did not appear to have taken up any of my references or questioned my experience. I had thought it strange at the time – now it took on gigantic proportions. Had he known all along who I really was? That Miss Black was an abbreviation of Miss Blackmore, who was in fact Miss Voisey?

And I thought of what had occurred between us last night after he had plied me with alcohol. Had he been deliberately, cold-bloodedly, leading me on – had he been subtly exciting my interest and arousing my emotions from the moment I arrived? Was I to have been his next victim? Was I too intended to pay for the sins of my father with my life? The very idea was unbearable – and not just because it meant I was in danger. No, what was tearing me apart like sharp knives slashing at the very core of my being was the thought that everything I had felt might have come about because Brad was deliberately manipulating me. That every smile was calculated, every touch cold as the grave.

Oh, I couldn't bring myself to believe it! I couldn't! Was I so naïve? But Rosalie, so much more worldly-wise than I, had been deceived. She too had fallen for his treacherous seduction – and where was she now?

Suddenly the four walls of my little room seemed to be closing in on me; more than ever, I felt it was a trap. I had to get out into the fresh air, I had to find Charles Winters and seek his help to escape, I had to leave this terrible place where tragedy might well have bred madness and wickedness such as I could scarcely conceive of. And yet still my foolish heart did not want to believe any of it. Still I hoped with every fibre of my being that I was wrong. That Brad was innocent of any crime, innocent of any elaborate plot to gain his revenge. That he had felt as I had felt last night. That once again I might be in his arms . . .

Those last, faint, desperate hopes were to be short-lived.

I struggled down the stairs, my ankle still painful when the weight went on to it, but, I thought, a little better able to support me – though that might have been because I was so desperate to escape, so preoccupied with other matters that I paid less attention to it. I struggled down the stairs and outside. The air was fresh on my burning face, cooling it a little; I breathed it in and tried to steady my jangling nerves.

'Miss! Miss!'

I turned. It was one of the estate workers. Through a haze I saw his ruddy cheeks and rough clothing – calico shirt, rushy-duck trousers.

'Were you calling me?'

'Aye.' He loped towards me. 'I've just been up on the ledge. Mr Brad asked me to make sure those stone urns were safe, seeing as what happened last night. Would you tell him I can't find anything amiss? The stone looks safe as houses to me.'

'I'll tell him,' I murmured automatically.

'But I did find this, which I'm sure he'll be glad of.' He held out his hand. In the palm I saw something glinting in the sunlight.

'One of his cufflinks, by the looks of it. Silver, too – and worth a month of my poor wages, I shouldn't wonder. I don't know how it got there, I'm sure, but lost things often do turn up in the darnedest places. Will you give it to him?'

My heart seemed to have stopped beating. I took the cufflink from him and the cold silver seemed to burn my skin like a brand.

Brad's cufflink on the ledge from which the urn had fallen last night and so nearly killed me! Oh dear God, it could mean only one thing.

The urn had not fallen because the ledge was unsafe – hadn't this man just told me it was 'safe as houses'? It had

174

fallen because Brad had caused it to do so. He had been on the ledge last night – he must have found some excuse to leave Charles' company for a few minutes and gone on to it through the library window.

Without a doubt, Brad had tried to kill me.

Once, as a child, I fell from a tree I was climbing when a branch broke, sending me crashing to the ground to land flat on my back. I remember still the way the impact knocked all the air from my lungs so that I had to gasp painfully for breath, the shock waves that reverberated through my body, and the stunned sense of disbelief at what had happened that numbed my senses. It was like that now. Except that there was pain as well – not physical pain, but a searing agony deep within me – my heart? – my spirit? – and fear too, real fear, sharper than any I had felt in my life before.

Brad had tried to kill me and make it look like an accident. Had I been right in thinking he may have known my identity all along, and intended to make me, too, pay for the torment and death of his beloved Alex? Or was it simpler than that – that he had quite simply been driven mad by grief and was unable to bear the thought of any woman, wife or governess, taking her place at Upton Stowey and caring for her child, even though he knew someone must. Did he attempt to find care for Janine, only to be so overcome with disgust that another woman was replacing the little girl's mother that he was driven to make away with her?

Or was there some other motive altogether? I saw again his angry face when he had discovered me beside the open door of the room that was always kept locked, and heard his accusing voice: '*I suppose you've been in there too, poking about?*' He had not believed me when I said I had not, I felt sure, and when Sir Harry told me about the disgusting pictures, I had assumed Brad was angry because he was afraid I had seen them. But was it possible there was something else hidden away behind that locked door? Something that would incriminate him? Something that Rosalie had seen – and so sealed her fate?

I did not know. Despite my best efforts, I still really did not know anything. Why, I could not even be sure that the terrible story Sir Harry had told me was entirely true. He had seemed lucid enough whilst he was telling it – surprisingly lucid, given his usual wanderings – but how did I know that he had not confused fact with fiction, embroidered the story over the years and come to believe that certain events, which were no more than his imaginings, had actually taken place? No, I had gained very little information, and certainly none that would stand up in a court of law, and if I was honest with myself, I could not see that I was likely to now. I was totally out of my depth – and I was in real danger. Though it hurt my pride to admit it, I had failed. Now it was time to beat a retreat – whilst I still could.

At least I had one piece of evidence against Brad; I glanced down at the cufflink in my hand and, in spite of everything, felt another bolt of sadness, for I could seem to see that silver disc at his strong wrist. But resolutely I thrust the vision aside. Charles would no doubt be able to say Brad had made some excuse and left him alone in the drawing room at about the time the urn fell; together with the statement of the estate worker that he had found the cufflink on the ledge, it just might add up to enough to persuade the authorities to investigate further.

And there was Rosalie's letter. I cursed myself for not having brought it with me – clearly, though I thought I was at the end of the road, I had not been quite ready to give up when I left my room, or I would certainly have done so. But I was ready now. If I had believed that staying here would achieve anything, then whatever the risks, I would have stayed. But I did not believe it. I would be placing myself in mortal danger for nothing. And besides . . .

I could not bear to be in Brad's company knowing what I did about him. I could not look at him across the dinner table and know that the man who had stolen my heart was in fact a murderer. Most of all, I could not bear to have him continue his treacherous seduction of me – the touches that set my senses aflame, the smiles that made my stomach turn over, the gentle teasing that warmed me and made me laugh. I could not bear it, for I knew that I could not trust myself not to respond. Even now, Brad held me in his spell. No, I

176

must leave before he returned. I could not see that I had a choice any longer.

Somehow I struggled back to my room, retrieved the letter and hid it in my bodice as I had done before. Somehow I struggled back down again.

To my dismay I met Dolly in the hall.

'Where d'you think you're going, Miss?' she demanded accusingly.

'I need some fresh air,' I said. 'I'm going for a little walk.'

'On that foot? You should be resting it.'

'It's much better,' I lied. 'Your treatment was most efficacious, Dolly.'

She puffed with pride and I made my escape.

I headed for Charles Winters's cottage. Where else could I go? I did not imagine I would be lucky enough to find him at home at this time of day, and I had discounted the idea that he was hiding a secret lover there – the woman I had thought I had seen had been no more than a figment of my inflamed imagination, a trick of the light, and the reflection of the trees in the window pane, I felt sure. So, the cottage might well be empty and the door locked, but if so I would just have to sit upon the doorstep and await his return.

I limped along the path and emerged from the trees. The cottage indeed looked deserted. But to my surprise, as I approached, the door swung open. So Charles *was* at home, I thought, relieved. I was not to be reduced to sitting outside for goodness knows how long, afraid every moment of discovery.

The door had been opened, but Charles did not emerge. He must have opened it to let in some light and air, I supposed. I tapped upon it and called his name.

And was answered by a woman's voice.

'Imogen! Come in. I've been expecting you.'

Puzzled, I took a step into the cottage. It was dim inside, and my eyes took a moment to adjust to the light. But a single ray of sunshine, slanting in through the open door behind me, seemed to illuminate her so that she stood out against the gloom like a music-hall artiste in the spotlight. Dark hair tumbling to her shoulders – a gown of emerald green – the woman I had glimpsed in the window. She had not been a figment of my imagination at all, but flesh and blood. I stood staring at her, lost for words.

'Do close the door, my dear,' she said, 'and let me look at you. It's been so long. And you have quite grown up.'

Breath caught in my throat. But still I stood there, mute and disbelieving.

'Don't you recognize me, Imogen?' she said. 'It's me – it's Rosalie.'

Fifteen

Rosalie. Yes, I could see now that it was indeed her. Ten years older, of course, but still unmistakeably Rosalie. The dark flowing hair. The bold eyes. The wide red mouth. Rosalie – not dead by Brad's hand, or anyone else's, but very much alive. Shocked as I was, puzzled as I was, a bolt of fierce joy lifted my spirits.

'Rosalie! Oh, Rosalie! I don't believe it! We thought . . . Miles and I . . . we thought that something terrible had happened to you!' I went towards her with the idea of hugging her, but she made no move to reciprocate and I stopped, feeling a little awkward. 'But what are you doing here?' I asked. 'I don't understand.'

'Hiding,' she said.

'From Brad? Were you in danger from him? Is that it? Did he threaten your life?'

She smiled a little. 'Oh Imogen, it's such a long story! Why don't you sit down, my dear? Your poor foot must be paining you dreadfully.'

'You know about my accident?' I said foolishly, for I realized at once that Charles would have told her of it.

'Oh yes.' She crossed to the door, closing it, turning the key and removing it from the lock – so that Charles could open it with his own key when he returned, I supposed, but no one else – some unwelcome visitor – could get in and endanger us. 'It was fortunate for you that you were not killed.'

'It was indeed. But Rosalie . . . I have discovered that it was Brad who engineered the accident – pushed the urn off the ledge when I was almost directly beneath.'

Her eyes narrowed. 'What makes you think that?'

I opened my hand to reveal the silver cufflink nestling in my palm.

179

'A workman found this on the ledge this morning. It's Brad's. It proves he was out there last night.'

Rosalie took the cufflink from me, examining it.

'Oh yes, it's Brad's all right.' She smiled again, a rather smug, satisfied smile. 'Important evidence, I think, that he is a dangerous man – and a devious one. I'll take it for safe keeping. It will yet see him swinging on the end of the hangman's rope.'

In spite of everything, my stomach clenched at her words.

She crossed to a bureau in a dark corner beside the hearth, slid open a drawer and deposited the incriminating cufflink inside.

I thrust aside the terrible image that had assailed me of Brad swinging lifeless from a gibbet.

'I can't believe you have been here all the time,' I said. 'I thought there was someone here when I came to the cottage before, but . . .'

'Oh yes, I very nearly gave myself away, didn't I?' Rosalie said. 'It was careless of me. But I was curious to know what you looked like nowadays – after all, you were only ten years old when last I saw you – and my curiosity got the better of me. I couldn't resist peeping out of the window.'

'If only you'd made your presence known to me!' I said. 'I was so worried about you, Rosalie – as is Miles. How could you remain here and send him no word that you were safe . . . ?'

I broke off as I said the words, a sudden thought puzzling me. Rosalie was hiding in Charles's cottage; Charles was supposedly not only Rosalie's devoted friend and ally, but also Miles's. He was to have provided the link between me and Miles. So why had he not told Miles that his sister was safe and in hiding under his roof? And if Miles *did* know, why had he led me to believe that he was worried out of his mind for her safety? Had he thought it was the best way to persuade me to come here and try to uncover the evidence they were seeking? But if no harm had befallen Rosalie, then why were they seeking such evidence at all? It made no sense.

And another thing – why had Rosalie hidden from me before, yet opened the door to me so readily this morning?

And why had she said she was expecting me? There was something very strange going on, and the suspicion that I had been used in some way occurred to me.

'Did Miles know you were here all the time?' I asked directly.

She looked at me almost pityingly.

'Do you really need me to answer that, Imogen?' I did not, but she continued anyway, confirming my suspicion. 'We thought it was the best way to involve you. We needed you here – an independent witness – to uncover the evidence against Brad. And you have done well.'

Suddenly I was angry.

'How dare you and Miles deceive me so!' I demanded. 'Have you no idea what you've put me through? And why are you so anxious that evidence against Brad should be discovered anyway? He has done you no harm . . .'

I broke off. Quite suddenly I knew the answer to that, too.

Without knowing it, Sir Harry had told me as part of the terrible story concerning Alexandra. Raymond was his son; Sir Harry had disinherited him in favour of Brad, his nephew. Now, if Brad were to be found guilty of the murder of his wife and hanged for it, there would be no one to inherit the estate. When Sir Harry died – in the not-so-distant future, judging by his precarious state of health and the decline he had suffered in the last few years – Raymond would step forward and go to the courts in an effort to establish his own right to inherit. Illegitimate he might be, but with no other contender, they might well find in his favour. And Miles, his son, would be next in line.

But in any case, Rosalie was Brad's wife. If any hitch occurred, then maybe *she* would contest the estate.

Sir Harry had been right, it seemed. Rosalie had married Brad to satisfy her father's obsessive desire to get his hands on the inheritance he believed was rightfully his. And I had been dragged into their schemes, an unwitting accomplice. A puppet.

I scrambled to my feet. My heart had been broken, my life endangered, and all so that the man who had abused and broken Alexandra could achieve his twisted ambition.

'I think,' I said coldly, 'that it is time I left. I don't want to quarrel with you, Rosalie – you are, after all, my half-sister. But that is what will happen if I stay here a moment longer. I don't like being made a fool of, so I'll simply leave and go home to Devon.'

I turned for the door; Rosalie's voice, cold and hard now, stopped me in my tracks.

'Oh no, Imogen. You have not fulfilled your purpose yet. You are not going anywhere.'

I swung round. Rosalie was still beside the bureau in the fireside nook, but now something glinted in her hand. A little pistol which she had no doubt removed from the drawer. And it was pointed directly at me.

'Don't try to leave,' she said again. 'The door is locked in any case. But just to be sure . . .' She swung the pistol tantalizingly, then pointed it once more at my heart.

'I don't want to have to shoot you, Imogen. It's too soon. But make no mistake, if I have to, I will. Now, why don't you sit down again and I can tell you how clever we have been.'

I was shaking now from head to foot, mostly, I think, from the shock at the change that had come over Rosalie. This was the girl I had thought of as my sister, the girl I had put myself at risk for because I had cared so much about her. But also, of course, I shook from fear. It is not a pleasant experience to have a gun pointed at your heart and Rosalie's words echoed in my brain. *I don't want to have to shoot you . . . it's too soon . . .* What did she mean by that?

'What do you want of me?' I asked, striving to keep my voice level.

'Oh – we'll decide that when Charles gets here,' she said lightly. 'He shouldn't be too much longer. And I'm sure he will have ideas of his own.'

'Charles is in this with you.' It was a foolish thing to say; clearly he must be involved, since Rosalie was hiding here in his cottage. And had I not had my doubts about him already? Some instinct had warned me that he could not be trusted.

'Of course,' she returned smugly.

'And what are these ideas of his that you mention?' I whispered. 'Ideas for what?'

She shrugged. 'Oh, for how you should die, of course. It would have been nice if the urn had despatched you last night – the evidence had been so carefully laid to prove Brad's guilt – but then, things do not always go according to plan. There will be other ways – and we still have the cufflink, which Charles managed to purloin without Brad noticing it had gone. The estate worker will testify he found it on the roof, no doubt, and the falling urn will be seen as Brad's first attempt to make away with you. And there will be something else to tie him to your eventual demise, that you can be sure of. Charles is still in a position to engineer evidence against him. He is a useful ally indeed.'

In spite of my fear and confusion, in spite of the desperate situation in which I found myself, I felt a fierce pang of joy. Brad had not been the one who had tried to kill me – he had been framed! He was not the one threatening me now . . .

'My demise,' I said aloud. 'You intend that I should die then.' My voice was strangely calm and flat.

'I'm afraid so,' Rosalie said regretfully. 'It's all part of the plan, you see. To ensure that this time Brad cannot wriggle out of it. We need him to be convicted of murder, and this time I feel sure he will be. What jury will find him innocent in the face of all the evidence against him? It will not only be for your murder that he stands trial. His past crimes will be brought before the court too. One wife dead in suspicious circumstances, another missing and presumed, from her letter to her brother, to have been in fear of her life . . . Where is my letter, by the way?'

The paper scratched at the soft skin between my breasts, evidence of her treachery and the extent to which I had been tricked.

'You think I would tell you, now that I know the purpose for which it is intended?' I said defiantly.

'Oh well, no matter. It will be found after your death . . . in your drawer, I believe Charles said. He will, of course, testify that you had found it but refused to allow him to take it to the authorities until you had gathered further evidence, thereby placing yourself in mortal danger. And if it is not found, then I shall simply write another letter which Charles will plant where it is certain to be discovered. Your death will, I think, clinch the matter. Yet another woman from Brad's household to die violently and mysteriously. It will be far too great a coincidence for him to be able to explain it away. Oh, he'll hang right enough. And Upton Stowey will be ours.'

'How can you do this, Rosalie?' I burst out. 'We lived as sisters.'

She shrugged. 'Very easily, my dear. You are nothing to us – you never were. Just our father's wife's brat.'

My throat felt tight; there was a terrible weight around my heart. 'He was my father too, God help me!' I said bitterly.

She raised an eyebrow. 'Oh, I don't think so. Not according to Raymond.'

I gazed at her. 'But Grandmama said . . .'

'Your mother told them that story to excuse her marrying Raymond, as I understand it,' Rosalie said carelessly. 'She believed it would be more acceptable to them. But it was a fabrication, I am sure. And if Father had believed you to be his own child, it's possible he might have been less willing to go along with our plan, though one never knows. The inheritance means everything to him. And of course to me, for one day it will pass to Miles.'

'Are you saying that this dreadful plan was yours and Miles's?' I asked.

She smiled, almost proudly. 'We thought of it a long while ago, when it became clear Brad was not going to stand trial for Alex's murder as we had hoped he would. But I am the one who found a way to make it work. If I had not been clever enough to captivate Brad . . . persuade him to marry me . . . it would have been a great deal more difficult. And it helped, of course, that Charles is in love with me too. He went along with our schemes willingly enough when I promised that he and I would wed once Brad has been convicted of three murders and hanged for it.'

'You intend to marry Charles?' I asked, surprised.

Rosalie laughed. 'Of course not! I love Miles! He and I are as one, and have been since we were little more than children.'

My skin crawled. 'You and Miles . . . ?' I whispered, horrified. Dear God, the family was debauched beyond belief. With enormous relief I harked back to what Rosalie had said a moment ago, for suddenly, in spite of the terrible danger I now knew myself to be in, it seemed the most important thing in the world that I should not be part of this sick and evil brood.

'If Raymond was not my father, do you know who was?' I asked.

'Oh, a Porlock man, I believe, with whom she had become involved. Now, what was his name? Oh yes – Tom Pearce, that was it. I remember because it's the same name as the man in the song about Widdicombe Fair.'

I could scarcely believe that whilst waving a gun at me Rosalie could talk lightly about folk-songs! But I was very glad she did. At least now I knew my father's name.

'He was some milksop who was too soft to leave his own wife, though he was prepared to dally with your mother. That's what Raymond has always said. Abandoned as she was, she was ripe for the picking when Raymond took a fancy to her. A disgraced woman with a child . . . no one else would look at her, but I believe Raymond found it quite titillating.'

'My poor mama,' I whispered. Left to her fate by one man, betrayed by another. And killed by his depraved actions as surely as if he had plunged a knife into her heart too, if what Sir Harry had told me was to be believed.

'Oh, she brought it upon herself,' Rosalie said carelessly.

The anger began to rise in me again. 'As you would say I have brought upon myself whatever it is you plan to do with me!' I said spiritedly.

'Oh, you were just a convenience,' Rosalie said. 'A little ornamentation to the plan. We might have been able to pull it off without you if Miles was able to convince the authorities that for Brad to lose two wives was a little more than careless, though of course my body would never be discovered since I am still very much alive. No, we needed another victim and that is where you came in, my dear. And why you have to die. Brad may wriggle and try to get assistance for his cause in high places, but no one will be prepared to champion him with such a weight of evidence against him.'

I shivered at the cold-bloodedness of it all, cringed to think how readily I had fallen in with their plan. I had come to Upton Stowey like a lamb to the slaughter. But it was Brad I was thinking of now – Brad who would be trapped by their lies, brought to justice and made to pay the price. And little Janine, too, who would not only be orphaned, but have to live with the stigma of knowing her father hanged for murder.

'How can you do this to an innocent man and his child?' I demanded.

'Innocent? Brad? He is guilty of stealing my father's inheritance!' The light of zeal shone in Rosalie's eyes.

'He did not steal it!' I retorted, trying to ignore the pistol that was still levelled at me. 'Raymond brought about his own downfall by his depraved behaviour. He would be Sir Harry's heir now if he had not dealt in obscenities and subjected Alexandra to the most dreadful indignities for his own ends.'

Rosalie looked at me thoughtfully. 'You seem to know a great deal, Imogen. Are you in Brad's confidence?'

'No,' I said shortly. 'And I think you should know, Rosalie, that Sir Harry is a good deal more lucid where certain matters are concerned than you might think. He remembers very well why he disinherited Raymond, and he does not believe Brad was responsible for Alexandra's death. He may well yet ensure that his estate is placed well out of Raymond's reach whether you succeed in getting Brad out of the way or not.'

Rosalie's eyes narrowed. 'What does he know about Alexandra's death?'

'What do you?' I countered.

She smiled. 'Oh, I suppose there's no harm in telling you that now, since you know everything else, but you will not live to pass on the information. Raymond despatched her, of course. She was no further use to him; in fact, she was becoming a liability. She was supposed to be smoothing the path for Raymond to regain favour with Sir Harry, but instead she told him everything. He rode over here and launched a tirade at Raymond. Raymond had his revenge, though. He slipped a burr under the saddle of Sir Harry's horse and the beast bolted and threw him. Unfortunately the poor animal ran into a delivery wagon and died as a result.' There was a note of regret in her voice now – clearly she was more concerned regarding the demise of the horse than she was over the loss of any human life.

'Sir Harry, as one might expect, survived,' she continued. 'As they say, the devil looks after his own.'

'Tell me what happened to Alexandra,' I said. I was anxious to keep Rosalie talking, but also it was strangely important to me that I should learn the truth.

'As I say, she was disposed of,' Rosalie said coolly. 'Raymond could not be sure who she would confide in next. He couldn't risk that. He sent for her, telling her Sir Harry had met with an accident and needed her, then he drove her down to Exmoor, which of course he knew well, strangled her with his silk scarf, leaving no marks upon her neck, and hid her body. He was lucky – the snow came early that year, and it was the following spring before her body was discovered. By then there were all manner of rumours regarding Brad's culpability, started, of course, by Raymond himself, and we hoped that might prove enough to be his undoing. But he survived somehow, due mainly to Sir Harry's patronage, I think. So we had to decide upon another way of making sure the blame was laid at his door. First I, his new wife, would disappear in suspicious circumstances, then you, his governess, would be found murdered. Three women from his household, all apparent victims of a deranged killer. Not even Sir Harry's influence will be able to save him this time.'

So – I knew everything now. From beginning to end, all the terrible things that had happened had been an elaborate plot which Raymond believed would regain him the inheritance he aspired to. Like Alex before me, I had been nothing but a pawn in their evil game – the final move to trap Brad. I knew everything – and much good would it do me.

'You are evil, Rosalie,' I ground out. 'To think that I admired you and wanted to be like you!'

She laughed. 'Don't you wish you were like me now? Wouldn't you like to be the one with the winning hand?' The little pistol glinted as she waved it, then retrained it on me.

'No!' I said emphatically. 'Not if it meant stooping to your levels of wickedness and depravity.' But even as the words left my lips I could not help wishing that I was the one holding the pistol and pointing it at her. I swear I would have been sorely tempted to pull the trigger. It would have been no more than she deserved.

'You were always a pathetic child, and you are pathetic now.' She glanced towards the window. 'Ah – your ordeal is almost over. Here is Charles now. He'll be glad you made it easy for us by coming here. Now all we have to do is decide how you are going to die so as to best incriminate Brad.'

It was what I had been waiting for. Though it might mean my time left on this earth was short, yet it also offered me a small window of opportunity for escape. For a brief moment when Charles came into the cottage, the door would be open. If I could somehow distract Rosalie, then perhaps I could make a run for it. It was a far-fetched hope indeed, especially given my injured ankle, but it was the only one I had.

I waited, every muscle tense, until I heard Charles's key in the lock, then I leaped up, pretending to look out of the window.

'Who's that? There's someone with him!'

As I had expected, Rosalie's eyes went to the window and I launched myself towards the door. But even before I reached it I heard her voice, as sharp as any pistol shot. 'Sit down, Imogen, or I'll shoot.'

I had anticipated that, and I was fairly certain the very last thing she wanted to do was to shoot me here, now, with her little pistol. Not because she had a single qualm about killing me, but because the bullet would clearly have come from a lady's gun, not at all the sort that Brad would be likely to own. And in any case, I had nothing to lose. She intended I should die anyway. I ignored her and ran to the door. Charles was blocking my way. I aimed a kick at his shins and tried to duck between him and the doorpost.

To no avail. He stopped me easily, grabbing me by the shoulder.

'Imogen! Well, well.'

'Hold on to her, Charles,' Rosalie ordered. 'She mustn't be allowed to escape now – time is running out. And besides, she knows too much.'

188

'Really?' Charles' dark eyes bored into me. 'What does she know?'

'I know that you have been deceiving me!' I spat into his face. 'I know why you refused to take Rosalie's letter from me and deliver it to Miles. It was never intended for Miles at all, but planted to add weight to the evidence against Brad. It had to be discovered here by the investigating officers. And I know too that you tried to brain me last night with a stone urn, and very nearly succeeded. And now – now, you intend to try again. You will be a murderer, Charles. A murderer! And for what?'

His eyes flicked to Rosalie.

'You don't think she loves you, do you?' I cried desperately. 'You can't be such a fool as to think she is really going to marry you? She is using you, just as I have been used!'

'Don't talk such nonsense, Imogen!' Rosalie grated.

'It is not nonsense!' I was fighting now for my life, and I knew it. 'She doesn't want you, Charles! Her lover is her own brother!'

I saw the look of startled disbelief come into his eyes, but before I could say more, Rosalie was across the room in a few short steps. She raised her hand and hit me full in the face, the force of the blow jerking my head back. Pinioned as I was by Charles, I could do nothing to defend myself, and as she slapped me yet again, so hard that my teeth rattled, I believe I would have fallen had he not been holding me fast.

'Be quiet!' she grated at me. 'Hold your tongue!'

She raised her hand yet again, and I winced in anticipation, but to my surprise Charles intercepted her, catching her by the wrist.

'Stop that, Rosalie! There's no need . . .'

'There is every need! I have wanted to do that since she was ten years old – wanted to slap her prissy little face! Do you know how my father used to look at her? Oh, I know what he wanted to do all right – and he would have, too, if her grandparents had not taken her away. I know what he wanted to do to her – and never once did he look at me that way. Never once!'

Sickness rose in my throat; I could taste bile, and not

189

simply from the violence of her assault. Rosalie was saying that Raymond had had it in mind to treat me as he had treated Alex – was grooming me to succeed her, perhaps. But if that was not bad enough, Rosalie was actually jealous. She was jealous that it was me and not her who featured in his perverted plans. And she had compensated by seducing her brother instead – if he had taken much seducing. Dear God, was there no limit to the depths to which they would stoop, the depraved behaviour they seemed to accept as part of normal life?

'You are pathetic!' I screamed at Rosalie. 'Oh, I'd rather be dead than live as you do! Your evil father did not want you, so you took your brother. You are beneath contempt.'

Charles relaxed his hold on me a little.

'Is this true, Rosalie? You and Miles . . . ?'

Her eyes were wild now. 'What does it matter? I'm yours now, Charles. Soon we shall be together and you will be rich beyond your wildest dreams too. All this – ours. Once we've disposed of this . . . strumpet, and seen Brad hang for the crime. How shall we do it? Suffocation, perhaps? Or strangulation, as Papa strangled Alexandra? The choice is yours, my love. Only let's do it quickly. She is annoying me.'

'And how will you explain your finger marks on her face?' Charles demanded.

'What?' For the first time, Rosalie seemed a trifle disconcerted.

'The weal you raised when you struck her.' Charles' voice was grim. 'Look – the mark is already reddening.'

'Oh – those who find her will believe it was Brad who marked her face.' But Rosalie sounded less sure of herself suddenly.

'They will not. Brad's hand is far bigger than yours, Rosalie. Why could you not contain yourself? We'll have to wait – keep her here until the marks fade.'

'No! Kill her now or I'll do it myself!' She caught me, pulling me back into the cottage, and I felt the cold steel ring of the pistol against my forehead. 'I'll do it myself, I swear it!' she repeated.

The door slammed shut and suddenly, without knowing

how I got there, I was on my hands and knees on the floor and gazing up into Rosalie's crazed face.

'We've come too far to fail now!' she said passionately. 'Upton Stowey is ours by birthright. And I intend to ensure we inherit whether you will help me or not, Charles!'

Cold horror enveloped me. I had, it seemed, reached the end of the road. I closed my eyes, trying to curl into a ball there on the floor – as if that would save me!

And then, quite suddenly, there came a hammering on the door. At first I thought it was only the sound of my own heart, reverberating in my aching head. Then the door burst open again and I heard the sound of the most welcome voice in the whole world.

Brad's voice.

'Rosalie! Imogen! What in the name of heaven is going on here?'

Sixteen

For a moment everyone in the room froze, so that we resembled nothing so much as a display of waxworks. In that moment I did not have time to wonder why he had come here to the cottage or how much he knew. I could only feel an enormous rush of relief, as if somehow, now that he was here, he could miraculously make everything right.

He was staring at his missing wife, eyes narrowed in puzzlement, features set in stone. He seemed almost oblivious to the pistol she still held in her hand; perhaps coming into the dim cottage after the bright sunshine outside he did not at first see it.

'So – you were here all the time,' he snarled. 'You thought to make a fool of me. And you, Charles . . . what is your game?'

He took a step towards his estate manager, the legendary temper of which I had heard so much suddenly apparent in the curl of his lip, the flash of his eyes and the balling of his hands to fists.

'Brad! Don't! She has a gun!' I gasped, trying to scramble to my feet and falling back again.

'Yes, Brad, I have a gun! Stay where you are!' She raised it to point at him, then swung it towards me. 'You too! Don't move, you little fool!'

'Rosalie . . .' Charles raised a hand, and it was his turn to have the barrel pointed in his direction, before she swung it back towards Brad, seemingly uncertain which of us she most needed to threaten.

She had, I realized, finally taken leave of her senses, and it made her even more dangerous than the cold, calculating Rosalie of a few moments ago.

Brad realized it too, I believe, for he stood stock still, both hands raised cautiously.

192

'Don't be a fool, Rosalie.' His voice was level now. 'Give that gun to me.'

She laughed, a mad cackle. 'Oh no, Brad. It's your turn now to do as I say. What are you doing here anyway? You shouldn't be here! But no matter. You are in my power now. All of you! Do you know how good that feels? Very soon Imogen will be dead and you will be charged with her murder – and Alex's too. Then Upton Stowey will be my father's, as is his right, and after that – Miles and I will inherit. Don't you think I've been clever?'

'I think, Rosalie, that you should give me the gun before you do something you will regret.' Still his voice was admirably level.

She laughed again. 'Regret? Oh no, Brad! You are the one who will live to regret ever coming here and stealing our inheritance.'

'Rosalie . . .' He took a step towards her, hand outstretched.

'You think I'd give up so easily after all I've done to gain my ends?' she demanded. 'Marrying you . . . shutting myself away in this dark little cottage . . . pretending to be in love with Charles . . . oh no!' She wheeled, dragging me up by my hair and placing the gun once more against my temple. 'Stay where you are, or I'll shoot Imogen now and be done with it!'

'For the love of God, Rosalie – this has nothing to do with Imogen!' Brad entreated her. 'Do whatever you wish to me, but let her go. She is just an innocent.'

'You think so?' Rosalie sneered. 'Perhaps, Brad, you should know the truth about Imogen – and her real name. Imogen is not Miss Black, the governess, as you believe. In reality, she is Imogen Voisey, my stepsister.'

I saw the startled look come into Brad's eyes – and the accusation.

'I'm not in league with her, Brad!' I cried. 'I didn't know she was hiding here in Charles's cottage. It's true that I am who she says I am, but the reason I came here was to try and discover what had become of her. She and Miles deceived me totally!'

'It was so easy!' Rosalie could not resist crowing, and this time I was glad of it, for it confirmed to Brad that I had no part in her wicked scheme. 'You are right, Brad, she is an innocent. And a fool. But that won't save her. She has to die. It's all part of our plan.'

I saw Brad's jaw tighten, but the calm he maintained was impressive.

'What do you want, Rosalie? Just name your terms. Let Imogen go and we'll talk about it.'

'I've already told you what I want!' she exclaimed. 'Upton Stowey, of course! It's ours by right – mine and Miles's and Raymond's. Why should you have everything? What have you ever done that that old fool made you his heir? It should be ours – and it will be!'

Brad's face was stony, unreadable. 'If that's what's behind all this, then it's easily resolved. What do I care for Upton Stowey? It's nothing but bricks and mortar and land. Put that gun down and let Imogen go, and you can consider it all yours.'

Her eyes gleamed with triumph, then her lip curled once more.

'It's not yours to give though, is it?' Her voice was full of bitterness. 'Sir Harry is still the landowner. He's not dead yet.'

'Then talk to him,' Brad urged. 'Plead your case. He may well listen.'

'He would not. He turned against Raymond – his own son. He disinherited him and threatened him, and enjoyed doing it.'

'Then if he does not and I remain his heir, I will make it all over to you when the time comes,' Brad said. 'Whatever you want. But don't drag Imogen into it. This is not the way to get what you want.'

'It's the only way! Don't you see? I shall shoot Imogen and you will be hanged for it, Brad. Charles and I will testify that we saw you shoot her, shall we not, Charles?' Her voice had risen triumphantly, as if she had already achieved her ends.

My eyes skittered to Charles. He looked, I thought, a trifle uncertain.

'Why should he?' I managed. My voice sounded choked, for my throat was pulled taut by Rosalie's grasp and I was

194

afraid to move lest the gun should go off. 'Charles is not included in your plans – you told me as much. He'll perjure himself and send an innocent man to the gallows, and all for nothing.'

'Be quiet!' Rosalie commanded. 'Charles does as I tell him.' She started for the door, dragging me with her. 'We'll do this outside – in the park. Open the door for me, Charles.'

Charles made no move and she pushed it open herself.

'Rosalie . . .' Brad took a step towards us. Rosalie fixed him with her mad stare.

'Don't try to stop me, Brad, or I swear . . .'

'Papa! Papa!'

I did not see Janine running towards the cottage, for Rosalie was between me and the door, and I do not believe Rosalie saw her either, backing as she was. But there was no mistaking the piping voice. My blood ran cold. Dear God, that Janine should come upon a scene such as this! And with Rosalie crazed as she was, it was even possible she might turn upon the child . . .

But even as the terrible thoughts raced through my brain, the whole world went mad around me. At the time I was aware only that the pressure on my throat suddenly eased and something hard struck me in the face. And then there was the sharp crack of the pistol, followed by Janine's shrill scream. Rosalie gasped, a rasping sound that I can hear even now in my nightmares. I swung round, half falling back into the room, and saw Rosalie crumpled in the open doorway. A dark stain was spreading across the bodice of her emerald green gown, her face contorted into an expression of utter shock. And Charles, who I now know had taken the chance offered by the diversion created by Janine to knock the gun from my temple – it had been his forearm which had struck my face – Charles was on his knees beside her.

'Rosalie! Oh, my love . . .'

Rosalie's eyes were wide but oddly glazed. Blood was beginning to pool on the flagstones beside her.

'Why?' she whispered. 'Oh Charles, why . . . ?'

'It had to end,' he murmured back. He sounded utterly broken; without doubt he had loved her very much – or at least been completely under her spell. But in the last resort he had been unable to see murder done. At the end he had realized the object of his passion was an evil woman driven mad by obsession. And one who had used him, too, as she used everyone who came within her clutches.

Janine was still there in the doorway, looking down at Rosalie, her face a picture of stunned puzzlement.

'I told you I saw her!' she was saying. 'The day of my accident. I told you she was in the copse . . . Oh, Rosalie – Rosalie . . .'

'Janine!' I rushed to her, hiding her face in my skirts. And suddenly Brad was there too, with his arms around both of us.

In spite of all the horror that had gone before, in spite of the fact that I was shaking now from head to foot, in spite of the fact that the girl I had believed to be my sister lay dying at my feet, I felt I had come home.

I had come home, and nothing could detract from the fierce joy that rushed through me to dispel the darkest terrors and doubts. I felt sadness, of course, that the treasured memories of my childhood days had been so sullied by the knowledge that the Voiseys were a crazed and evil brood; sadness for my mother, that she too had been so deceived by them, and for the terrible betrayal that had brought about her death; sadness for Alexandra and her wasted life, a bright shining light dimmed by the wicked and depraved behaviour of one man and, in the end, snuffed out as mercilessly as a spent candle.

I even felt a little sadness for Charles, led astray by his passion for a wicked woman. In truth, I knew all too well how easy it was to be driven by the vagaries of the heart, for I had myself been unable to control my feelings for Brad, even when I had believed him guilty of the most dreadful crimes.

But I could not feel sadness for Rosalie, nor for Raymond and Miles, who must now face the justice they so richly deserved.

But at that moment, in the circle of Brad's arms, I knew only that the nightmare was over. The man I had fallen in love with was guilty of nothing – my instincts had been right all along.

196

And he cared for me, too. No words were needed for me to be more certain of it than I had ever been of anything. I had come to Upton Stowey to find evidence that would bring him to justice, and instead I had found love. A love that I knew without doubt would last a lifetime.

'Thank goodness you came to Charles's cottage this morning!' I said to Brad.

It was evening, and we were in the drawing room. Janine had been tucked up in bed, seemingly none the worse for what I would have imagined to be a terrible experience for child. Instead, she seemed almost to be treating it as an adventure. Perhaps, I thought, we had managed to keep the full import of what had happened from her, and I certainly hoped so, for to see Rosalie shot dead before her very eyes could have scarred her sensibilities for life. Unbeknownst to her, Dolly had been settled in a chair outside her door, just in case she should experience night terrors, but so far there was no sign of any such thing occurring. Brad and I had both looked in on her and she was sleeping as peacefully as a baby. How resilient the young could be!

Sir Harry, too, had retired for the night. He too was utterly unfazed at the turn of events. 'I always told you that woman was no good for man nor beast,' he remarked mildly. Brad had decided not to acquaint him with everything I had learned for fear of upsetting him, and Sir Harry did not ask.

Now Brad and I were alone, and at last I had the opportunity to ask him about the details that were puzzling me.

'Truly I dread to think what would have happened if you had not,' I went on. 'I would be dead, and you might well be in custody charged with my murder. It was such a fortunate chance that you happened to call to see him.'

'Fortunate, yes, but not so much a chance,' Brad said.

I frowned, puzzled, and he went on: 'Dolly told me the estate worker had found one of my cufflinks on the ledge this morning and given it to you. Since I knew that I had not dropped it there, I knew it could have been deposited by only one other person – Charles Winters. I remembered he had excused himself from the drawing room at the time when the urn fell, and I realized that not only must he have been the one responsible for the so-called "accident", but also he intended to frame me for it. I did not know why, of course, but I intended to find out. And when Dolly also told me that she had last seen you hurrying towards his cottage, I was very afraid for you. He had, after all, made one attempt on your life – who was to say he would not make another? I was, I admit, totally puzzled as to the reason, and I have to confess it crossed my mind that you might have been involved with him all along. Your arrival here in response to my search for a governess was, well, shall we say fortuitous, to say the least.'

Colour rose in my cheeks. 'I am so sorry that I thought for a moment that you might have harmed Rosalie,' I said. 'But I had no reason to doubt what Miles told me and . . . well, I do feel very guilty about deceiving you too. Can you forgive me?'

'Is that a question you need to ask?' Brad took my hand in his. 'What you did was very brave and selfless. You were not to know . . . You thought you knew them, Imogen, and you did not know me. I cannot find it in my heart to blame you. Rather, I blame myself. How could I have been so blind? How could I have been such a fool as to be taken in by such an evil woman?'

'The Voiseys are past masters at deceit,' I said. 'And it is easy to be wise after the event. I can see now that I should never have agreed to do what Miles asked. Grandmama warned me of him and I did not listen. I should have known something was wrong when Miles outlined such an intricate plot, and I should have refused to be a part of something so secret and underhand.'

'But you were concerned about Rosalie,' Brad comforted me. 'Indeed, it is to your credit that you were prepared to go to such lengths for the sake of the girl you believed to be your sister. And you certainly could not have been expected to know how evil the family were. You were only a child when you lived with them.'

'Rosalie always seemed so bold and brave to me,' I said. 'I admired and looked up to her. Though I have to confess I never cared much for Miles. And the very fact that neither of them had ever attempted to contact me in the intervening years should have alerted me. If they had cared about me, surely they would have made the journey at least once or twice? But it certainly never occurred to me that they cared so little that they could plot my murder to gain their own ends.'

Brad swore. 'If only I had known what they were up to! And if only I had known all those years ago, Alex would not have died as she did. Oh, why did she not confide in me?'

His expression was so tortured, his voice so full of his agony, that it wrung my heart. He had loved her so much, and by being named as Sir Harry's heir he had inadvertently brought about her death. It was a terrible burden for him to have to bear.

'Why did she tell Harry and not me?' he agonized now.

'She was ashamed, I expect. And afraid, too, of what you might do,' I said.

'I'd have killed the bastard without doubt,' Brad said grimly. 'But how could she think I would blame her for one instant? She was just a child when he defiled her – an innocent. Dear God, I can scarcely believe even now what he did to her!'

'If you did not know about the pictures, why were you so angry when you thought I had been in the locked room?' I asked.

'Because her things are there,' he said simply. 'I could not bring myself to throw them away. Her gowns, packed into trunks, her riding crop, even a doll she brought with her when we wed, which she said had slept on her pillow since she was a child . . . Barbara, she said her name was . . . I couldn't bring myself to throw them away, but I couldn't bring myself to look at them either. And certainly I did not want anyone else handling them. Harry suggested they be locked away there, and so they were on the day we buried her. They have been there ever since.'

'And will remain so,' I said.

'No.' Brad reached for my hand. 'No, the time has come, I think, to move on. Alex has been avenged now – she can rest in peace. She was my first love – I always thought she would be my last. But now . . . it would not be right, Imogen, to ask you to live with her ghost.'

199

Warmth was spreading through my veins.

'To live with . . .?' I repeated. 'What are you saying, Brad?'

His face softened, he smiled, that smile that right from the first time I saw it had captivated my heart.

'Well, I am asking you to marry me, of course! Imogen – dear, brave, foolish Imogen – I know you may think it far too soon. But will you do me the honour of being my wife?'

The happiness spread in me like a starburst. Too soon? Too soon after our meeting? Or too soon after Rosalie's demise? No – never too soon! And another thought occurred to me. Brad had not thought to dispose of Alex's belongings when he had wed Rosalie, but now . . . At last I truly believed that he had been telling the truth when he said he had married her solely to provide a mother for Janine.

'Imogen?' Brad said urgently. 'I know it may not sound an attractive prospect to you given my past history. And I realize you would have to take on Janine as a daughter . . .'

'I love Janine,' I said. 'She would certainly be no deterrent to me, quite the reverse.'

'Then . . . I swear I shall do everything in my power to make you happy. If there is anything you want, just say the word and it is yours. Only say you will be my wife.'

'Of course, Brad. Of course I will!' I whispered.

It was a long time before we continued our conversation.

'There is one thing I would like, Brad,' I said much later.

'Anything.' His voice was languid, molten as his eyes. 'What is it?'

'Well, two things, actually.' I smiled. 'I'd like you to come with me to Devon and formally ask Grandpapa for my hand . . .'

'Well, of course!'

'And on the way there or on the way back, I would like to go to Porlock and see if I can find my father.'

I could see that he was taken by surprise. 'Your father?'

'Rosalie told me that he lived in Porlock. It would not be so far out of our way to make a detour, would it?'

Brad hesitated, his eyes narrowed, and for a moment I thought he was going to refuse me, though for the life of me I could not understand why. Then he said: 'Are you sure about this, Imogen? Do you think it wise?'

'Perhaps not – but when have I ever been wise?' I countered. 'All my life I have wondered about my father – who he was, what he was like. Then for a little while I thought it was Raymond – and you can imagine how I felt about that when Sir Harry had told me what sort of a man he was. Now . . . I would very much like to learn what I can, and perhaps meet him – if he is still alive, of course.'

'But it would seem his family know nothing of you,' Brad cautioned. 'If he kept your birth a secret from his wife then it would cause no end of trouble and heartache if you were to suddenly arrive on the scene – a grown woman claiming to be his daughter. He might very well deny you, which I feel sure would only upset you all over again. Don't you think it best to leave the past where it belongs?'

'It is not the past to me,' I said stubbornly. 'It is the present and the future. It is who I am. And I don't mean to go blundering in with the truth. I just want to see him, that's all. And any true brothers and sisters I may have. I have just been robbed of the only family I ever knew, remember.'

Brad sighed. 'Very well. If it means so much to you. I just don't want to see you hurt again, Imogen.'

I slipped my hand into his. 'With you beside me, Brad, nothing can hurt me now.'

We went to Devon, taking Janine with us. I would have very much liked to take Sir Harry too, for I thought the trip might do him good, but he refused good-humouredly: 'I'm too old to travel far these days. Dolly will look after me well, never fear. And I like to be here with my memories.'

Miraculously, he seemed to be a good deal clearer in his mind these days, I thought – though he still rambled in the past, he no longer confused me with Alex, and it occurred to me that sharing the weight of guilt which had so troubled him had lessened the fog of confusion.

Janine, of course, was excited about the journey – almost as excited as she had been when we told her the news about our forthcoming nuptials.

'I am so glad you won't be going away, Imogen!' she

cried, hugging me.

I was a little apprehensive as to what Grandmama and Grandpapa's reaction might be, but I need have had no fear. They instantly took to Brad, and were happy for me – and for themselves.

'We've always worried so about you, Imogen,' Grandmama said. 'I am glad to say you have chosen well – unlike your poor mama. It's a great relief to us to know that you will be settled and happy.'

'And you know you can come to visit us as often as you like,' I assured her.

Grandmama smiled. 'I don't know when that will be. Your Grandpapa has just begun work on another memoir and you know how that absorbs his time.'

'Then you will just have to persuade him to put it aside,' I told her.

On the way home we made the detour that I had asked for and stayed overnight in the inn at Porlock.

I have to say I was charmed by the place, the steep hill dipping from the moors to the little harbour, and I hoped very much that my mother had enjoyed some happiness here. But if I had hoped to meet my real father, I was doomed to disappointment. When I mentioned his name to the landlord, it was to be told that he had moved from the area many years ago, returning to his wife's native Cornwall.

'Ah, Tom was a good man – best doctor we've ever had in these parts,' the landlord said and I lapped up the information. My father – a doctor! I had been very afraid that he might have been an art dealer like Raymond, though I could not believe he could have been depraved.

'He's been sorely missed these last ten years and more – a medical man of his calibre you don't forget so easy,' the landlord, a talkative soul, went on. 'But he was a dark horse, too, if I'm not mistaken.'

'A dark horse?' I repeated, hoping to elicit further information.

The landlord needed little encouragement. 'There were secrets in his life, I feel sure, and I always believed he had a dalliance with a Devon girl who used to come to stay in the village. More than a dalliance, perhaps. There were times when he looked like a man torn in two. She died, I heard. Very sad. After that he was never the same, and I reckon his heart was broken, and maybe he blamed himself for breaking hers. I don't know. Whatever, the family left Porlock and I reckon it was to make a fresh start.'

'Did he have children?' I asked, anxious to know if I had siblings I had never met.

The landlord's eyes narrowed as if it had suddenly occurred to him that I was taking rather more than a casual interest in his one-time doctor. But still he could not resist telling me what I wanted to hear.

'There were three boys and a girl. All still children when they left, though they'd be grown now. A good family, as I say. They were sorely missed here in Porlock.'

I nodded, smiling faintly. 'I'm glad to hear they were held in high regard.'

'So why are you so interested, if I might ask?' the landlord said, looking at me intently.

I knew I had said too much.

'My parents spoke of them, that's all,' I replied.

'Do you want to go to Cornwall now to track down your father?' Brad said when we were alone.

I shook my head. It was enough that I had seen the place where no doubt I had been conceived, and knew that my father had not been of the same evil ilk as Raymond, but a respected member of the community. He must have suffered too, I thought, torn between his duty as a husband and father yet loving my dear mama, and my heart ached for them both – imprisoned and tortured by a love which could never be. But I no longer needed to upset lives in a quest for brothers and a sister who did not even know of my existence. I had a family of my own now – Brad and Janine and Sir Harry, as well as my dear gentle grandparents who had sacrificed so much for my good.

It was more than I could ever have wished for.

'Let's go home, Brad,' I said, smiling into his hazel eyes. 'Everything I could ever want is there. Let's just go home.'

50736042484988
Tanner, Janet.
Dangerous deception /

MAIN   NOV 3 0 2006